"MEGHANN?" BRUCE LIFTED HER CHIN WITH A LIGHT TOUCH of his finger. The tenderness in his eyes was heart wrenching. "Ah, Meg...what you do to me."

His hand cupped her face, and the gentle touch sent shivers coursing through her. He was going to kiss her and she was glad. She wanted him to do it. Now. Here. with no one around to see them.

But even as she leaned toward him, his hand fell away, and he turned back to grip the steering wheel.

Then, without a word of explanation, he turned the key in the ignition.

Mortified, Meg sat there, gripping her hands together in her lap. She was such an idiot! Why would he even think about kissing her? She was a friend, nothing more. Someone he'd promised to help.

The sooner she got that through her stupid head—and her foolish heart—the better off she'd be.

♛ *Palisades Pure Romance*

Newlywed GAMES

MaryDavis

Palisades is a division of Multnomah Publishers, Inc.

NEWLYWED GAMES
published by Palisades
a division of Multnomah Publishers, Inc.

© 2000 by Mary Davis
International Standard Book Number: 1-57673-268-1

Design by Chris Gilbert
Cover photograph of newlyweds by Tim MacPherson/Tony Stone Images
Cover photograph of family by Jim Cummins/FPG

Scripture quotations are from *The Holy Bible,* New International Version
© 1973, 1984 by International Bible Society,
used by permission of Zondervan Publishing House

Also quoted:
Holy Bible, New Living Translation (NLT)
© 1996. Used by permission of Tyndale House Publishers, Inc.
All rights reserved.

Palisades is a trademark of Multnomah Publishers, Inc., and is registered in the U.S. Patent and Trademark Office.

Printed in the United States of America

00 01 02 03 04 05 06—10 9 8 7 6 5 4 3 2 1 0

To the Lord who made all this possible.
To my husband. You have always stood
behind me and believed in me. Moine!
And to my mom and sister.
Thanks for your encouragement and help.
A special thanks to my editors, Julee and Karen,
for all their help and hard work.

Someone might argue,
"If my falsehood enhances God's
truthfulness and so increases his glory,
why am I still condemned as a sinner?"
Why not say…"Let us do evil that good may result"?
ROMANS 3:7–8

Prologue

BRUCE HALLOWAY HAD LOOKED UP WITH A START WHEN HE heard the ruckus outside his office window. It sounded like an all-out war with all the shouting and crying going on. He pushed out of his leather executive chair and moved toward the window to see if he could break up the commotion.

Meghann? What on earth are you doing?

His office, located on the first floor of the Palace Hotel, overlooked a small grassy patch with a dogwood tree and a flower bed. One of his employees, Miss Meghann Livingston, rose on some sort of stepladder from the center of the excited crowd that had gathered around the tree.

Was she out to break her pretty little neck?

With the thinning fall leaves, he could see a small gray kitten perched up in the tree. From what he could discern, the terrified cat belonged to the crying little girl and it had been chased up the tree by the still barking corgi, who apparently thought he could climb up after his prey.

When Meghann reached for the frightened, cross feline and was hissed at and clawed, Bruce made a bee-line for the chaotic group. He reached them just as Meghann captured the kitten. It took all his skills, but he managed to soothe the little girl, calm the distressed maid, who was acting as baby-sitter, and appease the agitated dog owners all while keeping his fearless employee from tumbling from the rickety ladder with needle-sharp claws in her neck, hand, and shoulder.

Back in his office with Meghann, Bruce said, "Why didn't you come ask for help?"

"It was just a poor, defenseless, little kitty, hardly anything worth calling out the cavalry for."

He took her wounded hand and turned it over, sur-veying the damage. She had multiple scratches on both sides of her right hand and forearm but nothing that was bleeding much. "Hardly defenseless." Leave it to Meghann to jump in and try to take care of the situation.

He sat her on the couch and retrieved a wet wash-cloth and first-aid kit from the private restroom off of his office. He sat next to her and gently cleaned her wound-riddled flesh. She grimaced at the pain but didn't complain or cry out.

As he sat ministering to her injures, touching her warm, silky skin, it felt as if jolts of electricity coursed through him. What he really wanted to do was pull her close and wrap her in his arms, but with great effort he restrained himself.

He had made a point to keep a professional dis-tance from all the female staff, this one in particular. From the moment he was introduced to her and shook her slender hand, he felt some sort of unexplainable connection he hadn't been able to shake. So he put extra effort into keeping their contact minimal and strictly business.

But now he feared his resolve was quickly dissolving with her sitting here, letting him treat her scrapes. He also feared she was far too intriguing to avoid any longer.

It was the middle of December and the fresh blanket of snow that had covered the ground the night before had melted in the strong Colorado sun. The Palace Hotel's Christmas party was winding down by the time Meghann had joined the festivities. She hadn't cut her shift short like so many others had. No, Meghann stayed at the front desk until her shift was over, allowing her coworkers to enjoy the party. He was starting to have a nice conversation with her over a cup of eggnog when a sultry voice from his past brought him up short.

"Bruce Halloway!"

It could be none other than Charmaine Altman. His ex-girlfriend was a stunning five-foot-eight glamorous platinum blond, not a flaw to be seen…on the outside anyway. He wanted to ignore her in hopes she would go away but knew that would be rude, and so, he turned to her. "Charmaine." He had thought he had gotten away from her for good.

"You are a hard man to track down."

But you still managed it.

She extended her slim manicured hand to him with

her long blood-red nails. He wasn't about to take her hand, and he stretched his arm around Meghann's chair. "I've been here." He hoped she wasn't going to make a scene.

"Who's this?" she said as if she had only just noticed Meghann sitting with him. "The latest flavor of the month?"

Bruce's lips tightened. "She's a friend." But he hoped she would become more.

Those perfectly sculpted brows arched. "A friend?" She turned her gaze on Meghann and studied her. "Since when do you have *friends* of the female persuasion?"

Meghann shifted in her chair uncomfortably. She hadn't missed Charmaine's malicious tone or piercing glare.

"I know you can do better than this. She's hardly anything worth getting jealous over."

He heard Meghann take in a quick breath and sensed she would like to give Charmaine a piece of her mind, but Bruce was faster. "That's enough!" He stood face-to-face with his adversary. He could put up with a lot by the grace of God but not her insulting Meghann, a true beauty.

Charmaine took a step toward him. "I always could get a reaction out of you." She raised a haughty brow, obviously pleased with herself.

He stepped back, refusing to let this woman get to him. Why couldn't she leave him alone? He wondered what Meghann thought of their exchange and was almost afraid to turn to her, but he did.

"Let's go." He held out his hand to her. "I'll take you out for dinner." He figured an all-out retreat was his best defense before Charmaine got really ugly, or he said something he would regret. He wasn't sure Meghann would accept the invitation because their relationship had always been strictly professional, but she rose and went with him without hesitation, most likely to escape any more of Charmaine's tawdry remarks.

They had almost made their escape when they were sidetracked in the lobby, and Bruce had to excuse himself to take care of some business. The business took longer than he anticipated, requiring an immediate trip out of town. On his way back to tell Meghann he would have to put off their dinner engagement, Charmaine waylaid him in the hall.

"I must say I didn't expect you to abandon your little *friend* so soon, but I can't say I'm sorry about that."

"I haven't abandoned Meghann." At least not yet. He wasn't about to tell Charmaine he was going to have to cancel on Meg. "I'm in a bit of a hurry." Mostly to get away from her.

She batted her lashes. "I thought maybe we could get together."

"No." He tried to step around her, but she expertly slid herself in his path.

"Well, then a drink...for old time's sake."

He looked her straight in the eyes. "I'm really not interested."

She held up her hands. "You can't blame a girl for trying."

He was relieved when she sidestepped out of his

way, but then was caught off guard when she tripped and clutched at the front of him to regain her balance.

She pasted on a sweet, innocent smile. "Pardon me."

As he grabbed her to set her aside, Meghann opened the door and witnessed them. His eyes locked with hers for an instant, and as clearly as if she had shouted it at him, he could read in her disbelieving eyes, *You used me!*

He hadn't. Never in a million years.

Embarrassment and hurt flamed to her face, then she ran away.

"Meghann, wait!" He shook Charmaine off and hustled after Meghann. He searched for her but couldn't find her anywhere. Why did she have to choose that very moment to come down the hall? She didn't understand. How could she with the damaging evidence?

Meghann, where are you? Let me explain, please!

Several months later, Meghann shifted in the hard chair as sounds gushed in from the hospital hallway, battering her. A straight-back chair with what little padding it offered did not make for a good bed. She didn't know what time she drifted off or how much sleep she got, but apparently enough to make her stiff. She moved slowly to her mother's bedside, trying to work out the kinks in her shoulders. Her mother had collapsed two days ago and slipped into a coma. Meghann had insisted on staying through the night against the hospital staff's recommendations. She wanted to spend every last minute with her mom.

Beep...beep...beep.... The monitor continued to measure out each beat of precious life.

Contrary to the doctor's prediction, her mother lasted through the night. That had to be a good sign.

Thank you, Lord!

"Good morning, Mom."

Heavy lids fluttered open. "I've had better," her mother rasped out.

"You're awake!" Tears sprang to Meghann's eyes. Her prayers had been answered.

"I woke up some time ago. The doctor and the nurse have both been in to poke at me while you slept."

Meghann sat on the edge of the bed and smoothed back the hair from one side of her mom's face, feeling more like the parent instead of the child. "Why didn't you wake me?"

"You looked so peaceful sleeping there." Her mother patted Meghann's hand. "It reminded me of when you were a baby and I would slip into your room to watch you sleep."

A heavyset nurse that Meghann recognized from the day before entered the room. The nurse picked up her mother's chart and looked at Meghann. "I see you've woken up, too, and have seen the good news for yourself." The nurse scratched something onto her mother's chart. "It seems she's pulling out of this."

This? Don't they even know what's wrong with Mom?

"Congratulations on your new marriage."

The nurse was looking right at Meghann so she could only assume the woman was speaking to her. "Marriage?"

"I heard you tell the doctor you just got married."

When did I tell the doctor that?

"Did I ruin a surprise?" The wide-eyed nurse tucked her multicolored pen back in her uniform pocket.

Meghann searched her brain for conversations with the doctor the previous day. Had she mentioned marriage? Only when the doctor told her to talk to her mom and give her something to fight for. She had told the doctor the thing that would make her mom happiest would be if she told her she had just gotten married. The nurse must have only heard a piece of the conversation. Why didn't some people get their facts straight before pouncing on every bit of gossip they thought they heard? Meghann opened her mouth to set the record straight when her mother's tired voice stopped her.

"Oh, darling, I'm so happy for you."

Meg's protest died in her throat with her mother's smile and bright eyes. Did her mother really look better or was it her imagination?

"It must be that nice young manager you're always talking about."

"A-assistant manager," was all she could manage to say. Did she really talk about him that much?

"My daughter always tried to play down her relationship, but a mother can tell. I knew she was hiding something." Her mother turned back to her then. "His name's Bruce, right, honey?"

Her affirmation came out as a squeak, then she cleared her throat with a nod. "Bruce Halloway."

"Meghann Halloway. Doesn't that have a nice sound to it?"

Meghann thought so. But exactly how did she suddenly become Mrs. Bruce Halloway? More important, how did she tactfully become unmarried to her boss?

The doctor came in then, giving Meghann the chance to collect her thoughts. Her mother looked so invigorated with the news of her marriage. She would be disappointed to find out it was all a misunderstanding.

The doctor brought her out of her thoughts. "Whatever you're doing, keep it up. She's improved since I was last here, but she's not out of the woods yet."

Keep it up? But...but...it's not true!

She looked from the doctor to the smiling nurse to her ill mother. A weak smile pulled at Meghann's mouth.

I guess I'm married...for now.

One

"I'M GOING TO KILL MY MOTHER!"

"No, you're not." Meghann's friend Jennifer tried to console her, but she knew better.

Slouched on her gingham-covered sofa, Meghann Livingston rolled her head to the side with a sigh and gave her friend a weary pout. "Yes, I am going to kill her. When I tell her I have no husband, she will collapse again...only this time at my feet."

Meghann's mother had recently been released from a Florida hospital after being treated for what the doctors were calling overexhaustion for lack of a better, more accurate diagnosis. Truth was, they didn't have a clue what was wrong with her mother. Other than a slight potassium deficiency, all the tests came back negative. Even the CAT scan revealed nothing.

Meghann shook her head. It just didn't make sense. A person didn't just faint and slip into a coma for no reason. But that's what her mother had done. It had been a terrifying time, but thankfully her mother seemed to be recovering. And the doctor had said she should take it easy and rest or the next time could be worse.

The next time?

No! If Meghann could help it, there would be no next time. Only one thing could be worse than *almost* dying, and that wasn't going to happen. Her mother was all she had.

Why were you driving yourself so hard, Mom? Was she that lonesome? So much so that she had to fill her every waking moment?

It was no wonder Meghann had said what she had, that she'd tried to give her frighteningly ill mother some hope…some shred of something to hold on to. No wonder she'd avoided setting the misconception straight and lied through her teeth. It was everything her mom wanted for her.

Her mom thought it was unreasonable for her daughter to still be single at twenty-five. *"What is wrong with all the men these days? Are they all afraid to commit?"* Her mom's questions played over and over in her mind. Meghann just hadn't found the right man yet.

That isn't true. She had found him. She planned to invite him over for a home-cooked meal but had to postpone it when her mother collapsed. And now she was in a bind. Her mom was on the mend and coming to visit her under the guise of meeting a nonexistent husband, and Meghann had the unfortunate task of breaking the bad news to her.

"I have to let her down easy." Meghann said to her friend, then sat up with a start. "I've got it! You tell her. Maybe it wouldn't be such a shock coming from you." She raised her brows in hope.

Jennifer shook her head. "You take life far too seriously. Why are you making this so hard?"

Because it is hard.

"It's really quite simple." Jennifer's dark eyes blazed with delight.

Meg stared open-mouthed at her friend. "Simple?"

This she had to hear. True, Jennifer could reduce almost anything to simple terms, even Einstein's theory of relativity. Take out all the difficult-to-understand stuff and whatever is left, if anything, must be right. But what Meghann had done wasn't difficult to understand, just stupid. Crazy. Totally wrong.

And utterly impossible to get out of.

"Care to explain how telling my mom I'm not really married to Mr. Right and not killing her in the process is...*simple?*"

"Yep." Jennifer's nod was firm and her smile broadened. "You don't."

Meg frowned. "I don't what?"

"You don't tell her you're not married."

Meg came up off the sofa, disturbing her black Lab at her feet. "I thought you were going to help me!"

Jennifer laid a gentle hand on her arm. "I am, Meg, more than you know. Look, your mom's not really well yet, right?"

Sinking back onto the couch again, Meg nodded. "Right."

"But thinking you're married and settled has been a big help for her, right?"

Meg's midsection twisted at the playful sparkle in her friend's eyes. "Right..."

"And telling the truth might send her into a relapse, right?"

Meg fixed her friend with a glare. "Is this supposed to be helping me?"

Jennifer sighed. "All I'm saying is that you keep up the ruse for now. I mean, what's more important? Making sure your mom gets better or making yourself feel better by telling the truth?" She came to kneel beside Meg. "Really, who are you hurting? You'll tell your mom the truth when she's strong enough, but for now, go along. It's what she's always wanted, so why not give it to her for a while? Honor thy father and mother and all that."

Meghann hated to admit it, but for once, Jennifer sort of made sense.

Lying to your mother was wrong, regardless of your intentions. How can continuing the lie make it better?

Meghann knew the question was valid. Knew the lie was wrong. *But what else can I do, Lord? What if I tell her and it's too much for her, too hard on her heart?*

No. She couldn't take the chance. Meghann rubbed a hand over her eyes, trying to wipe away the ache. "So how do I explain the absence of my supposed husband while Mom is here?"

Jennifer's triumphant grin did little to ease Meg's worries. "I've already thought of that. He's on an extended business trip. And you get one of the guys from the hotel to call you now and then to talk with you. Trust me, your mom will buy it."

"I don't know, Jenn."

"Trust me."

Meghann waited expectantly, scanning the travel-worn passengers exiting the terminal gate at the Colorado Springs Municipal Airport. Person after weary person emerged and donned a smile as their eyes met their waiting party.

The flow of people through the door stopped. No, that couldn't be everyone. Her mother would have called if she had missed the flight. She glanced nervously at her watch, straightened it on her wrist, then glanced back to the empty doorway. Her eyes darted around the crowded waiting area, searching face after unfamiliar face. Another small wave of travelers coming through the exit caught her attention. There, she saw a familiar form at the back of the group. She let out a sigh of relief when she caught her mother's gaze. At the sight of her daughter the smile in her mom's eyes spread across her weary face. The two embraced for a long moment.

"I was beginning to wonder if you were on the plane. I had almost given up," Meghann said, stepping back slightly. Though some of her mother's color had returned from when Meghann saw her a few weeks ago, she still looked drained.

"Everyone jumps up and tries to stampede off the plane as if the folks who came to meet them will be gone before they can get there. I wasn't afraid you would leave without me—" a teasing smile lifted her mother's lips—"at least not until you thoroughly searched the plane."

"And interrogated the crew." She became more serious. "You look good…better, anyway. How are you feeling?"

"I'm fit as a fiddle," Gayle Livingston said with upturned hands. "I've been given a clean bill of health."

Her tired eyes and haggard look belied that. "Mother…"

"Okay. I'm worn-out and cranky and could use a nap. Are you happy?" Her lips pulled into a thin line. "I know I will vastly improve just being away from those moody doctors and here with you and Bruce."

She let the reference to her nonexistent husband slide. For now. "I still can't believe your doctor okayed this trip so soon." She had toyed with the idea of moving back to Florida but couldn't bear to part with Colorado unless absolutely necessary. Springtime in the Rockies was beautiful when everything budded to life.

At first her mother had balked at Meghann's offer for her to come for a visit and rest but she had stood firm in insisting. Her mother would only overdo it again and wind up right back in the hospital. Finally, her mother had agreed, but Meghann's relief was short-lived when her mother also reminded her she had a husband her mom was eager to meet. Now she wondered at the wisdom of having her here.

"I'm supposed to get plenty of R&R, but you already know that. I won't lift a finger." She held out her carry-on bag to Meghann. "I'm prepared to be pampered," she finished with a regal air of sophistication.

Meghann took the bag and slung it over her shoulder, wrapping her other arm around her mother's slender shoulder. She could feel more bone than was healthy, but it was good to see her mother looking enthusiastic. If only it were for something real!

She looked down at her mother and said lightly, "To baggage claim?"

The older woman nodded, then looked forward and pointed. "To baggage claim." The two marched arm in arm through the terminal, winding in and out of the throngs and down the escalator. They stopped by carousel 4, where her mother's bags were scheduled to appear, and stood near the motionless conveyor belt.

Content didn't quite describe her mother's attitude, happy maybe. She looked like the cat that got the canary. "What's got you smiling so?"

"I thought maybe Bruce was parking the car and would meet us down here. Where is that husband of yours? Didn't he come with you? Or is he working late and will meet us at home?"

She couldn't avoid a direct question. "Yes, well, about Bruce. He's on a business trip." And that was actually the truth.

"Ooooh. I was looking forward to meeting him." The disappointment in her mother's voice tore at her heart. "I guess it will have to wait. When will he return?"

"I'm not exactly sure, but I wouldn't expect to see him while you're here." There. She hadn't lied…not really, and she'd still avoided the truth. Avoiding the truth was not the same as lying, was it?

"Mercy! I'm going to be here a whole month. He certainly won't be gone the entire time?"

"As assistant manager, he doesn't have a whole lot of say in the matter. Besides, it wouldn't be good for his career for him to say no." Meghann couldn't look her mother in the eye while she talked about Bruce, so she studied a kidney-shaped stain on the gray carpet. She glanced up when her mother spoke again.

"But does he really have to be gone the whole time I'm here? A whole month? Can't he sneak home for a few days? I'm beginning to think I'll never meet him!"

That's the plan, Mom. "I'll ask again. Maybe it can be arranged."

Her mother gave her an understanding smile. "Well at least you can tell me all about him."

Meghann let out a deep breath. "He's wonderful, Mom." More truth. Bruce's self-assured demeanor gave him the ability to calm most everyone's anxieties; nothing ever seemed to rattle him. He took even the most frustrating circumstances in stride, handling problems both big and small with grace and seeming ease. And he treated everyone, from the hotel's manager to the maids, with the same degree of respect and consideration.

He wouldn't ever have gotten himself into a situation like this. He certainly wouldn't have lied to his own mother....

A verse from Proverbs she had once memorized, jumped to the forefront of her mind. "The Lord detests lying lips but delights in men who are truthful."

The words pierced her heart, and she knew the Lord couldn't be too delighted with her at the moment. She turned to her mother, her mouth open, ready to confess. Then she looked into her worried, pale face, the frail hands and arms, and knew she couldn't. "Bruce would be here if he could, Mom. He tried everything to get out of going." She knew it wasn't going to be easy to evade her mother's persistent questioning but hadn't expected it to start before they even left the airport.

"I know. I just don't understand why they couldn't send someone else." The disappointment was evident in her voice. "Isn't it the manager who's supposed to take all the trips?"

"Mr. Phenton does go on some trips, but he doesn't like to travel and says it is good for Bruce to learn all he can about the hotel business."

Standing back from the crowd huddled around the motionless machine, they waited in strained silence. Then her mother excused herself to go to the restroom. Meghann reached for the offered claim stubs just in case the conveyor-belt beast decided to offer up the luggage. She watched her mother retreat into the crowd.

Her conscience pricked her to tell her mother the truth, but she pushed the notion away. What was the real harm anyway in letting her mom believe what she wanted to believe? It made her happy, and with any luck she would regain her strength. Then Meg would tell her.

And in the meantime, when her mother was so anxious to meet her husband? Well, it was not going to be easy to placate her, but Meg would do it. Somehow.

Lord, please heal her quickly and give me the strength to endure.

"Do you have the time, sir?"

"Quarter past six," Bruce Halloway said to the man passing by and grabbed his garment bag and briefcase.

As he hurried through the airport, a particular honey-blond caught his attention, her hair pulled back in a braided rope down her back. It took him only a moment to recognize her. He would know her anywhere, especially looking down. That's the way she looked at work behind the front desk when he would study her. She was also wearing that blue floral dress he liked so well. Though conservative, it flattered her figure. The warm place inside him that she had unknowingly claimed jumped to life.

He had fought the urge to date her because of his position as her boss. But he couldn't resist looking for other ways to spend time with her on the job. In the process, he'd found out they had a mutual love for the historic old hotel they both worked in.

That discovery came when he was on a search-and-seizure mission to locate some old hotel records. He was trying to recount the hotel's complete history. Meghann knew where she thought some old records could be and offered to show him where they were. Her eagerness to help him—or any of her coworkers no matter how detestable the task—piqued his interest. Her servant's heart mesmerized him to the point of distraction. He could have gotten directions from her and gone alone, but he couldn't pass up the opportunity to be with her.

The dim lighting in the musty room gave a dreamy aura to all that was there. While rummaging through dusty old boxes, they stumbled upon an aged scrapbook someone had kept on hotel events fifty-some years prior.

Meg gasped, and he'd turned to her, surprised at

the delight on her face. The fact that she was so excited at their find warmed him. They whiled away nearly an hour regarding the scraps of yesteryear's mementos. Page after yellowed page offered tokens of history, voices sounding across time, a library of bygone days. They stood with the book opened on a stack of cartons and sifted through the pages of time.

One such vintage page captured them both and Meghann squealed with delight. "A masquerade ball!"

Her enchanting voice awash with enthusiasm tickled his senses and stirred a deep longing in his heart. A longing that was fueled every time he was around her...and even when he wasn't.

Together they came up with a plan to resurrect the Palace Hotel's annual masquerade ball; a tradition that had ceased thirty years ago.

Laughing, letting themselves get lost in their inspiration, they'd thrown out ideas for decorations, invitations, and costumes.

He'd grinned at her glowing face. "What would you suggest for me? Something with chain mail and shiny steel? I always fancied myself a knight." He held his hand out in front of him as if he clutched a sword. "Saving damsels in distress." He was thinking of her tangle with a cat up a tree last fall.

Meg shook her head. "No distressed damsels for you." Her sweet voice brought him back. "You would be the regal prince presiding over the whole affair. Of course, there would be many maidens there, but none in need of rescuing. Your duties would fall to far duller things than slaying dragons. You would have the daunting task of entertaining and dancing with all the ladies."

If you were one of those ladies, I would dance with every last one to have the honor of dancing with you. "Then whom would you be? The fair Cinderella?"

A stillness settled around them in the hushed silence and she whispered, "Maybe."

Standing there, looking down at her, those brown-green eyes shining up at him, the urge to kiss her nearly took control of him. Instead, he swallowed and mustered the will to step back. "We should get back to work."

But the spell she had over him didn't diminish when they stepped from the past back into the present.

At thirty, his life was quite comfortable. He knew where he was going and what he wanted. The only thing lacking was someone to share his life and grow old together with. And Meghann seemed to be the one God kept bringing to mind. Or was it his heart? He wasn't completely sure…but this he knew, employee or not, he was going to ask her out and see where it would lead.

He strode over to her, now standing in the airport baggage claim. "Meghann Livingston."

She looked up with a start. Her eyes widened. "M-Mr. Halloway."

"Please we're not at work, call me Bruce." She just stared up at him, dazed, looking like she swallowed something wrong. Since the horrible scene that Charmaine caused at the Christmas party, Meghann had been cool toward him, and he had backed off on pursuing her. But it was a new day, and she stood before him as pretty as ever. Even though she didn't seem to know what to say to her employer outside of the hotel, he figured he would give a stab at small talk and work up to asking her out. "Have you been out of town, too?"

She looked down at the claim tickets in her hands. "No—these aren't mine," she said in a guilty tone, glancing off in the other direction, then back at him nervously. "My mother just came in."

He drew in a slow, even breath to hide his disappointment that she wasn't at least a *little* happy to see him. Had he wasted too much time and waited too long to ask her out? Maybe her interest in him had only been in his imagination…. "Where is she? I'd like to meet her." He scanned the crowded baggage claim area.

"No!"

He raised his eyebrows at her abruptness, and a dull red filled Meghann's slim cheeks.

"I mean, she went to the restroom. She's been ill and needs rest after her flight. I don't want to overtax her; besides, I don't want to keep you. I'm sure you are probably very busy, with a lot of things to do. I'll see you at work tomorrow, well, bye then."

Her words gushed out in one breath, and Bruce felt the need to breathe for her.

"You can go now."

Her firm words and determined, almost panicky, wide eyes left no doubt: this was a brush-off. He could take a hint when slapped in the face with it.

"Bruce?" a woman's voice called out to him. "Is that you?"

Meghann's eyes widened even more, which he

hadn't thought possible. "No! Tell her no!" She swung around, forcing a smile as she did so. Her sweet perfume greeted his senses, momentarily entrancing him.

His eyes searched out the unfamiliar voice and found an older woman approaching them. She had the same honey-blond hair as Meghann and was a couple of inches shorter—he guessed around five-foot-two. Bruce looked at the woman next to him. Unmistakably mother and daughter, except the younger Livingston had gone stark white.

Mrs. Livingston's joy-filled eyes lit on him with pride etched in her soft wrinkles. They were a mother's eyes. Even though he hadn't been introduced yet, he liked this woman. He saw no reason to deny who he was. What harm could there be in meeting Meghann's mother? Then he would grant her request to depart. "Yes. I'm Bruce Halloway."

"I *knew* it was you. Meg has told me so much about you. I think I could have picked you out in a crowd even if you weren't standing next to my daughter." Her eyes misted, and she pulled a tissue from her pocket to dab at them. "You don't know how much it means to me to have you here."

"Mom…" The single word held a heavy note of dread.

Meghann might not want him there, but he saw no reason to be rude to her mother. He put down his briefcase and garment bag and extended his hand to her. "I'm pleased to meet you, Mrs. Livingston."

"Please, call me Mom," Mrs. Livingston said proudly.

"Mom!"

At the strangled word, Bruce glanced at Meghann. She looked positively ill. And was now beet red. He turned his attention back to the older woman. Something was up. Just what, he wasn't sure. While one woman had clearly tried to get rid of him, the other was so happy to see him she was on the verge of tears. What could his employee possibly have said to her mother to make her so emotional about meeting him?

"At least call me Gayle," the older Livingston woman said. "We're family now."

Family?

He looked to Meghann for an explanation. She stared open-mouthed at her mother.

Apparently unaware of her daughter's discomfort, Gayle continued, "I was so disappointed when Meg said you would be away my entire visit. I knew you would make it if you were everything Meg said you were. And here you are. Do you mind if I give my new son-in-law a hug?"

"Mother!"

So that was it.

Understanding washed over Bruce. For some reason Meghann Livingston had told her mother they were married. He knew he should be put out. Even angry. But he wasn't.

Not even a little.

For one thing, he knew the kind of pressure parents, especially a mother, could put on a son...or daughter...to get married.

For another, he was inordinately pleased Meg had

chosen him. He managed to hold back a smile. Maybe he had a chance with her after all. He eyed the red-faced young woman, then turned back to her mother. "It would be my honor to give you a hug…Mom."

Two

MEGHANN CHEWED ON HER BOTTOM LIP AS SHE STARED AT the suitcases passing in front of her. Her knotted stomach told her that her little white lie was spinning out of control. Fast. She had to regain control without upsetting her mom. Mr. Halloway hadn't said anything yet, for that she was grateful, but tomorrow she would probably lose her job. She couldn't do what she'd done and not expect repercussions. He wasn't *ever* supposed to know about this. Ever!

She knew exactly how he felt when he found out they were supposedly married because she had had the same sinking, confused feeling. Maybe if she explained it all—well, almost all—he would understand. How could she have let Jennifer talk her into this?

Simple? This was anything but simple.

Recognizing a bag coming toward her, she reached out for it.

"Let me get that for you." The deep voice caressed her ear, and all her senses came alert, her flesh tingling at his nearness.

She looked up into Bruce Halloway's smiling face. He reached around her and grabbed the handle of the suitcase before the conveyer carried it away. As he leaned past her, she stared at his short wavy brown hair as his woodsy cologne, the smell of outdoors, wafted passed her nose.

"Thank you." She barely managed the words around the humiliation. The butterflies swarming inside her fluttered and for an instant as their eyes connected she wished her lie could come true.

"You're welcome. Any others?"

"One more, larger than this." She couldn't bear to look at him any longer. She could only imagine what he must think of her. How was she going to get out of this? She could confess and risk her mother relapsing but shuddered at the thought. It was too soon. She had to tell her mother something to get Mr. Halloway off the hook—fast.

"Mr. Halloway, I'm so sorry for this…misunderstanding."

"Now, you really should call me Bruce. After all, we *are* married." A smile pulled at the corners of his mouth, softening his strong jaw. Did *anything* catch him off guard or ruffle his feathers?

"I can explain."

He made a tsking noise. "A wife shouldn't keep such secrets from her husband."

How could he tease her at a time like this? This was serious. "Please let me explain."

"I look forward to every word of your explanation. I'll bet it's quite entertaining. Is this one your mother's?"

he asked, reaching for the matching suitcase.

How could he be so calm in the face of calamity? At the question, another frenzied situation came to her mind....

She'd found herself in the middle of a scrap between two guests' pets: a kitten and a corgi. A wild chase had ended up with her balancing on a stepladder and reaching up a tree for the terrified kitten. But the creature's hissing and claws hadn't been on her mind. No, what she'd been thinking was why couldn't the angry beast have picked any *other* tree? Why the one in front of this window? The window to Mr. Halloway's office! She'd hoped desperately that her boss was otherwise occupied.

No such luck.

He showed up and had taken control with ease, calming all the agitated guests and even seeing to Meg's scratches—her thanks for saving the panicked kitten. It was so like him to fix everything so everyone was happy.

And his gentle ministrations to her wounds ministered to her heart as well. She had hoped it would be a turning point for them and he would ask her out, but he didn't. She supposed it was wise of him not to fraternize with a subordinate.

"You aren't going to say anything to my mother then?" she asked, coming back to her current dilemma.

Gazing into her upturned face, he winked at her. "Your secret is safe with me."

"Thank you. I promise to think of something to get you out of this mess."

As he bent down to get the suitcases, she thought

she heard him softly say, "No rush."

He hoisted the two bags and returned to her mother. He lifted his garment bag over his shoulder, tucked his briefcase under one arm, and gripped the two suitcase handles firmly. "Which way to the car, kitten?"

She looked up at him sharply, his smile endearing with a teasing glint in his eyes.

Kitten?

"I-I thought you…had to…to go into work? Shall we drop you off at the hotel?" There. That would get him out of this. She breathed a sigh of relief.

"Heavens, no. Work can wait until tomorrow. Family is more important than shuffling a few papers, darling." He gave her another charming smile.

Darling? For the life of her she couldn't figure out why he was playing along. All she could do was stare at him and drink in his alluring smile.

Her mother interrupted her thoughts. "You may be as surprised to see your husband as I am, but you can gawk at him at home. His arms are going to drop off if he stands there much longer."

"Oh, yeah, the car. This way." She shook off the romantic cobwebs in her mind as she picked up her mom's carry-on bag and headed for the parking garage, leaving Bruce and her mother to follow in her wake.

This couldn't be happening to her. This was a dream—No, a nightmare!—and she was going to wake up. How had she gotten herself into such a mess? Who would have known one little, itty, bitty, tiny lie would turn into this? Now it was out of control.

This *was* a nightmare.

She heard voices behind her and remembered she was ignoring the people with her. She slowed her pace to let them catch up. The smell of exhaust fumes inside the dim parking structure turned her already turbulent stomach. Or was it this whole, fabricated situation that had put knots there?

"You saved my life, you know," her mother was saying to Bruce.

"How did I manage that?"

Meghann fell into step beside her mother, desperately wondering what she could do to stem her mother's words.

The answer was clear: absolutely nothing.

"Cutting the engagement short. Rushing the wedding. I just wish I could have been there. The doctors said my chances of making it were quite slim. But you already know that. Meg told me it was your idea to marry before she came out to see me in the hospital. It put my mind at ease to know she had a good man to take care of her. Then I thought about the grandchildren I would never see. I'm convinced wanting to see my grandchildren pulled me through." She looked up at Bruce with a mischievous grin. "I'd like to order up half a dozen, one to be delivered within the year, maybe?"

"Mother!"

"You have talked about children, haven't you?" She turned to Meghann. "How can I be a doting grandmother with no grandchildren to dote over?"

"We're going to wait a while," she said through gritted teeth and rolled her eyes.

"With the wedding being so hurried we thought it would be best to wait before having children," Bruce added. "I'm traveling a lot right now. When my job settles down, I promise we will discuss it. I don't want Meg to go through a pregnancy by herself."

"I have something to say about your traveling." Her mother waved her index finger in the air.

"Mother!"

"It's not healthy for a newly married couple to be apart so much." She held her hands up in front of her. "That's all I wanted to say. I won't bring it up again."

"Here's the car." Meghann pointed to her seven-year-old cream Honda, then glanced up at Bruce. His smile told her he was still taking this all in stride. Calm, cool, and collected, while she was a nervous wreck inside. They couldn't have reached her car any sooner for her sanity.

Meghann opened the trunk for him, then the front passenger door for her mother. When her mother was seated, she went back to help Bruce with the bags. He put in his garment bag, then closed the trunk.

"All set," he said, turning to her with a devastating smile. "You going to drive or shall I?"

She took a quick breath to give strength to her weakened knees. His smile distracted her to no end. "I-I'll drive. I'm afraid that only leaves the backseat."

"That suits me fine." He held open her door for her, then climbed in the back and stretched his long legs across the back seat floor—filling it as completely as he'd filled her thoughts and heart.

"I should be the one sitting back there."

Meg's mother looked over her shoulder at Bruce, and he marveled again at how much she and Meg resembled one another.

"Nonsense. I'm quite comfortable. I'm just going to get a little shut-eye, if you two don't mind me being so rude." He folded his arms and leaned back against the corner where the door and seat met. "It was a long flight." He yawned and closed his eyes.

Bruce listened to the two women in the front seat. No, he wasn't tired. He feigned sleep to collect his thoughts and keep his supposed mother-in-law from asking him something he couldn't answer. Like when were they married, or where did they meet? He could answer the easy stuff like favorite color or flower. He had found out as much about Meghann as he could without her knowledge. But if her mother asked something more personal like shoe size or, heaven forbid, a birthmark only a husband would know about. No, he couldn't risk it.

Why did you risk getting involved at all?

He frowned at the question. To help Meg, of course…to avoid humiliating her in front of her mother.

By lying?

By playing along. He hadn't told any lies…not really. He just hadn't come out with the truth.

A sin of omission is still a sin….

It was too late to back out now. If he was going to do so, he should have at the beginning. It would hurt both women if he changed his story now. No, better to go along, at least for now.

But even as he presented his case, he knew it wasn't the whole truth. There was something more to his involvement in this charade. It opened the door to something he'd longed for: the chance to get to know Meghann.

As her supposed husband, he could do what he longed to do for so long. He could hold her hand whenever he wanted, or caress her cheek. He could test the waters, so to speak, find out if he was right about the nudgings he thought he was getting from the Lord that Meghann was the woman for him.

If things went the way he thought they would, then this masquerade would just be a preamble to the real thing.

He had instantly liked Mrs. Livingston with her smiling eyes. And maybe his helping out would go a long way in the young Miss Livingston's forgetting the incidence with Charmaine at the Christmas party and his quick unavoidable departure.

His thoughts drifted back to that day. The party had been the perfect opportunity to approach Meghann. Her shift was over and he'd invited her out for dinner. He hadn't counted on Charmaine Altman showing up, playing her petty games again to trap him. Nor had he anticipated that Meghann would get caught in the crossfire.

Then George had delivered the bad news of yet another unwanted trip. Only because it was utterly vital for the hotel had Bruce agreed. He lost a prime chance to take Meghann out and spend time with her. And Charmaine couldn't have timed her little mishap any better if she had known Meghann would open the door at that exact moment.

He prayed during his flight that Meg would let him explain and would understand. He started to write her a letter several times but knew he had to apologize face-to-face. Between his travel and her extended vacation, he managed to squeeze in a brief apology. It in no way made up for the misunderstanding. She accepted it, but he wasn't convinced she really believed him. Now three and a half months later, the look on her face still haunted him.

If only he hadn't had to rush off on that business trip, things could have been different for them. If only he had found her to explain. If only Charmaine hadn't shown up, playing her petty little games. If only...if only...

With the traveling completed and things calm at the hotel, he'd hoped to finally make it up to her. She must think him such a cad. When he saw the look on her face at the airport, he hadn't thought twice. He'd jumped in, wholeheartedly. She'd gotten herself into a fix, and he would do all he could to help out. It was the right thing to do, wasn't it?

Really? The right thing to do? In whose eyes?

He pushed the thought away with a slight shake of his head. From what he'd picked up, Meg had told her little tale about them for a pretty good reason. The least he could do was go along with it. For now.

And if at the same time he could get to know her better, and she him, then that was even better. Who knew, by the end of her mother's visit he might even manage to win Meghann over.

At least, he hoped so.

Three

NORMALLY, MEGHANN LOOKED FORWARD TO ARRIVING home. Two huge elm trees dwarfed her cozy one bed-room rental cottage, blanketing her yard with shade in the summer but offering very little shade now. The early signs of the new buds were beginning to show. In the fall when everyone else complained of all the leaves to rake, she relished it. From her two elms and even some of the neighbor's leaves, she had plenty to make a pile big enough to jump in. Azalea and rhododendron bushes along with other higher bushes and shrubbery formed a fence, and she was able to imagine herself in the country except for the traffic noise. It was her mini-sanctuary.

Today was different. Today her mother and her make-believe husband were both coming home with her. Talk about having your worst nightmare come true....

Meghann's unease grew as she pulled into her gravel driveway. Now what? She parked the car and the trio stepped out.

"I'll get the bags while you unlock the door."

She nodded at Bruce's seemingly casual words. The look in his eyes confirmed what she'd thought: He was trying to be as cautious and strategic about this as he could be. He didn't want to give her away.

After unlocking the trunk, she went and opened the gate. Across the yard bounded a big black blur. Oh, no! How could she have forgotten about Lucky? The Labrador came to a halt, barked twice, then wagged her tail.

"Hello, girl."

The happy canine wagged her way over to her owner. Meghann scratched her head, praying the dog wouldn't give Bruce away. As friendly as Lucky was with people she knew, strangers sometimes made the Lab nervous.

"Say hello to Mom, Lucky," she said, purposefully using the dog's name for Bruce's benefit. Lucky wiggled over to Mrs. Livingston and jumped up on the older woman.

"Off, Lucky." Meghann tried to nudge her away with her knee. "Get off."

"Off!" Bruce's voice was stern and low. Obediently, the dog turned toward him.

Meghann had gotten Lucky to be sort of a sentry, but this was one time she didn't want to be guarded. She was about to say something when Bruce's next command came.

"Sit!"

Lucky instantly obeyed. Her tail continued to wag, brushing across the brittle winter grass.

The dog's response amazed Meghann. All that time and money spent on obedience training and she had never gotten that quick of a reaction. Maybe if she had put more heart into it and kept up with it instead of letting it slide, Lucky would obey her as well. Meghann watched, fighting a surprising twinge of jealousy, as Lucky stared up at Bruce with wide, attentive eyes.

"She certainly knows who's boss around here," Meghann's mother said.

A weak smile pulled at Meghann's mouth.

Bruce lowered the suitcases to the ground. Lucky eased up but stopped with another firm word from Bruce. "Stay."

The Lab wiggled in anticipation. When he had put his load down, Bruce knelt three feet in front of the smiling dog, who looked like she was going to jump out of her skin.

Bruce waited a moment longer, eye-to-eye with the canine, before releasing her. "Good girl," he said in an even, calm tone. "Okay, come."

The Labrador shot off her spot and bounded toward the man, knocking him over and licking his face.

Meghann was aghast. But Bruce just laughed and wrestled the happy, energetic dog for a minute. She couldn't help smiling at the playful pair.

"That's enough," Bruce said. "Sit."

Lucky sat, awaiting her next order.

Bruce rose and brushed the dog hair and dry grass off his expensive looking suit. Meghann hoped it wasn't ruined. Of course, she'd pay to have it dry-cleaned, but she fought a groan at the idea of having to pay for a new suit.

This little charade was turning costly. On many fronts.

"Your dog missed you," Mom said. "I think she would like her *daddy* to be around more."

"Mother!" Meghann spoke to her mother's back as she hurried up the porch steps. Meghann felt the heat rush to her face. *Daddy?* Reluctantly, she turned to see Mr. Halloway's reaction. His head was ducked down and she could swear the man was doing his best to hide a smile. Well, at least somebody could smile about all this. She was too mortified to comment and simply unlocked the door in silence.

"I like him," her mother whispered so only Meghann could hear, then stepped over the threshold. "I couldn't have chosen a better son-in-law myself."

Meghann rolled her eyes. Good heavens. How on earth was she going to keep her mother from making such comments with Mr. Halloway around? She had to get rid of him before her mother totally embarrassed him. And her. He had been a good sport to go along with this charade so far, but she couldn't expect him to do it indefinitely.

Not that you'd want him to…right?

Of course not! The last thing she needed was Bruce Halloway in her home, acting like he cared about her, smiling at her like she meant something to him.…

Liar. You love it.

Pressing her lips together, Meghann went inside. The small bedroom and dinky bathroom were off of the cozy living room. From any one spot the whole interior could be viewed. The furnishings were by Goodwill, garage sales, and curbside rejects. With a little paint everything matched, more or less. Some red and yellow fabric to cover what couldn't be painted finished off the cheerful decor.

Bruce came in behind them, hauling the luggage. "Where do you want these?"

"My mom's suitcases go in the bedroom." Meghann crossed the room and opened the bedroom door. Thankfully she had made her bed this morning. Bruce took the bags in and did a quick surveillance of the room.

"I can't take your room, honey. Where will the two of you sleep?"

As far from each other as possible.

"I'll be fine on the couch," her mother finished.

"Mom, you will not sleep on the couch. It's not very comfortable, and you need your rest. Doctor's orders." Besides, sharing a bedroom with Bruce Halloway was definitely out of the question! This little charade could only go so far, for heaven's sake.

Her mom opened her mouth to protest but was stopped by Bruce's voice directly behind Meghann. "We insist you take the bedroom. We won't take no for an answer." When Bruce said *we* the first time, he put his hands on her shoulders; with the second he had given her shoulders a gentle squeeze. His touch sent a little ripple through her.

As quickly as the dog had obeyed, so had her mother. Did he always get his way? She knew she worked extra hard to complete any tasks he gave her, as many others at the hotel did. He had merely to suggest something needed to be done and people fell over each other to do it, some making real ninnies of themselves. He was just the kind of guy people wanted to please.

But how far would Meghann go to please him?

Later that evening, Meghann grew tired of her suppose-to-be protector lapping up every bit of attention Bruce Halloway gave her. "Come on, Lucky. It's time for you to go outside for a while." She patted her hip and headed for the door.

Lucky jumped up and trotted two feet toward the door, then turned back to Bruce and gave a little whine.

Oh, brother. Now *her* dog was asking his permission!

Bruce looked up from where he sat in an over-stuffed chair, his briefcase open on the floor before him. "Go on, Lucky," he said, pointing toward the door.

Meghann went out with Lucky to check her food and water. Lucky raced around the yard, then stopped by her owner and nudged her hand.

Meghann knelt down and scratched the dog behind the ears with both hands. "Some watchdog you are. A stranger comes in the yard, and you beg for his attention. Are you trying to impress him? Flirting per-haps?" She sighed. "Or is it because you've heard me talk so much about Mr. Halloway that you feel like you already know him?"

She settled back on the grass, shaking her head. "I have really gotten myself into a pickle. Who would have thought one little lie could become so complicated?"

"Your refuge looks strong, but since it is made of lies...the enemy will come like a flood to sweep it away...."

The words struck home and Meghann blinked against sudden tears. What had she done? How could she have talked herself into this mess? Whatever made her think that lying could bring about any good?

Lord, I'm in so deep here. What can I do?

The Lab's ears perked up as she looked past Meghann and bound away, sending her sprawling.

"Sit. Stay." There was no mistaking the deep, lulling voice. And here she was in a dress, sitting in the grass. Bruce was at her side in a heartbeat. When he reached over to help, she noticed how strong and masculine his hand felt as it swallowed hers. Bruce pulled her to her feet, then walked her over to the towering elm tree in the middle of the still brown-yellow yard.

"How do you get her to obey so quickly?" This was good, a delay from a more serious matter they needed to discuss. She couldn't put it off forever, but for now she would take the reprieve.

"When a dog jumps up most people say *down*, which is the command to get a dog to lie down. You said *off*, which is the correct command, so I assumed you had taken her to obedience school."

"How come when I ask her to do something she ignores me?"

A smile tugged at his mouth. "Your answer, my dear, is in your question."

Her heart quickened at his endearment, but she clamped down on the pleasure sweeping through her.

He probably calls lots of women 'dear.' It's probably only a friendly, casual gesture that means nothing at all to him. If she could only convince her pounding heart of that, maybe she could remember to breathe. "It is?"

"You *ask*, ever so sweetly, I might add. Lucky is not ignoring you; she is simply answering you with a definite no. Like a child, she must be told what to do, firm but kind."

He gave the dog a few commands in demonstration, and then coached Meghann to do the same until Lucky obeyed her almost as quickly as him. "They say 80 percent of training a dog is training the owner."

"How do you know so much? Do you have a dog too or something?" She realized how little she knew about this man.

"Or something." He smiled and hesitated a moment. "I once dated a dog trainer. She wouldn't go out with me until I learned the basics."

"Oh." She looked down, not meaning to pry, but wondered if he always got what he wanted. From what she had seen, he did.

"Hey, don't look so bothered. It was a long time ago." He stepped closer, taking her hand in his, their fingers laced together.

"W-what are you doing?" Emotions swept over her at the intimate connection, at the way their hands seemed to fit together so perfectly. Swallowing hard, struggling to get control of her jumping pulse, she backed away—right against the mighty elm trunk.

With an easy smile Bruce rested his forearm on a low branch beside her, boxing her in. Did he sense her impulse to flee? "Meghann." His voice was low, deep…and about as beguiling as anything she'd ever heard.

Oh, help!

He tugged on her hand gently. "We need to talk."

She knew that. But for the life of her, she couldn't respond. It wasn't what she had to say that was unsettling her. As a matter of fact, she couldn't really remember *what* they needed to talk about! No, it was how close they were—the warmth of his hand on hers, the sweetness of his breath fanning her cheek—that was sending her senses spinning.

She made a lame effort to free her hand. It was a token tug, just enough to show protest but not enough to succeed. How long she had waited and wished for this kind of interaction with him. But this was just all too strange—too sudden and unexpected. Besides, they weren't alone. Her mother was here.

Her mother and Bruce. Under the same roof!

Jennifer, what have you gotten me into?

No, not Jennifer. Meg was honest enough to admit she'd done this to herself. But what she didn't know was how one dealt with a situation like this. How did one cope? How could she calm her racing heart? She never planned to have her mother and a fake husband to deal with. Her mother was going to be hard enough. Actually she never planned any of this, it all sort of happened. First the nurse, then her mother and Jennifer, and now Bruce was tangled up in her deception. Where would it all end? It certainly couldn't get any more complicated than this.

Lord, help me cope with this bizarre situation.

He raised their intertwined hands with a little squeeze. "I hope you don't mind—" he looked from their hands back to her face—"Your mom may see us. If it were my mother, she would peek out more than once. I'm assuming we want to give the illusion of a happy couple? Unless we are having troubles. But then if you went to all the trouble to fabricate a marriage, it should be a happy one, and your husband would, of course, be perfect. I will do my best to fulfill that role—" he dipped his head in a token bow—"and keep up the image of a happily married couple. Any objections so far?"

His mischievous smile told her he was teasing, and she could feel her face flush. The only objection she had was that it wasn't real.

"So, tell me how I came to be the son-in-law of that charming woman inside?" He raised his eyebrows. "Unless you know another Bruce Halloway who looks just like me? I assume I am the Bruce Halloway you told your mother about."

He was definitely *the* one. Meghann could feel her cheeks heat more, if that was possible. If only she could sink into the ground and hide…just how red had her face become? She couldn't be any more embarrassed and so took a deep breath and began. "When I was ten my father died."

The smile faded from Bruce's face, and she saw earnest regret in his eyes. "I'm sorry." His sincerity loosened some of the knots in her nervous stomach. Compassion was something she could use right now. And understanding…a lot of understanding.

"Mom never remarried. There was insurance money for us to live on but not enough. We always managed to get by, though. We were a real team." She smiled remembering all the ways she and her mother had scraped along, making ends meet. They'd been each other's world for a lot of years. "I loved being at home, but the time came when I needed to leave, to be on my own. Understandably, it really bothered my mom to have me move away. We were close and still are. She kept pestering me about who I was dating and when I was going to settle down and get married. So I..." She cleared her throat, shifting, afraid to meet his gaze. "I finally had had it with her questions and the fifth degree every time I called, so I made something up to appease her."

His dark brows arched slightly. "Something?"

"Yes, well, I told her I was dating someone."

The brows rose another fraction. "Someone?"

This really was too much! Bad enough to have to tell him all this, but the way he was watching her, with that teasing gleam in his eyes.... She perched her free hand on her hip and shifted from one foot to another, feeling uncomfortably like a child caught in a prank.

"Fine. You. I told her I was dating you. I'm sorry, I didn't mean to use you or lie about it, but she sounded so worried and I'd just reached the end of my rope. I saw you every day at work and...well...your name just came out. But it was just to put her mind at rest! She's really lonely without me around, and she's so worried I'll be alone." Meghann was horrified to hear the quaver in her voice. She was not going to cry! "I just want to make her happy."

The nonjudgmental look in his eyes put her at ease a little as she went on. "I was about to tell her that we— I mean, that my pretend boyfriend and I were breaking up when she suddenly became ill, and this nurse overheard something I said to the doctor and completely misunderstood." She shook her head. "There she was, congratulating me in front of my mom on my recent marriage. Mom was so happy; her eyes were alight with hope…it was the first spark of energy I'd seen in her. So I let her believe it—just for a little while until she was stronger, then I'd tell her the truth. I figured it wasn't hurting anyone, and it was actually helping her, so I let it go on."

She couldn't stand the tenderness she saw in his eyes, or the slight smile on his generous lips, so she looked down at her feet, hurrying to finish her explanation.

"I know I should have told her the truth, if not before then certainly when we met at the airport. But I'm just so afraid…." This last admission came out on a hoarse whisper, and Meghann fell silent, struggling with the tears that wanted to overcome her.

"Afraid?"

At his gentle prodding, she looked up and met his gaze. "I don't want to lose her. I'm afraid if I confess now the shock will be too much for her; she may even relapse. She may seem strong, but she's not. Not really. I can see how tired and frail she is beneath that smiling image she puts out." An errant tear finally escaped, and Bruce caressed it away as she drew in a shuddering breath. "I didn't see the harm in continuing. It's already helped her so much. I never thought for one minute you would get caught up in this."

He started to speak, but she held up her hand, hurrying on. "But don't worry; I have a plan. Tomorrow you can get called away on another business trip and simply don't return. Mom's happy just having met you."

Bruce was silent for a moment, and she wondered what he was thinking. Probably that she was a scatter-brained nitwit.

"I can play the doting husband and son-in-law for a while," he finally said. "How long is your mother staying?"

What? Did she hear him right? He actually wanted to continue to go along with this farce? Her fantasy image of him would, of course, play along...the imaginary Bruce would sweep her into his arms and make everything right...even propose to her for real. But this was the *real* person. He wouldn't be able to or want to play along as long as her mother was to be here. "A month." He would change his mind now. That was okay. She was touched by his offer anyway.

"Oh, a whole month." His voice had a thoughtful tone to it. He was quiet for a few moments, probably trying to figure a way to get out of it. She would let him off the hook.

"I think I could arrange that."

She blinked several times. Had he really said what she thought he'd said or was she just imagining it? "You...you can't be serious."

"Sure, why not?" He shrugged his shoulders.

Why would be a better question. "Why would you

do this for me?" Bruce hesitated and glanced away. When he looked back at her, he seemed to be choosing his words with great care.

"I have a mother, too," he said simply.

Duh. "Don't we all."

He smiled. "What I'm saying is that I understand how much pressure a mother can put on a child to get married and settle down."

Meghann frowned. This just didn't make sense. He should be running for the door, frantic to get out of this mess. "I'm sorry if your mother is as pushy as mine, but that doesn't—"

"Look, Meg." He released her hand and took a step back. "I'm doing this for reasons I'd rather not say right now." He ran a weary hand down his face. "Let's leave it at that."

A multitude of questions assaulted her as she stood there, staring at him. Why would a man like Bruce Halloway possibly want to go along with her idiotic farce? And why didn't he want to tell her his reasons?

Maybe he's in some kind of trouble. What do you really know about the man, anyway? Or maybe he's setting you up…creating an IOU to cash in later?

She dismissed the cynical thoughts. Bruce wasn't like that. She was sure of it. Then why…?

There's always the remote possibility that he harbors some feelings for you.

Her eyes widened a fraction. That possibility, remote or not, sparked hope in her.

His hand reclaiming hers jarred her out of her thoughts. "Now suppose you fill me in on our meeting and courtship. I want every last detail."

She swallowed hard, remembering all she'd told her mother.... Had she actually thought her humiliation was complete? How silly of her.

It was just beginning.

Four

"Mom, you need to get quality rest. You can't get it on the couch. This thing is not comfortable." Meghann's mom still hadn't gone to bed, and it was getting late. She knew her mother had to be tired from her flight and needed rest.

"But where will you two sleep? It makes more sense for me to be out here."

No, nothing about this made sense.

"It will be a bit crowded with all three of us on it," Bruce said, standing beside Meghann with his arm hooked around her waist.

"I meant you two should have your bed." Mom glared at Bruce with a don't-get-smart-with-me-young-man look.

"No. We've already made up our minds. We've got first dibs. It's up to you whether or not you take the bed, but if you don't, you'll have to scout out your own floor space."

Her mother threw up her hands. "You win, but I don't have to be happy about it."

Bruce smiled at the older Livingston woman then leaned forward to kiss her on the forehead. "We'll figure out something better tomorrow. I promise."

Yeah, like you taking a sudden extended business trip! Meghann smiled at the thought.

"I'm going to hold you to that promise." With that, her mother disappeared into the bedroom and shut the door.

Meghann quickly turned away to make up the couch before he turned around.

"Does this fold out?" His whisper was right behind her.

She unfolded one of the blankets that had been piled on the chair. What was he thinking about all of this? "No." She hoped he didn't notice the slight quiver in her voice.

"That will make things interesting." He helped her smooth the blanket.

"You can have the couch, Mr. Halloway." Meghann spoke in the same hushed tone he was using. She added the *Mr. Halloway* to remind herself who he really was. "I'll sleep on the floor."

He clasped her hand. "I can't let you do that."

She froze, not knowing what to say. If he envisioned anything more than a curt good night, he was in for a surprise. She might be in a bind, but she wasn't *that* desperate. Pulling her hand free, she grabbed up the other bedding and spread it out on the floor away from the couch.

Before she knew it, Bruce came up behind her, swept her up in his arms, and deposited her, sputtering and speechless, on the couch. Then he retrieved the blanket and pillow from the other side of the room, laid them on the floor parallel with the couch, and stretched out. "Good night, *Miss Livingston.*"

"Good night." She laid her head back, noting his use of her surname.

She glanced down at him, taking in the stiffness in his back, feeling miserable. He was probably mad at her now. He'd been so kind, so willing to help her out, and how had she repaid him? By being curt and suspicious.

He had her so confused every time he looked at her with those molten brown eyes or smiled at her; and his touch sent shock waves through her scrambling brain. He easily made her forget that her mother's health and a rapidly building lie had brought them together and nothing more. She had only spent a few hours with him, and she was already incapable of thinking straight. What would more time bring? Complete brain failure? If she didn't watch her step—or in this case, her emotions—she would be throwing herself in his arms before the week was out.

He was most definitely going on a business trip—tomorrow!

Meghann dried the mirror with the towel that had moments ago been wrapped around her head. She ran her brush through her wet hair. She had to figure out how to walk out of the bathroom with no makeup, her hair wet, dressed only in her robe, and act like it was perfectly natural with a man in her house who slept only a few feet from her last night.

He was so close she could hear him breathe, yet far enough away to be safe. She had lain there thinking about him and the fix she was in. The fix she'd gotten them both into. How had it all gotten so complicated, so out of control? One little lie: "Yes, Mom, I have a boyfriend." Now she was playing house with a man she liked but really didn't know that well.

She felt guilty enough for lying to her mother. But those feelings were quadrupled when she let herself think how she'd gotten her boss—her *boss*, for heaven's sake!—caught up in this. If only he hadn't shown up at the airport....

Fifteen minutes one way or the other and their paths wouldn't have crossed. All he'd had to do was take a slightly different route.... All she'd had to do was go to the restroom with her mother.... Why couldn't she have accompanied her mother, then Bruce would have kept walking and no one would be the wiser. Simple decisions that had resulted in disaster.

Why, Lord? Why has something so small and harmless grown so unbelievably complex and overwhelming?

"The wrath of God is being revealed from heaven against all...who suppress the truth..."

Meg stared at herself in the mirror. God's wrath. Had she brought that on herself? Was she only getting what she deserved for her deception?

But I did it for my mom....

You did it for yourself.

She looked away. No point in arguing about it. What was done was done. There wasn't anything she could do about it now except keep up this act.

She pulled her thick lavender robe tight around her and eased open the door, wanting to know where he was before she waltzed out. She couldn't hear his voice or see him. All she saw was her mother curled up on the end of the couch reading while sipping a cup of tea.

"Where's Bruce?" She hoped to make the question casual but her tone sounded forced even to her own ears.

Her mother looked up. "He left a few minutes ago, and said he would see you later."

"Oh." Meghann darted into her bedroom and dressed. She put on her makeup in record time and wolfed down a bowl of cereal. She was at work a full half hour early and paced in the newly remodeled employee lounge. It wasn't that she wanted to be at work so soon; the fact was she was avoiding her mom. She felt more and more guilty about lying and was afraid of what her mom might ask her about Mr. Halloway. Questions she couldn't answer but should be able to. It was easier when she only had to remember her own lies. Now she had to match his as well. Where was the simplicity in this?

She wondered if he was here at the hotel. How would he act toward her? She was so wrapped up in her thoughts that she almost arrived late at the front desk.

Meghann had been at work for nearly two hours when Mr. Halloway—she had to make herself think of him that way now—passed by the front desk and did a double take. He frowned as he strode over with purpose. No doubt that purpose was her. She shifted uneasily. No doubt about it: she was in for it. He was going to tell her what a flake she was.

"Ms. Livingston, I'd like to see you in my office."

Here it came. She smiled up at him, doing her best to exude confidence and graciousness. "Now?"

"If you're not too busy." A shadow of annoyance crossed his face.

She glanced down the length of the empty counter. Where was the swarm of guests when you needed them? "No."

He walked across the lobby to the door leading to the offices and waited for her.

"Oooh, you're in trouble now," her coworker Peter said in a low voice. "I wonder what he wants to see you about."

Meghann had a good idea and swallowed hard. She would undoubtedly get a tongue-lashing for marrying him without his knowledge but she sure couldn't tell Peter that. She just shrugged her shoulders and followed in Bruce Halloway's wake.

He held open the door for her, motioning for her to go first down the hall. She stopped at his office door and started to reach for the knob but pulled back. In her hesitation he reached around her to open it and let her enter ahead of him.

Walking behind his uncluttered, massive mahogany desk, he waited for her to sit before easing himself into his burgundy leather chair. From a drawer he pulled out a file and began surfing through the pages, shaking his head. She sat there, tapping her fingers on her wrist, jiggling her foot, feeling for the entire world like a kid who'd been sent to the principal's office. She felt the flutter of butterflies congregating in her stomach.

Why didn't he just get it over with? The waiting had to be worse than what was to come. Though he really didn't have much right to be mad at her. He had refused her offer out. Maybe a night on her hard floor had changed his mind. If not, she would insist on him feigning a trip. She would stand up for herself and hope she didn't get fired.

When he leaned back in his chair, studying her, her small measure of courage nearly evaporated. "What am I going to do with you?" The corners of his mouth turned up slightly.

Caught off guard by his question and light demeanor, she stared back at him. "Do with me?"

"Do you know what this is?" He held up the file he had perused a moment before.

She shook her head.

"Next week's schedule."

She frowned. Had he really called her in to discuss the schedule?

"You're working all week."

So? She *always* worked the day shift, Monday through Friday.

"Do you have any time off while your mother is here?"

Why did he sound so irritated? "Just…just my normal days off."

"Why don't you take your vacation time while your mother is visiting?"

"I took all my vacation days when my mom was in the hospital. I've also used up all my personal days and my sick days. I don't have any time left to take."

Bruce shook his head. "I'm finding someone to replace you."

Meghann leaned forward. "Please, Mr. Halloway, I *need* this job!"

"I'm not firing you," he said gently. "Just getting someone to fill in for you this afternoon. You will have every day off while your mother is here."

"I can't. I've already taken all the time I'm allowed."

"What kind of son-in-law would I be if I couldn't get my wife time off while her ailing mother was in town?" He spoke as if he were addressing an errant child. She felt like an errant child. "No arguments. You will take the time." He wasn't angry with her for her lie, only irritated at her lack of time with her mother. A puzzling man indeed.

Meghann bent her head down, then looked him in the eyes. She had to put a stop to this. "I can't, Mr. Halloway. I can't afford to have that much time off."

His expression changed from irritation to compassion. "You will be paid your regular wage. And what happened to calling me Bruce?"

"Mr. Phenton would never allow it."

"Which, the pay or the name?"

She grimaced. "Probably neither one."

His chuckle was low and resonant and filled her senses as completely as it filled the room. "I'll talk to George. And I have the owner's ear. It won't be a problem, trust me."

This whole thing was already a bigger problem than she ever imagined. But the owner? What would Bruce tell him or her? *"The ding-a-ling we put in charge of the front desk needs a month off to straighten out her personal life."* And he not only had met the mysterious new owner but also was evidently chummy with him.

"Mr. Hallo—" she stopped at the abrupt raise of his brow. She couldn't help it with him seated behind that huge mahogany desk, he just looked more like a Mr. Halloway than Bruce.

"Bruce." It felt strange to be so familiar with him at work. "Time off really isn't necessary. My mom needs rest more than anything, not me hanging around. I don't want the new owner to think I'm unreliable."

"A compromise then. You come in a few hours each day and we can tie up any loose ends on the masquerade ball. Then you can take the rest of the day guilt-free."

Guilt-free? It took all Meghann's will not to laugh out loud. Not likely.

The bell jingled over the door as Meghann entered the small computer repair shop where Jennifer worked. There was a computer and two monitors on the counter, and inside the glass front counter were computer guts she supposed. Various other computer parts and debris cluttered the floor along the far wall.

A six foot, three-hundred-and-something pound sandy blond hulk with a beer belly hanging over his belt stepped out from the back room. This must be Dan.

Meg had heard Jennifer speak of him and her other boss.

Dan plucked the donut from his mouth and smiled. "May I help you?"

"I was looking for Jennifer Zimmerman."

He disappeared into the back, and a moment later Jennifer popped through the doorway. "Meg! What brings you here? No, wait, it doesn't matter." She waved her hand, then called toward the back room, "I'm going to lunch."

Dan appeared again and looked at his watch. "It's a little late for lunch."

"The book work is almost done, and I'll finish the invoices when I return. Can I go?"

He braced his hands on the counter and leaned forward with a teasing glint in his eyes. "Only if you'll marry me."

Jennifer smiled back at him. "Thanks. I'll see you later." She headed for the door.

"One of these days you'll say yes," he called after them.

"Not if she marries me first," came a voice from the dark reaches of the back room that could only be Michael.

Jennifer waved a hand over her shoulder as she pulled the door open with a jingle.

"You have a regular fan club," Meghann said, stepping out into the sunshine.

"They've made up this schedule for taking me out so it's fair. I feel like a dog bone being fought over."

Meg grinned. "And you love every minute of it."

Jennifer's smile was smug. "Absolutely."

They went up the street to the bagel store, got a bagel each, and found a quiet table in the corner.

"So, did your mother buy your story? Does she believe your hunk-of-a-husband is away on business?"

"No."

Jennifer's disappointed expression almost made Meg laugh. "No! Why not? Didn't you explain it was last minute and urgent?"

"I was going to but it all fizzled away when Mr. Halloway showed up at the airport when I was picking up my mom."

Jennifer's mouth hung open. "You're kidding. What happened?"

She explained briefly the embarrassing scene at the airport and all that had happened since then. "What am I going to do?"

"Nothing."

Meghann looked up at her sharply. Obviously Jenn had recovered from her earlier shock. She was smiling and looking utterly pleased with the situation.

"It's perfect, Meg."

"Perfect? It's a *disaster!*" Was the woman totally insane?

Jenn picked off a piece of her bagel and waved it around as she spoke. "No. It's like a sign from God or something."

How could anyone possibly figure Bruce Halloway and her mother under Meg's roof as a sign from God?

"Don't you see? With both of you there it's more convincing, like having a corroborating witness. And you can't get much more corroboration than from the hubby himself." She nodded firmly. "It was meant to happen this way, Meg. I know it. Why else would Bruce have shown up at the right time and agree to play along? Your mom's happy, right?"

"Yes, but—"

"But nothing. She will get better because of it. And as long as she is getting better you know this is what God wants. Trust me, it's best for your mom not to say anything right now. She's just not strong enough yet."

Though Jenn went to church semiregularly, she never seemed to have any trouble with bending the truth. Maybe that should have been her first clue not to listen to her. But she had to admit, her mom did seem better, stronger, and was overjoyed at Bruce's presence. Bruce. Why was he doing this? What reasons could he have that he didn't want to tell her?

"I don't know, Jenn. I'm so confused."

"You may not know, but I do. Trust me. You couldn't ask for things to work out better."

It sounded good…it really did. But Meghann was having a hard time believing it. If things were working out so well, so perfectly according to God's design, why did she feel so terrible?

Five

"WELL, NOW THAT YOU'VE BEATEN ME UP ON THE COURT, DO you want to talk about it?" Kurt said. Kurt Hill was a thinning sandy-haired man, smaller than Bruce but fast on his feet on the racquetball court. He was an associate pastor at a church Bruce didn't attend. He had met Kurt at a prayer breakfast nearly a year ago and respected the man and his walk with the Lord. They'd hit it off and now had a once-a-month racquetball game.

"Talk about what?" Bruce dried his face with his towel and draped it around his neck.

"Whatever it is that's eating you."

Sometimes Kurt's insightfulness was downright irritating. "How do you know if a woman is the right one for you?"

"Nothing simple with you, is there, Bruce?"

Life could be complicated and complex. He wanted to make the right decisions now that he was a Christian. Before becoming one two years ago, he had made so many wrong choices in his personal life. He didn't want to make those mistakes again. Picking up his gym bag, he held open the door for Kurt. Once outside the court, they took a seat on a bench, both straddling it, facing one another.

"I didn't even know you were dating anyone, Bruce."

"I'm not…not really." Where did he start to explain this situation? "It's complicated…very complicated."

"Anyone I know?"

"I doubt it."

"You meet her at work?" He raised his eyebrows in interest.

"What does *that* have to do with anything?"

"Nothing." He shrugged a shoulder. "Just curious. Are you going to ask her out?"

Though they had been out together, technically he hadn't asked her out since the Christmas party; even then he didn't really ask her. "I've been spending a lot more time with her recently." Now *that* was an understatement.

Kurt gave a knowing nod, but what was it he knew? "People have varying opinions on finding a spouse, someone to spend the rest of your life with," he began. "Some people think that God has put many choices out before each of us, and we are to choose the one we like best, so to speak. But if you choose someone outside this pool, you could find yourself regretting it."

"Outside? How do you know if someone is outside this choice group?"

"Anyone who is not a believer is definitely outside the group. But when it comes to your choices among those who share your belief in Christ…well, you just have to pray about it." He paused then went on. "I know some folks believe that there is only one right person for each of us, and if we don't marry that one person, we are forever outside the will of God. And some believe God can bless you no matter who you marry."

So far this wasn't helping much. "And you, what do you believe?"

Kurt drew in a long breath, seemingly reluctant. Bruce knew his friend well enough to figure he didn't want to force his opinion on Bruce, that he wanted to let him make up his own mind. But that was the problem. Bruce just wasn't sure. He met Kurt's gaze. "I'd really like to know, Kurt."

He nodded. "I look at it this way. God is not bound by time. He already knows who you are going to marry, if you marry at all."

Bruce was surprised that it should hit him so odd, the thought of not marrying Meg. He had never really thought of marrying her, at least not yet. But the idea of not marrying her was…what? Well, suffice it to say he didn't like it. Not one bit.

"If you are praying and reading your Bible regularly, you are more likely to be receptive to God's promptings. If you continue to have feelings or leadings about this person, then take action and see if you still feel the same way or if you feel like you have just made a big mistake by asking her out."

Take action? He almost laughed out loud. He'd certainly done that, though he doubted it was what Kurt had in mind.

"How do I know if these are leadings or just my own desires?"

"Maybe God has put those desires in your heart."

"What if you choose not to follow these leadings and go a different way?"

"If you're seeking to be obedient, if you're submitting your own will to God's in prayer, I don't think that will happen." He paused. "This woman must be special to have prompted you to ask."

"It's just a feeling I have. Which confuses me because I thought we weren't supposed to go by our feelings."

"Test them against the Word of God. If they stand up, maybe it's not a feeling as much as a leading."

"Thanks, Kurt. I appreciate all your advice."

He smiled. "Don't mention it. I'll keep you in my prayers. One of these days, I'm going to get you to cross the threshold of my church."

"Thanks, but I like the church I attend."

"They're lucky to have you, buddy."

Bruce smiled, wondering if Kurt would still feel that way if he told him what he'd been doing. Playing husband to a woman he hardly knew...a woman who had captured his heart, yes, but still one he didn't know well. But he wanted to. Heaven knew he wanted to.

Lord, help...

It was all he could think of to say.

It was late afternoon when Bruce pulled into the gravel driveway and gave an approving smile at Meghann's cream Honda parked there. He practically had to throw her out of the hotel. He literally escorted her out of the building to her car and watched her drive away. She couldn't accept he was giving her so much time off.

He felt uneasy about opening her front door without knocking, but he knew he couldn't knock. So he grabbed the doorknob, took a deep breath, and swung it open.

A warm feeling washed over him as he stepped across the threshold into the cheery atmosphere. It was so characteristic of his impetuous make-believe bride. He found he liked coming home to this cozy, welcoming setting with a beautiful wife waiting for him. The desire for this to be real jumped to life in him.

Meghann and Gayle were in the kitchen. "We are just starting dinner. It won't be ready for a while."

He crossed over to them and produced a variety bouquet of flowers to his pseudo-mother-in-law, who rewarded him with a pride-filled smile. He scored some points there.

With a kiss on her cheek, he handed Meghann a big bouquet of yellow carnations and red roses set in a spray of baby's breath.

Taking them, she put her face to them and drank in their sweet scent. "They're gorgeous. Thank you." She turned appreciative eyes on him. His heart thumped harder in his chest.

"Yellow carnations, your favorite color and favorite flower in one." He smiled at her surprise that he knew.

She raised her eyebrows. "And the roses?"

His smile broadened but it was Gayle who

answered. "Everyone knows what a red rose means."

Meghann turned to her mom, but Bruce kept his eyes on her, not that he could take them off her.

"Love, daughter. And from the looks of that bouquet, he loves you a great deal."

Meghann's cheeks highlighted pink, and he noticed she avoided looking directly at him as she retrieved two vases to put the flowers in. He knew she knew the roses were for show and still she blushed. He also knew how to get Meg to look at him again and break the awkward tension. "Pack your bags, ladies. I have good news."

Lucky got up from where she had been resting, trotted over to him, sat down, and stared up at him. Bruce scratched her head. "Sorry girl, you're not invited."

"What are you talking about?" He could hear a note of alarm in Meghann's voice, but she was looking at him with those glorious green-brown eyes.

"We are going to my apartment."

Her mouth dropped open; fortunately her mother was behind her and couldn't see the stunned look on her face.

"You have your own apartment?" Gayle said, perching her hands on her hips. Her tone was a mix of surprise and anger.

He was amused by both women's reactions. Without thought of how either one would react, he had decided that his apartment made sense. "Yes. Unfortunately, my apartment is no place for Lucky." He reached down and patted the dog's head. "And this cottage is too small to accommodate all my things. So, until we find a bigger place that's suitable for Lucky, we have two residences."

Meghann's mother accepted his explanation readily enough. "I won't say a thing. Not one thing about having two places."

Bruce held back a grin. The woman didn't have to say it. Disapproval all but dripped from her voice.

While dinner was cooking, Meghann stared mindlessly across her backyard that spring had not touched yet while her mother repacked her suitcases for the trip to Bruce's apartment.

Her life was in turmoil and her insides resembled a novice's poor attempt at Boy Scout knots. What could Bruce be thinking, inviting her and her mother to his place? Certainly he wasn't expecting them to share a room…and a bed. She wanted to ask but was afraid. What if that *was* what he had in mind? It would break her heart. She didn't want him to be like that.

Please, Lord, don't let him be thinking that.

"You wanted to speak to me?"

Meghann sucked in a quick breath. He'd come up so quietly, she hadn't heard his approach.

"At least, I assumed that's what the glare you sent me before you retreated out here meant."

She took the soggy tennis ball from Lucky's mouth and threw it across the yard. The dog ran after it without a care in the world. Meg wished she were so fortunate. He couldn't really expect her to just move in with him.

She let her gaze travel from the dog's hind end

sticking out from a bush to meet Bruce's gaze.

"If you're worried I might try to take advantage of you or the situation, I assure you I won't. You have my word."

Thank you, Lord. She breathed a sigh of relief. "How did you know that's what I was thinking?"

Her hand flew to cover her mouth. She couldn't believe she'd said that out loud. But Bruce just smiled.

"It's written all over your face and body; the worry lines across your forehead, your mouth drawn into that thin line, your stiff stance."

She tried to relax, but in truth it was difficult with all that was going on.

"I can easily slip out after your mother goes to bed and be back before she wakes up."

"I don't want to kick you out of your own place. Where will you go?"

"It was my idea, remember? I'm sure I can make some sort of arrangement at the hotel."

"I know you don't want to disclose your reasons, but I can't help but wonder why you are doing all this. You could pretend to go away on a trip and make this easy on yourself. It makes me wonder what's in it for you and what you want."

"I just want to do this for you, no strings attached. Isn't that enough for you?"

No! She wanted specifics, details. Still, she could see that this tight-lipped Bruce Halloway wasn't likely to give her any more than that, and she wasn't exactly in a position to insist.

"I guess so. Of course." It would have to be.

After dinner was cleaned up, Meghann and her mother finished packing.

"It would have been easier to go on a business trip," Meghann whispered, handing Bruce her suitcase to put in her car trunk.

"But not nearly as much fun," he said with a smile and closed the trunk.

She reached in her pocket and plopped something unceremoniously in his hand before retreating to the driver's seat. He looked at the circular gold wedding band in his palm. It had a fine, etched design around it. He smiled at the back of Meg's head as she sat alone, her posture stiff, waiting to leave. She had thought of everything, even a ring for him. As he slipped it on his finger, he noted the perfect fit. Had she bought it when she bought hers or did she run out and get it just today?

He could tell he had ruffled her feathers a little, but that was okay. He kind of liked having her off balance so he could be there to steady her.

Meghann followed Bruce and her mother, keeping a close eye on his silver gray Infinity Q45. How could an assistant manager at a hotel afford such a car? Was Bruce moonlighting?

She studied the automobile in front of her, fighting the growing anxiety. What were her mom and Bruce talking about? Why couldn't her mom have ridden with her? She pressed her lips together. They were probably talking about her. She bit her lip, wondering what they were saying. Was her mother asking him all sorts of questions? Embarrassing questions?

Another possibility occurred to her then, one she desperately hoped was not true. What if her mother had figured out it was all a lie?

Dread filled Meghann and she wished Bruce would drive faster. She wouldn't be able to relax until she was able to grill them both and knew everything was okay.

"Here we go, ladies." Bruce swung open his apartment door and gave a courtly bow.

Meghann walked in behind her mother. The apartment was spacious and lavish on the top floor of the nicest building in town. The living room was furnished with a forest green leather couch, two matching chairs, and an ottoman. A black lacquer dinette with six matching chairs and a china hutch graced the dining room. Her whole house would fit in the living/dining room combination, and the kitchen was larger than her bedroom. There was an alcove off the kitchen that was probably designed as a breakfast nook, but he had a roll-top desk with a notebook computer on it, bookshelves, and other office equipment. All the windows were shrouded in dramatic black and white crepe panels.

She helped her mother settle into the guest bedroom. It had a four-poster cherry bed with matching nightstands, armoire, and mirrored dresser. It was a gorgeous room. If this was the guest room, she wondered what Bruce's room looked like and quickly shut the thought out.

She looked around the living room. Here she was at his ritzy apartment with a gorgeous view of the city and mountains from his tenth-floor balcony. The carpet was plush and looked new, the furnishings luxurious. Everything was upscale, bold, dark, and masculine. She felt a sudden wave of embarrassment that he had been in her little hovel. He slept on the floor, no less. How could she have done that to him? She had lied, that's how. Started one little lie that had become a monster. If she could stop it, she would. But how when he refused to go away?

She let her troubled gaze roam the room once more. An assistant manager must get paid more than she realized to afford a place like this. Either that or he was getting money from another source.

A pretty generous source at that…not many ways to make this kind of money legally.

"There you are."

She spun, a guilty flush filling her cheeks at the suspicious thoughts she'd allowed a moment ago.

Fortunately, Bruce didn't seem to notice. "I've put your suitcase in my bedroom."

The implications of that statement hit her full force. He hadn't changed his mind about his promises to her, had he? Coming here was a bad idea, a really bad idea.

"I was just looking around. You have a very nice place." She hoped her voice didn't give away her nervousness as she followed him into the room.

The master bedroom was furnished much the same

as the other bedroom, but instead of cherry it was black lacquer, sporting its own bathroom and a to-die-for walk-in closet.

Now it was just him and her in his bedroom. She stared into her opened suitcase on the end of the bed. Absently rummaging through it for the fifth time, she wondered how best to tell him it was time for him to vamoose. If she kept busy, she could hold her anxiety at bay.

"I emptied these two drawers for you," Bruce said behind her.

She froze and didn't say a word. Her stomach clenched into one huge knot.

Bruce came up beside her. "It would look suspicious if your mom noticed you were living out of a suitcase."

"I forgot my nightg—pajamas." She rifled through her suitcase once again. "I can't believe I did that. I usually forget my toothbrush. Well, it's not like I've never forgotten them, but more often it has been my toothbrush." She opened her cosmetic bag and produced her toothbrush. "See here it is. I have my toothbrush. Uh-oh. I don't have my toothpaste. I forgot my toothpaste, too. I packed in such a rush; I guess I wasn't very careful. I wonder what else I forgot. I hope I didn't forget anything else." She dug deep in her suitcase like it was a matter of life or death that she find out if she forgot anything else.

"You can use my toothpaste," Bruce broke in. His voice did not suggest any emotions.

He turned away and she fell silent. What was he

thinking? She was rambling like an idiot. She knew it but couldn't stop. She hadn't expected to feel so nervous; after all, he said he would be leaving. She hoped he meant it. She heard a drawer open, then close a moment later.

He appeared at her side again. "You can wear these."

Her hands, of their own volition, reached out and accepted the men's blue silk pajamas. Her thank-you got caught around the lump in her throat.

"I'm going to go wash up," he said, and entered the master bath.

Meghann stared down at the blue silk in her hands, biting her lip, wondering what he'd do if she bolted for the front door and just went home. Because she wanted to do exactly that.

More than she'd ever wanted anything in her life.

Bruce hadn't heard any noise from the bedroom and had taken longer than normal in the bathroom to make sure he didn't catch her indecent. Tapping on the door, he said in a hushed voice, "I'm coming out." He heard no protest; in fact, he heard nothing at all. He rattled the doorknob to make his intention known and opened the door slowly.

A smile crept across his face when he saw her curled up on the far side of the bed. Her head was on his pillow and her feet conspicuously hanging off the bed as if to keep her shoes off the bed. He moved around the end of the bed to stand beside her. She still held the pajamas he had given her cradled in her arms.

He debated whether or not to wake her. She was so tired and the situation was terribly awkward. The contrast of her dainty form against the dark, harsh background appealed to him but seemed out of place. He looked around the room and surveyed the rest of his apartment. After being in Meg's wonderful house, his place suddenly resembled more of a show room than living quarters. This was definitely a bachelor's apartment. Unlike Meg's charming, cozy place, there was not a hint of anything feminine here, except this delicate flower asleep on his bed. The picture was too lovely to disturb.

Slipping off her shoes, he carefully eased her feet onto the bed and pulled the forest green and burgundy comforter over her. As he brushed back a strand of hair from her forehead, a warmth welled up from deep inside him, a sense of rightness. He wondered if a month would be long enough to satisfy his need to take care of her and gazed at her a moment longer before silently slipping away, closing the door softly behind him.

Six

MEGHANN WOKE SLOWLY, MOVING HER STIFF BODY AND rolling onto her back, stretching her muscles one at a time. She felt so snug and comfy…

She pried her eyes open, but they slammed shut. Concentrating hard, she managed to get one open and keep it open. With success, she proceeded to open the other one and focus.

This isn't my room, she thought with a yawn. *Where am I?* Suddenly her eyes snapped wide open. *Bruce Halloway's!* Reality crashed in on her and she bolted upright in bed. Quickly she scanned the room and the bed. Her heart raced. The clock read 7:22 A.M.

Man, what a sleep. Once she drifted off, she was out. Sleep depravation had certainly caught up with her last night.

The last thing she remembered was waiting for Bruce to come out of the bathroom after he had given her his pajamas. She looked down and found the blue silk in a puddle beside her. She was still in her clothes from yesterday; evidently she had slept in them. The bed was untouched except for the comforter over her. Bruce must have covered her. But where was he? More important, where had he slept last night? Had he left as promised?

She pulled back the comforter and stood. Making the bed with quick, hasty movements, she selected some fresh clothes and dumped the remainder in the two drawers Bruce had emptied. Changing in the bathroom, she ran a brush through her hair, and fixed her makeup.

If her mother were up and wanted to know where her son-in-law was, Meghann would tell her he went to work early. Her mom would believe that. Oh, but what if he arrived in jogging clothes or something? Did he even *go* jogging in the morning? Okay, so the truth. That's what she would tell her mom.

What a novel idea...

She grimaced at the sarcastic thought. At least in this, she could be honest: Bruce was already gone when she got up and she wasn't sure if he was jogging or at work.

Meghann left the bedroom with confidence but stopped in midstride when she entered the dining area. Bruce sat at the table reading a Bible.

His faith had always shown through at work, in the way he dealt with people, in the things he said and the kindness he showed. And the sight of him now, bent over the Bible, face intent on what he was reading, touched her heart deeply.

She must have made some little noise because he raised his head and his gorgeous brown eyes settled on her.

That heart-melting smile spread across his face. "Good morning, darling. Did you sleep well?"

"F-fine. And yourself?" Drat. Why couldn't she think straight when he smiled at her like that? Her brain went to mush and her legs felt like they were melting out from under her.

"Good." He stood and pulled out a chair for her.

She glanced around the apartment as she dutifully took the offered seat, thankful she didn't have to rely on her unstable legs to keep her up. "Thank you."

"To answer your question—" he began.

"What question?" She met his gaze. She hadn't asked any question.

"The one on your face." He grinned as she felt her face flood with heat. "I slept on the couch in my office at the hotel."

Quick relief swept her, accompanied by a twinge of guilt. *You should have trusted him.* With a sigh, she leaned her chin on her hands. "I'm really sorry for all the trouble I've caused you."

"It's not a problem." He shrugged off the apology and ducked into the kitchen. A minute later he returned with a plate full of sliced bagels and a variety of mini-muffins. He placed a glass of orange juice and a small empty plate in front of her. "Water for your tea will be hot in a few minutes."

Her gaze traveled from the food up to him. Where did he get all this? Last night he apologized for not having any food on hand. And how did he know she liked tea and not coffee?

His smile broadened as he tried to stifle a laugh.

"Don't ever take up poker, Meg. Your eyes are too expressive. It's as though your thoughts are right there, waiting to be read."

Only by you. No one else had ever understood her as well or as easily as this man. Why was that?

He took his seat, still smiling, then pushed his Bible forward and rested his forearms on the table, leaning toward her. "I stopped by the grocery store on my way home."

She shook her head, and this time the laugh escaped him. She gave him an all-right-that's-enough look. *Can you read that one, "darling"?* Surprise filled her when he sobered quickly—apparently he could!—but she could still see the amusement dancing in his eyes.

"I stopped by your cottage to check on Lucky," he said, obviously playing it safe with a change of subject. "She was snug in her doghouse. I couldn't feed her though. The door's locked." He pulled a key from his pocket. Meghann looked up at him questioningly. "It's a key to my apartment." He handed it to her. "For when you and your mom want to go out when I'm not here."

She took the key and slowly looked up to his eyes. It was her turn to read the question there. "You want a key to my place?"

"As your 'husband' I should have one. It would eliminate a potentially awkward situation."

She had to agree with his logic, but the past two days had already been filled with multiple awkward situations. What was one more?

"If you give me your key, I'll have a copy made."

Meghann shook her head. "You don't have to do that."

"That's all right," he said. "If you're not comfortable with my having a key to your cottage, don't worry about it. We'll work around it."

"No, that's not it at all." She reached out, putting her hand on his arm. "I already have a spare key. It's under the front lip of the porch by the top rail post on the right. But you have to watch out for spiders and crawly things." She shuddered at the thought and realized she was still touching his arm. As casually as her suddenly racing pulse would allow, she pulled her hand away and picked a couple of minimuffins and a half of a bagel from the plate. "I'll get it later when I check on Lucky." She meticulously spread cream cheese back and forth on her bagel until it was completely covered.

"You missed a spot." Bruce's voice broke in. The bagel came into focus, and she set it aside. She looked straight at Bruce and held his gaze.

"Mr. Halloway, is there anything I can do or say to get you to change your mind?"

"Call me Bruce," he said in a voice designed to disarm her, "after all, we *are* married." He gently lifted his eyebrows.

Oh no you don't. You're not going to distract me with charm.

Not completely, anyway. With pure force of will, she shook off the haze of attraction his tone had created and pulled herself together.

Kind of.

She stared at him, then frowned. She'd been saying

something…something important…what was it—

"You wanted to change my mind." His smile was broader now, and just a bit smug.

Crossing her arms with a huff, she nodded. "Would you *please* reconsider a business trip? It'd be simpler for everyone, especially you."

"But not nearly as much fun."

Fun! Her mouth went dry. "Won't you please go away?"

"Are you trying to get rid of me?" He leaned back in his chair, effecting a perfect wounded little boy expression.

Her reply was without hesitation. "Absolutely."

He clutched his chest as if a mighty blow had struck him in the heart. She was going crazy here and he was playing games! When she didn't laugh or even smile at his antics, he sobered. "Meghann, you aren't still worried I'll impose myself upon you, are you?"

"Let's see…you spent the night on my living room floor with a black Lab as a companion, and last night you slept on a sofa. I just have to wonder how long you will put up with it. You can't be sleeping well."

"You don't trust me?" He sounded mildly offended.

"No, it's not that."

"You don't trust yourself then? Should I be worried *you* will try to take advantage of *me?*"

"No. Yes. *No.*" She took a slow, deep breath. "I mean, I feel like I'm already taking advantage of your *kindness.*" How had the conversation gone astray so quickly?

"I'll take a room at the hotel, then. Will that make you feel better?"

No! "A month in a hotel room would be very expensive."

"There are generally always a few empty rooms. I'll use one of those until we fill up just before the ball and won't have to pay a thing. Feel better?"

Not really.

"Meg."

At the soft word, she focused on him, taking in the sincerity in his eyes, the slight smile on his lips. He reached out to give her hand a light squeeze. "Everything will work out. You'll see. Just relax."

She nodded, swallowing against the tears his gentle words had sparked. As though sensing she needed some time to herself, he excused himself and disappeared into the bedroom. A minute later, her mother came out of her room. Meghann hoped she hadn't overheard any of her conversation with Bruce.

Speaking of the devil, he reappeared a few minutes later, dressed in a crisp suit. "Sorry to desert you ladies, but duty calls." He came up behind Meg and rested both warm hands on her shoulders. All her senses came alert and she had to fight not to lean back against him.

"I'll go by the cottage and feed Lucky." When he leaned over her and kissed her on the cheek, she jumped.

He chuckled and grinned at Meg's mother. "She's still not used to me."

"I daresay it won't take much longer for her to be so," her mother said with a laugh.

That's exactly what I'm afraid of, Meg thought miserably. Kisses from Bruce would be all too easy to get used to....

He leaned down to whisper in her ear, "I'll brave the spiders and get the key." With that, he kissed her cheek again and headed for the door. "I'll see you this afternoon."

Meghann jumped up and rushed after him. "I'll walk you to the elevator." She practically pushed him out the door, and he looked down at her with a barely restrained grin.

When they stood in front of the elevator, she turned to him, straightening her shoulders. "I think I should change and go to work, too."

"Nonsense. You stay here and enjoy your time with your mother."

"I feel so guilty. It's not right. I should be working."

"Right or not, that's the way it is. Spend the day with her and come in tomorrow for a few hours." The elevator dinged and the doors opened. Bruce stepped inside but kept them from closing with his hand. "By the way, running after me to walk me to the elevator looked good."

She blinked at him. "Looked...good?"

"To your mom."

"That's not why I did it. You know that."

"It doesn't matter why, it only matters how it appears to your mother. Appearance is everything." He removed his hand and made a gesture as if tipping an imaginary hat. "Have a nice day."

She watched as the doors slid closed on his endearing smile. *Appearances. And you are so good at them.* If she didn't know better, she would swear he was in love with her. But then it was all in the way it appeared, wasn't it? Since he appeared to have deep feelings for her and nothing was as it seemed in reality, he wasn't in love with her. Right?

Bruce leaned back in his chair and propped his feet up on his mahogany desk. What had he done? What had he gotten himself into? He knew better than to get involved in this kind of deception. The Bible was clear on the consequences of lying, on the importance of living in truth.

But when it had come right down to it, a woman's gratitude had seemed more important than the truth.

Of course, this wasn't just any woman. It was Meghann Livingston! With any other woman he'd just have brought out the truth as kindly as possible, even if it caused discomfort or some pain. After all, he hadn't started the lie.

But when he'd looked into those eyes, seen the alarm on that sweet face…he hadn't thought twice. Just jumped into the fray, playing the gallant hero, joining the charade.

It had made sense then. But now…with every passing moment he teetered between the truth, keeping up the charade, and taking Meghann up on her mythical business trip.

The Bruce Halloway of three years ago wouldn't have thought twice about pressing his advantage with Meghann if he had ever found himself in a similar situation. He would have been more than happy to manipulate the circumstances to get exactly what he wanted, to charm his way back into his bedroom.

But he wasn't that man any longer. What was it Scripture said? He was a new man. Made new from the inside out. Must be true because what used to matter most was him, his desires and wants. And now what mattered most was helping Meg.

He wanted—needed—her to trust him, so in return maybe he could trust, too. There were too few people in his life, if any, that he felt he could truly trust. Instinct and life taught him to rely only on himself.

But there was something about Meghann that drew Bruce in. He found himself wanting to trust her, to tell her all about himself and his past, sordid though it may be.

Don't be stupid. Let people know too much about you, and they can and will use it against you.

No, Meghann wasn't like that; he knew it in his heart. Still, he just couldn't bring himself to risk it just yet. He had to be sure of his own feelings first. Had to be sure she really was someone he could trust. All he knew now was that he had never felt for another woman what he felt for Meg.

Of course, the easiest solution would be to follow Meg's suggestion, to pretend to go away on some business trip. But he didn't want to do that. No, what he wanted was to be near Meghann. And while their bogus marriage might have a lot of drawbacks, it did allow him that. Time with Meg.

Besides, they weren't doing this just as a lark. It was for Meg's mother. The woman was clearly still fragile, and if this would help her regain her health, then it was worth it, wasn't it? It wasn't as though he were toying with Meghann's affection. She knew as well as he that this wasn't real....

Even as he made the assertion, he saw again the way she'd looked at him this morning: the uncertainty, the questions swirling in those big, green eyes; eyes he could easily drown in....

He shook his head, then uttered a sigh. With any luck, down the road they would laugh about this, and they would draw closer together because of it. And when her mother was strong enough to hear the truth, he would be the first to tell her.

Who are you really serving? Meg's mom, or yourself?

Bruce stared at the wall. *Meg's mom,* he insisted. *This whole charade is for her benefit.*

"Christ suffered for you, leaving you an example.... No deceit was found in this mouth."

But He was never in this situation! What if I'd told on Meg? What if I'd told her mother the truth and she'd relapsed?

Do not use deception....

I didn't have a choice! But even as he said it, he knew it wasn't true.

The ringing phone interrupted his internal debate. He lifted the phone. "Yes?"

"Didn't we have a meeting at two o'clock?" George Phenton said over the line.

Bruce glanced at his watch: 2:20. "Yes, George, we did. I'm sorry. Time got away from me. I'll be right there."

Bruce grabbed a couple of files and marched down the hall to the general manager's office. George's secretary waved him to go on in.

George wasn't waiting behind his desk but was seated in one of the brown leather chairs flanking the matching leather couch, files strewn across the coffee table.

Bruce sat in the other chair and tried to focus his attention on the business at hand. But for the life of him, he couldn't keep his mind from drifting back to Meghann Livingston and her problem. She needed his help, and it was within his power to give it to her. Surely God wanted him to help her.

When he came back to the present, George was spouting something about the renovations. And he was sorry the work wasn't going to get done on schedule. Since when did anything get done on time? After they had hashed out what to do about the renovation problems, discussed the upcoming ball and various other hotel matters, George asked, "Is something on your mind?"

The question took Bruce by surprise. "Why?"

"You're never late for a meeting and time doesn't just 'get away from you.' You've only been half here since you walked in." George settled back in his chair. "What's up? Anything I can help you with?"

Bruce took a deep breath and thought for a moment. He did want advice, but how much should he tell? "Have you ever done something that was maybe technically wrong, but it was to help someone else?"

"The end justifying the means?"

"Something like that."

"This 'something' wouldn't be illegal or have anything to do with the hotel, would it?" George shuffled some papers and straightened a few files.

Bruce shook his head. "No, nothing illegal or to do with this place." He raised one foot and rested his ankle on the opposite knee, trying to appear relaxed. "It's...personal."

"Well, if it's not illegal and it's helping someone, I don't see any problems."

"But something doesn't have to be illegal to be wrong."

"If it's bothering you, then put it right."

Bruce slipped his foot down and leaned forward. "Then I hurt two people."

George, too, leaned forward, resting his forearms on his thighs. "Is it something you can live with?"

"I guess so." The truth was he couldn't just abandon Meg, but he wasn't so sure he could live with their lie for much longer, either.

"Then accept it, forget it, and move on."

He would try to accept it, but he could neither forget it nor move on, not when he was living with it daily. Meghann had become very important to him, and he felt a deep need to help her in any way possible.

If only the way presented to him didn't make him feel as though he were selling out on something even more important than Meg.

Lord, help me out here....

But there was no reply. Just silence—and a small but undeniable sense of divine displeasure.

Seven

MEGHANN AND BRUCE RETURNED TO HIS APARTMENT AFTER A Saturday afternoon visit to take care of Lucky while Gayle rested. Revived from her nap, she greeted them energetically. "What time do I need to be ready to leave for church in the morning?"

Oh, dear...church. Meg glanced at Bruce in dismay. The three of them couldn't show up at church together! Her mom would wonder why no one knew Meg was married and had never seen her husband before. A wave of guilt rushed through her for not having considered church services. She racked her brain for a reason not to go but came up empty.

"I've been wanting to check out Grace Bible Church. If you ladies are game, I'd like to take you," Bruce said.

Perfect. She sighed. *That solved that problem.*

"Fine with me," Gayle said.

He turned to Meghann for her answer. When she failed to respond, he nudged her gently. "Darling, is it okay with you if we go to a new church?"

"I'm sorry," she said, coming out of her daze. "That sounds great. I'd love to." Good thing she'd picked a man who thought so quickly on his feet for her make-believe mate.

And it doesn't hurt that he is handsome, wonderful, Christian, kind, considerate, thoughtful...

No, she admitted, it didn't hurt in the least. And the list could go on and on. Bruce Halloway was, in a word, perfect.

What a pity their relationship wasn't. Wasn't perfect. Wasn't...period.

Meghann turned away, suddenly depressed. This month had better go quickly, or she was going to need therapy to recover!

Going to a new church was harder than Meghann had thought it would be. From the moment she walked through the doors on Bruce's arm she felt oddly conspicuous, as though she was on trial. She wondered what the verdict would be?

A man who looked to be in his seventies greeted them. His name tag read *Bill Neilsen*. He was a friendly man who obviously enjoyed his role as greeter, but when he smiled at her, she felt as though he could see straight into her soul. As though somehow the wisdom of years could see beyond the facade.

He introduced them to another couple, Margaret and Frank, who in turn introduced them to their son and daughter-in-law, Frank Jr. and Sue.

"I could tell you two were newlyweds," Sue whispered to Meghann as the men exchanged pleasantries about their jobs. "You have that shy, self-conscious, new-wife look with the glow of young love still on your face."

It was more like that fear and trepidation, I-hope-no-one-guesses-we're-frauds look. As for the glow, nervous perspiration could account for that.

Was it her imagination or were people staring at them? She glanced around but no one seemed to have their eyes fixed on them. An occasional nod of acknowledgment and friendly smile but no overt attention.

Meghann couldn't wait to escape into the sanctuary, to get away from any prying eyes. Once in the pew, she found herself wedged between Bruce and her mother.

Singing the opening hymn wasn't nearly as refreshing as it usually was. That hymn was followed by another before the welcoming and announcements were made.

The Scripture reading was from Colossians 3:1–12. Meghann felt adrift without her Bible, but Bruce slid his over so it straddled both their laps.

As the man read, Meghann followed along until verse 9. Her brain came to a screeching halt. "Do not lie to each other.…" It echoed in her head over and over, louder and louder, until it was all she could hear.

Bruce cupped her elbow to bring her to her feet. Everyone around her was standing. She got up quickly and looked at the hymnal Bruce held open. The hymn was unfamiliar to her, but she found the place and joined in. Her voice trailed off on the second verse when one of the words was *lies*. When the song finally ended, she slumped back in the pew. This was going to be a *long* service. One where God's piercing darts of truth seemed aimed straight at her heart.

Meghann shifted uneasily as the pastor began to preach. The closer he got to verse 9 the more fidgety she became. Her mother gave her the look she had received many times as a child. It meant sit still and quit squirming.

"Do not lie to one another," the pastor quoted. Did he really say it louder than the rest or was it her imagination? "What about bending the truth? If it is not 100 percent the truth, it is a lie. Even Satan speaks truth 95 percent of the time. It's the 5 percent you have to watch out for. Though you may never get caught, it will eat you up inside. It will haunt you and hound you, plaguing your innermost being. If you are a child of God, He won't let up until you confess and make yourself right with Him and others."

How could she tell the truth now? Her lie was so big. It involved so many people. It was only supposed to affect her, but lies have a way of growing and being found out…and hurting people. She wanted to run and hide. To start over.

She breathed a sigh of relief as they exited the church. It was finally over. She always looked forward to and even longed for Sunday morning worship. It was life and breath to her. This morning it was all she could do to endure. The verdict was in—GUILTY!

Next Sunday she planned to be sick.

The weight of Meghann's lie pressed in on her and wouldn't let up. It kept nagging, "Thou shalt not lie. Thou shalt not lie." It wasn't exactly a lie. She hadn't come right out and said she was married to Bruce. Okay, so she didn't set her mother's misconceptions straight, but that wasn't the same thing. Was it?

She knew the answer before it came, but it came all the same.

It's still deceit.

Okay, but what about honor thy mother?

What about it?

This was honoring her. This was what she wanted.

No. She wants the real thing for you...just like you do.

That went without question. Meg's mom was so happy with this marriage...but it was a joy that lacked foundation. It wasn't right to let her go on thinking Meg was settled when she wasn't. Not by a long shot.

Though it would break her mother's heart, it was time to come clean.

When they returned to Bruce's apartment after church and brunch, Meghann wanted to get it over with.

"Mom, we need to talk to you." Meg glanced across the living room at Bruce. He was leaning against the dry bar. For someone who said he would stand behind and support her in this decision, he was certainly far enough away. At brunch when her mother was away from the table, he agreed to help her break the truth to her mother. She supposed she was alone in this. After all, it was her lie and it was up to her to tell the truth. "Actually, it's me. *I* need to tell you something…about Bruce and me."

"This sounds serious." Her mother sent a worried glance to Bruce.

"Well, it is."

"I'd better sit down." Her mother touched her hand to her chest and sank down on the couch, her breathing shallow and controlled.

A swift alarm pierced Meghann. "Mom, are you all right?" She moved to sit next to her, taking her mother's hand in her own.

Her mom patted the back of Meg's hand, but her face was definitely paler than it had been. "It's just a little spell. It will pass."

Bruce knelt in front of them with a glass of water. Meghann waved it away. "I'm not thirsty."

"It's for your mother."

"Oh," she said and quickly took it. Her mother rested a shaky hand on top of Meghann's as she took an assisted sip of water.

"Maybe you should go lie down." *Lord, please, don't let her relapse!*

"I'll be fine," her mother said weakly. "Now, what was it you wanted to tell me?"

Oh no. No way. Not now. Not after what had just happened. If anything happened to her mother because of her, Meg knew she couldn't live with herself. Now was not the time for making herself feel better. And after all, wasn't that why she'd been ready to tell the truth? To get it over with? To get out from under this feeling of guilt and being wrong?

Well, she'd just have to deal with it for now. Her mother was what mattered most. Meghann would wait a few more days, until she was sure her mother was stronger. "Nothing. It's not important. You go rest." Yes, a few more days, then her mother could handle it better.

"If you insist." Her mother held out her hand for assistance. Meghann helped her up and to the room. All of her intentions deflated. The weight of the lie settled solidly back on her shoulders.

Bruce watched as Meghann escorted her mother. He hadn't been sure until Gayle's last statement, that weak "If you insist" complete with a heavy sigh...all perfectly executed, perfectly designed to steal the color and confidence from Meg's face.

Remembering the fear he'd seen in Meg's eyes, he felt his jaw tighten and forced himself to relax. Gayle's 'spell' was just too convenient. He'd suspected it had more to do with Gayle not wanting to hear any bad news concerning her daughter than it did with the woman's health. And Meghann was playing right into her mother's hand, too close to see what was going on.

A spell of self-induced ignorance. That's what was happening. Gayle obviously had no idea what Meg had planned to say, but she'd picked up that it wasn't news she was going to like. So she'd cut the bad news posse off at the pass....

He didn't like the way Gayle pulled Meghann's

strings. For a moment he seriously considered marching into Gayle's room and confronting her, telling her he wasn't going to allow it, that he wouldn't permit her to play her daughter this way.

But the truth was, he didn't have the right to do any such thing.

If he were really Meg's husband, he wouldn't hesitate to stand up to Gayle. Gently, of course. And with as much kindness as possible. But with a firmness that let her know all the spells in the world wouldn't work on him—or on his wife. But he wasn't Meg's husband. Wasn't even her fiancé.

He was a fraud, nothing more. And that didn't give him the right to protect anyone...least of all the woman he was coming to care more for.

Eight

Ring-g-g.

That was the third time the phone had rung in the past ten minutes. Someone was anxious to reach Bruce.

"Are you sure you shouldn't answer that?" Meg's mother looked from her to the phone for the umpteenth time. "It may be important."

"No, Mom. It'll be business stuff. They know to call him at work." She hoped that were true. In any case, she just wasn't up to dealing with answering Bruce's phone. It would invariably involve deceit to cover herself, and she'd had more than her fill of that.

Besides, how would she evade the person on the phone while maintaining the farce to her mother, who was right here to hear her every word? Even if all of that miraculously worked out, she would no doubt cause some kind of trouble for Bruce.

She closed her eyes against the growing complications. Lies, lies, and more lies—where would it all end?

With Bruce gone, Meghann hadn't known what to do the first time the phone rang. She was glad when the answering machine picked it up. The volume was down so she couldn't hear who was leaving a message.

She decided to call Bruce and let him know about the calls in case they were important. As she picked up the phone to dial the hotel, a key rattled in the door. *He's home early.* Relief swept over her as she hung up the phone. The door swung open, and she turned to greet him…then stopped short.

It wasn't Bruce in the threshold. Instead, a short, round woman in her midforties stood there, eyes wide with painfully evident surprise.

"I'm sorry, miss. I didn't know anyone was here." The woman raised her brows and peered around the apartment, looking every inch the suspicious guardian.

Meghann stared at her, mind working frantically. Who was this woman and what was she doing here?

"That's *Mrs.,*" her mother said, coming alongside Meg, clearly intending to defend her daughter. "Mrs. Bruce Halloway."

Oh, good heavens! Meg didn't know who the woman was, but if she had a key, she obviously had a reason for being here. And she'd obviously know there was no Mrs. Bruce Halloway!

Before the stunned woman could react, Meg stepped forward. "Please call me Meghann." She walked to the door where the woman still stood. She didn't like the woman's skeptical look. "And you are?"

"Mrs. Barr. I clean Mr. Halloway's apartment. He never said anything about a wife to me," she said with pursed lips.

Oh, dear. She mustered up her most persuasive

smile, the one she used on particularly upset hotel patrons. "Likewise, I'm afraid he failed to mention you." Desperately, she pasted an isn't-this-a-funny-mistake? look on her face. "We usually stay at my place." The explanation didn't quite sound right, even to Meg's ears. She recognized the look in Mrs. Barr's eyes: It was the same one her mother had had when she found out they had two places.

"We haven't had time to look for a bigger place," Meghann explained, hoping to ease the suspicion from the woman's face.

"Humph. I clean now or not at all. I have another place to clean."

"Now is fine." Meghann stepped out of Mrs. Barr's way, and the round woman came in. *Please, please…* Meg bit her lip. *Don't let Mom think anything is out of the ordinary.*

But her mother seemed to accept the situation with aplomb, moving to sit on the couch, out of Mrs. Barr's way. With a relieved sigh, Meg went to join her, determined to corner Bruce when he came home and find out if there were any *other* surprises she should know about.

Twenty minutes after Mrs. Barr's arrival, Bruce sauntered in and set his briefcase by the entry table. "I'm off for the day." In contrast to Meghann's turbulent emotions, he seemed calm and relaxed. He handed her a dozen red roses and kissed her on the cheek.

Her frustration over Mrs. Barr's unexpected arrival faded as Meg buried her nose in the fragrant blossoms. She gave Bruce a quick smile and headed for the kitchen to find a vase.

He really was the most considerate man. She smiled as she eased the stems into the vase. She'd never received so many flowers before.

It looks good, remember? Appearances are everything.

Her smile faded. Of course. He wasn't bringing her flowers because he cared about her. It was to keep up appearances. But then, what did she expect? Did she think getting the man into this ridiculous situation would endear her to him?

No way. More than likely, Bruce couldn't wait to be free of her and their mock marriage.

She touched one of the soft, velvety petals, fighting the absurd urge to cry. She'd better enjoy the flowers while she had them. When the month was up, she could be sure Bruce's attention would be as well.

With a sigh, she carried the roses back into the living room and set them on the table. As she did so, she heard Bruce say, "Where would you like to go, Mom? What do you most want to do in our fair city?"

Her mother touched her fingers to her chest. "Me?" Bruce nodded. "Anywhere?" Bruce nodded again. "I would love to go for a nice, quiet drive somewhere. I've been cooped up too long. And it would give your housekeeper a chance to do her job in peace without an audience."

"Natalie's here?" He gave Meg a quick look.

She responded with a sharp nod.

"That's right. Today is her cleaning day." He considered Meg thoughtfully.

Before she could say anything, her mother rose and smiled at the two of them.

"I'll go change for our drive. You two decide where we're going to go."

Meg watched her leave the room, then turned her gaze back to Bruce. She opened her mouth, but he cut her off.

"I need to make a couple of quick calls while you ladies get ready." With that he made a hasty exit.

Meghann sat herself carefully in one of the dining room chairs and hunched over the table, cradling her forehead in her arms. Staring at her dim reflection in the shiny black table, she began making faces at herself to release some of the tension for the trouble she had caused everyone.

Bruce joined her a few faces later. "Where's your mom?"

"She's changing clothes," she said dryly and raised her head.

Mrs. Barr came out of the kitchen, heading for the bedroom.

"Good morning, Natalie," Bruce said.

She gave them a stern look and a curt nod while continuing on her way.

"You could have warned me you had a housekeeper coming!" Meg hissed at him once Mrs. Barr was out of earshot. "I didn't know what to do."

He looked at her, exasperation evident on his face. "I tried, but you wouldn't answer the phone. I called three times."

"That was you? How was I supposed to know?"

"Pick up the phone," he said gently.

"I couldn't just answer your phone."

"Why not?"

"Because."

"Because why?" he asked pointedly.

She squared her shoulders. "Because it wouldn't be right. Because it could be awkward for you as well as for whoever is on the other line. Because it would be like snooping or prying."

"Your mother must have thought it a bit odd that you didn't answer the phone."

"Well, what would someone think if they called you and a woman answered? What if your mother called?" She sniffed. "Unless women answer your phone all the time." Where had *that* come from? She shouldn't have said that but found she desperately wanted to know the answer.

"I'm ready," her mother said cheerfully, coming from the bedroom into the dining room, abruptly ending their conversation.

Meg searched his face a moment for the answer. It wasn't there. She would never know now because his love life was a subject she wasn't going to bring up again. She hadn't meant to say anything. It just shot out of her mouth. It really wasn't any of her business. And the sooner she resolved herself to that fact, the better off they both would be.

Bruce held the back door of his Infinity open for her mother, which blocked Meghann from getting in the front. After closing Mrs. Livingston's door, Bruce hesitated opening Meghann's door just long enough to whisper, "You are the only woman I've had in my apartment besides my own mother and Mrs. Barr."

He opened her door before she had a chance to respond. Her heart leapt with joy to know he didn't entertain a lot of women up in his apartment, but that didn't mean he didn't date or have a girlfriend.

They drove through the Garden of the Gods and spent over an hour at the visitor's center.

"Are you getting tired? Do you want to head back?" Bruce said to Meg's mom.

His concern and thoughtfulness for her mother's well-being touched her. It seemed so genuine, so sincere, she couldn't believe it was a part of maintaining appearances. Bruce really did care that her mother was doing well. And that meant more to Meghann than she cared to admit.

"I'm a little tired, but I don't want to go back just yet. Can we drive around a little longer?"

Meghann twisted in her seat to face her mother. "If you're tired, we should go back. You shouldn't overdo it."

"Nonsense. What's to overdo, sitting in a car and staring out the window? I'm not even driving. It's very soothing and I'm quite relaxed."

"But—"

Her mother held up a hand to stop her protest, then turned her pale face toward the window. Her eyes were droopy, and she just seemed plain worn out.

A touch on her hand drew Meg's attention. Bruce clasped her hand in his and gave it a reassuring squeeze. He smiled at her, and she eased back in her seat. That smile was her undoing every time! All he had to do was turn it on her, and her heart quickened and her muscles refused to cooperate.

"Where to, sweetheart?"

Sweetheart...If he only meant it. "Anywhere but the middle of town."

He lifted her hand and brushed his lips across it with a featherlight stroke. "Your wish is my command."

The feel of his lips on her skin sent a shiver coursing through her. Thankfully, he released her hand to steer the car out of the parking lot and back onto the road. She folded her hands in her lap, grateful for a chance to get her riotous emotions back under control.

The buildings shrank and slowly diminished into the more open countryside, then up into the trees that skirted the northwest edge of town. Meghann rolled down her window and drank in the sweet smell of the pines.

"Stop!"

Meghann spun around and a muscle in her neck felt like it snapped. "What is it, Mom? What's wrong?" She had thought her mother was asleep; she had been so quiet.

Bruce came to a quick stop on the side of the country road. Fortunately the car behind them was far enough back to swerve around them and not rear-end them.

"Turn around, turn around," Mom was staring out the window raptly.

"What is it?"

Bruce checked for traffic and made a U-turn.

"You'll see." Her mother's eyes were bright with excitement. "Turn, turn right here."

Bruce made the turn onto the dirt driveway and slowed to a stop.

"Ohhh, it's perfect!"

Meghann turned from her excited, cooing mother to study the sprawling Victorian-style house laid out before her. Though the house itself was settled in the middle of a large clearing, the forest circled it like a cozy blanket. The house was older but had a beauty, character, and charm all its own. The porch stretched across the entire front and wrapped around the length of one side. The roof, windows, and porch awning were edged with delicate gingerbread cutout. But it was the surrounding acreage that intrigued her most. Plenty of land for Lucky to run and play in, trees, and even a small stream. It was like being far out in the country yet close to town.

Her mother was right; it was perfect. Perfect for a couple in love, for newlyweds looking for a place to call their own.

Neither of which applied to her and Bruce.

"Mom, we aren't ready to buy a house."

"You will be soon enough. We can at least look and get some ideas. This is just like those houses you used to cut out of magazines when you were a kid. Look! Someone's even here."

There was indeed a grungy old white pickup truck parked out front with tools and lumber in the bed. Before she could object, her mother was out of the car. Meghann turned to Bruce for help, and all she got was a helpless shrug. The sight of this beautiful dream house made her mother happy, exhilarated, even robust. What could it hurt to have a quick look around?

Daffodils and tulips sprang forth from the still cold ground, among the evergreen bushes and stick bushes awaiting spring's kiss to bud and bare their leafy fruit. This yard would explode with life over the next few weeks, energizing everything around it. It had a life all its own, just needing someone to prune and pluck it lovingly.

There were a few poplar trees at the edge of the woods—she could tell by their distinctive white bark. A willow tree rested next to the rushing stream, the pine trees made an effective fence, and some scrub oak that could make anyplace look haunted. She'd have to wait until the leaves came out to figure out what the other trees were.

Wait? What are you talking about? You'll never see this yard in its spring or summer splendor.

There were no leaves yet for the gentle breeze to rustle, but she could feel it on her sun-warmed face as she closed her eyes and listened. The rushing of water and birds returning from their winter vacation filled the air. But no traffic noise.

Hands settled down on her shoulders, causing her to jump. She felt silly for starting at Bruce's touch, but she hadn't expected him. She was in her own world.

"I'm sorry for scaring you."

"You didn't scare me; I was just surprised. I forgot I wasn't here alone."

"You like it here, don't you?"

Meghann nodded, inspired by her surroundings.

"Who wouldn't? It's perfect. Lucky would love to have all this room to run."

"You want to have a look inside?" he asked. "Your mom talked the repairman into letting us in."

She shouldn't, she knew she shouldn't. What was the point? But her answer jumped past her lips: "I'd love to!"

Once inside the kitchen where Meghann's mother was waiting while examining the cabinets and appliances, the house took on a new charm. She wondered who the original occupants had been.

"I like this house," her mother said, closing the dishwasher. "They don't make houses like this anymore. This is just what you have always wanted."

"I like it, too." Bruce reached out to take Meghann's hand. Once again his touch warmed her. If only it were real...if only he wanted to hold her hand, to be close to her...if only his affection and smiles weren't all a part of the act.

She nonchalantly disengaged her hand from his and admired the kitchen cabinet's workmanship. If she were going to survive the next three weeks with her heart intact, she needed to keep as much distance between them as possible.

"It's nice," she said cautiously.

Bruce scrutinized her. "Nice? Just nice? What could you possibly find at fault? Not enough bedrooms? Kitchen too small? What do you want in a house, Meg?"

He was siding with her mother. Why would he push for her opinion on a house? This house or any house?

"It's just so big. We don't need a house this large." A quiet voice inside her was nudging her to tell the truth. "In fact…we don't need a house at all." With that said, she bit her bottom lip.

"But you said neither one of your current places was adequate to accommodate both your lives," her mother said.

"What is it you are proposing, dear?" Bruce said with great interest.

"I'm just trying to be honest here." She swallowed nervously, drilling him with a steely glare.

"Now is probably not the best time."

Meg's eyes widened at the pointed comment. "There is no time like the present," she shot back.

"Then, by all means, go on." Bruce crossed his arms over his chest and leaned back on the counter in resignation.

"Maybe you two could decide later," her mother said and took hold of the counter for balance. "I suddenly feel spent, like someone pulled the drain plug and all my energy swooshed out." She moved her hands in sweeping motion.

Meghann turned a startled look at her mother. She did look exhausted. Guilt swept Meg at the sight of her mother's white face. She'd been so caught up in her subtle debate with Bruce that she hadn't noticed how weary her mother was—and she'd missed her opportunity to tell the truth yet again.

She wondered why that last part didn't bother her as much as it should. "I'm sorry, Mom. Let's get you home."

Chicken! That's what she was. A big, fat chicken. She hated confrontations and avoided them if at all possible, and when her mother finally did hear the truth, sparks were bound to fly. She could count on it. It would be Fourth of July in April.

When Bruce came home midafternoon the next day, Gayle sat reading on the couch. Meg had left him a note on the entry table saying she went to check up on Lucky while her mother slept. If he had known, he would have stopped by just to be with her.

"I'm glad you came by while Meg is out. It gives us a chance to talk." Gayle put her book aside as he slipped the paper in his pocket.

"Something special on your mind?" He sat on the couch near her. The air around him filled with the faint scent of fine leather as the cushion settled. He hoped she didn't want to ask him something he couldn't answer. Now he really wished he had stopped by Meghann's cottage.

Gayle remained silent for a moment, staring across the room, gathering her thoughts.

"What can I do for you, Mom?" he asked, hoping to lighten her serious mood. She seemed to like it when he called her that. He wasn't disappointed. A smile spread across her face. She liked having a son-in-law to call her Mom. She seemed to like having him in particular as a son-in-law. Hopefully that affection ran in the family.

She took a deep breath. "I want to apologize."

Bruce could see she was honestly concerned about

some breech she believed she caused. "For what?"

She turned toward him before she began. "For pushing Meg. For pressing her. For wanting to see her happily married before I died. For wanting to hold my grandkids."

"Is that all?" he teased. "You should be ashamed of yourself."

"I mean it. I can see the strain between you and Meg. You two are trying to cover it up, but I can see that things are not as well and fine as you want me to believe."

Very perceptive. "Meg and I will be fine. All couples have to adjust to married life."

She gave a sorrowful sigh. "But if the wedding hadn't been so rushed, it would be different."

If there had been a wedding at all, it would be different.

"I know this must be hard on you, but I'm so glad my Meg found a man like you to marry. I know you'll take good care of her. It means a lot to me."

"It's nothing." *Literally.* "But I'm not sure what you mean by *hard.*"

"I can tell her feelings for you aren't as deep as yours are for her. I'm afraid to say that she may have accepted your proposal and married you for my sake. Maybe you sensed that and took advantage of the opportunity. I don't know. I don't really want to know. It can't be easy being in a one-sided love relationship."

A moment of silence stretched between them. "Don't get me wrong, Bruce. I have nothing against you. I couldn't have picked a better son-in-law. I just wish I had been patient and not pushed. Let you two come together in your own time, that's all."

She was being so candid with him, painfully so. What could he say to ease her conscience?

"The truth will set you free…"

He *wanted* to tell the truth but didn't quite know how to go about it. Blurt it out or ease into it? The last thing he wanted to do was cause some sort of setback in the woman's recovery…or to damage the relationship Meg had with her mom.

No, Gayle was Meghann's mom, and it wasn't his place to say anything. But he wanted to. Oh, how he wanted to. Instead, he settled for giving as much as he could.

"I would never take advantage of Meg." He almost added that he loved Meg too much to ever do anything to hurt her, but he stopped himself just in time. He wasn't sure if what he felt was the beginning of love or not. He did know he would do almost anything to make Meghann happy.

Drawing a deep breath, he went on. "I've waited my whole life for Meghann. I'm not about to lose her now." The words came out without forethought, but he realized they had a ring of truth to them. A loud ring, the more he listened.

Nine

MEGHANN WAS GOING TO DO IT. SHE WOULD TELL HER mother the truth. She had psyched herself up all morning and spent the afternoon practicing on Lucky, gathering her courage. She was ready. It was now or never.

She walked into the nook off the kitchen. "You, come with me."

Bruce looked up from his computer screen and grinned. "Me?"

"Yes, you."

"Just let me finish this one last e-mail, then I'm all yours, darling," he said with a wink.

Though his fingers flew over the keys, she wished he would go faster. Her courage was ebbing. If he didn't hurry, she would have none left.

"All done." He rose in one fluid motion and came toward her.

Already?

"What can I do for you?" His smile was warm and open, and she nearly forgot her purpose in coming. She forced herself to focus. "Help me tell my mom the truth."

His smile faded to uncertainty. "Of course."

"I'm really going to do it this time."

He bent his head forward slightly. "Okay. Let's go."

She didn't move. "I mean, she looked really good this morning, full of energy. I think she's ready to hear the truth."

Bruce leaned closer. "But are you ready to tell it?"

She could smell his spicy cologne. *Stay focused, Meghann.* She took a deep breath to clear her mind. It was the wrong thing to do. She only succeeded in getting a stronger whiff of his cologne. "Yes, of course I am. That's what this is all about. I wouldn't be asking you to help me if I wasn't ready."

"Okay then…" He cocked his head to one side.

"Okay then, what?"

"Are you just going to stand around talking about it, or are you going to do it?" An easy smile played at the corners of his mouth.

"I'm going." But she didn't. She just stood there, staring up at him, motionless. It was just that her feet didn't seem to want to move.

He put his hands on her shoulders, turned her around, and gave her a little push. He followed close behind to the living room where her mother sat.

"Can I talk to you for a minute, Mom?" Her stomach flipped end over end. She was finally going to put things right.

"Sure, honey." Her mother's gaze flickered from Meghann to Bruce and back again. Curiosity—and then concern—etched her features.

"Well, Mom—" she twisted her hands in her lap— "I'm not sure where to start."

"The beginning is usually best." Her mother's tone was quiet, but calm.

I was born in—no, that's too far back. It started when—no, no. Where exactly did this story begin?

"Mom, you remember back just before Christmas…" This was embarrassing. She should have done it without Bruce. She took a slow, deep breath. "…when I first told you about Bruce?"

Her mother looked worried. "Yes, dear, I remember. I was so happy for you. For both of you." Her mom smiled up at Bruce, then leaned forward with her coffee mug outstretched, to set it on the table in front of her.

Meg nodded and started to speak again, but just then the bottom of her mother's mug caught on the edge of the coffee table. A startled "Oh!" escaped her mother as half the dark brown liquid erupted from the mug, splashing on the table, the expensive leather of the couch, and the equally expensive rug.

"Oh no!" Meg jumped up, looking at Bruce. Bad enough she was ruining his month with these shenanigans, did she have to be responsible for ruining his apartment as well?

Her mother looked up at them, her eyes wide with distress. "I am such a clumsy old fool. I'm terribly sorry."

"It's okay," Bruce reassured her.

"I'll go get something to clean that up." Meghann ran to the kitchen and seized several yards of paper towels. She hurried back into the room and knelt down, doing her best to mop up the mess. But the tremor in her hands made the task more difficult than it should be.

This wasn't turning out right at all! She should have been almost finished with her tale of woe by now, almost free from this whole mess.

"I'm not normally so ungainly," her mom said as she reached for a paper towel. "Let me help."

"No, Mom. You just sit back on the couch. I'll get it."

"It's my mess."

"I said no!" Meg's words came out angry, and she hung her head. She took a moment to calm herself, then looked back up at her mother. "Just take it easy and rest."

"Meghann Rachel Livingston! I'm not an invalid. I am perfectly capable of cleaning up a little spill." Her mother hadn't spoken to her in that firm tone in years.

"You're supposed to rest. Doctor's orders."

"You act as though I have one foot in the grave."

Her mother's flip remark stirred her turbulent emotions even more. "Must I remind you that a little more than a month ago you *had?* You almost died." Her voice began to shake. "The doctor said you might not—" She swallowed hard. "They don't even know what was really wrong with you. It could happen again at any time."

The image of her mother on the precipice of death, balanced precariously, ready at any moment to fall in, terrified her. "I don't want to lose you. You're all I have." She grabbed up the wad of paper towels and rushed back to the kitchen.

Why couldn't things work out once in a while? Why couldn't she get the truth out? And how long would it be before she was able to stop worrying about and being afraid for her mother?

She threw the mass of soggy towels into the sink with more force than she'd intended, watching with dismay when coffee splattered all over the counter.

"What a mess!"

"Are you okay?" Bruce said from behind her.

She spun around and nodded her head. *Another lie.*

He studied her, and the understanding in his gaze made Meghann want to weep. "Your mom is stronger than you think."

Meghann shook her head.

"I was ready. I really was. You saw that I was starting to tell her."

He nodded. "I saw that, yes. And I saw your concern for your mother as well."

She rubbed a hand over her aching temples. "I just wish I could get it out, get it over with. She needs to know." She dropped her hand and met his gaze. "You deserve to be released from this whole, sorry affair."

The smile that tugged at his lips, the odd longing she saw in his eyes, warmed her, even as they broke through her defenses. She felt a tear sneak down her cheek, and he reached out to take hold of her arms and pull her toward him. She was too weary to resist. She let him fold her against his chest, resting there in silence.

When he spoke, his voice was tender, almost a murmur, "Meg, don't worry about me. I'm fine. Just relax. When the time is right, you'll know it. And the time will be right. You'll see."

She hoped so. Because she didn't think she could take much more.

⟨∞⟩

Gayle went in her room and closed the door. She stared down at her hands and closed them into tight fists to stop their uncontrollable movement, then looked up at her reflection in the mirror. She had tried so hard to keep the trembling in her hands from Meg. The doctor said the shaking in her hands could worsen over time. But she didn't want Meg to know. She didn't want to taint her happiness with having her worry over her mother.

No, there was no reason to tell Meg what was happening. She had enough to deal with. Though neither Meg nor Bruce had said so, she could tell things weren't right. The last thing she wanted to do was add to Meg's struggles. She couldn't do much about Meg's marriage, but she could protect her daughter from worrying about her health.

Later that evening after dinner, Meg was relieved to see that her mother's coloring was almost back to what it had been before her illness. She seemed cheerful and talkative—both good signs.

Bruce, on the other hand, was acting decidedly odd. His scrutiny of Meg had not wavered since she got back from playing with Lucky earlier. He'd been watching her, studying her. She wasn't sure she liked the extra attention.

He crooked his finger at her and walked through the French doors onto the balcony without so much as a backward glance to see if she was in pursuit. Of course she would follow, and it irked her that he knew. Maybe she would find out what was on his mind.

Bruce was leaning against the railing, looking out at the city lights. His sharp and confident profile was dark against the moonlight. The cool night air wrapped around her, but surprisingly Meghann didn't shiver. She moved to the rail a few feet away from where he stood. He shook his head but didn't turn to her. Did he know she was there? She was about to clear her throat to announce her presence when he spoke.

"Your mom was right," he said, then turned to her.

"Right about what?"

"You talk as if you're in love, at least when I'm not around, but you don't act it. You say the right things, but you don't do them."

Meg stared at him. "I'm not sure what you mean."

"Did you ever hear the old saying, 'Actions speak louder than words'?" She nodded. "Honey, if your actions are saying anything it's, 'he's got the plague.' It's as if you are trying to stay away from me."

She followed his pointed gaze and took in the distance she had unconsciously put between them. She could just imagine his reaction if she explained that it was just too hard to think straight when he was so near. "What am I supposed to do, jump in your lap?"

"It wouldn't hurt."

Meghann's mouth fell open—and when he laughed, she clamped it shut. He didn't really expect her to…to sit on his lap. She was having a hard enough time keeping what was real and what was not straight in her own head. "You can't really expect me to…I mean, I couldn't…Mr. Halloway—"

"That's it!" He slapped his palm to his forehead. "I've been racking my brain to figure it out." He removed his hand from his head and pointed at her. "You called me Mr. Halloway."

She could see by his expression that he had received some great revelation that she was not privy to, which pushed her beyond confusion. "Of course I called you Mr. Halloway. That's your name." *Isn't it?*

"Every time you talk to me you sound like you are addressing your boss."

"I am."

"No. I'm supposed to be your husband, whom you love and adore. Not someone you are afraid to ask for a raise."

Love and adore? She swallowed hard. Already her feelings for him had doubled, no quadrupled. She had to keep her distance or give away her feelings.

She latched on to the one safe thing he had said. "I'm not afraid to ask for a raise."

He raised his eyebrows in challenge and folded his arms across his chest. "Then ask."

"May I have a raise?" She tossed the question out without hesitation. Of course he'd say no.

"How much?"

"What?"

"How much of a raise do you want?"

He was being ridiculous. Well, fine, she could be ridiculous, too. "A hundred dollars." She smiled. "A week."

"Why do you think you deserve a hundred-dollar-a-week raise?"

Enough was enough. "I suppose I don't, so let's drop it."

"Let's not. I'm interested in what you think your assets are."

Assets?

He must have realized how that sounded and quickly added, "In regard to the hotel, that is."

She licked her lips and took a breath. "I've been working there for three years and am due for a raise. I'm rarely sick and never late. I've put in a lot of extra hours working on the masquerade ball and…"

I think I'm falling in love with you.

"And…" he prodded.

. She swallowed hard around the sudden lump in her throat. "I think…"

He held her gaze, and something flickered deep in the depths of his eyes. He took a step toward her. "You think…?"

"I think I'm…"

Another step closer. Now she could feel his breath on her face. Her throat went dry, her head was spinning. *Oh, help…*

"You think you're…?" His hand slid along the railing, coming to rest beside her arm. She could feel the warmth of his skin where it rested against her.

Think, Meg! For the love of Pete, think of something *to say.* "I think I'm…worth more! Yes, I'm worth more than I'm getting paid." She shook her head and blinked. "Worth far more…than I'm getting now—getting paid now."

His easy smile returned. "Done."

Meghann went slack jawed. "You can't be serious."

He gave her a nod. "I agree with your reasoning. You are a valuable employee. You have just successfully negotiated a raise, one of the hardest things for an employee to do. Now can you relax around me?"

She eyed him suspiciously. "Mr. Phenton will never approve it."

"I'll talk to George."

"No, don't!"

He raised his eyebrows again.

"You've already gotten me all this time off with pay. I don't want you to get in trouble on my account."

"I can get around George Phenton."

"Oh, please, Mr. Halloway, don't." She didn't want him to get fired. "You have done so much for me." She noticed he was shaking his head but continued anyway. "I appreciate everything you've done, really I do." She couldn't stand it any longer. "Why are you shaking your head? Don't you believe me?" She *was* a known liar to him, so why should he believe her?

"You called me Mr. Halloway again."

Meghann let out a heavy sigh. "Well, that's who you are. At least, that's how I think of you." *How I have to think of you if I'm going to survive this whole thing!* "I know you are supposed to be my husband." She felt a little twinge inside when she said *my husband.* He would make a wonderful husband. "But you're not."

The words came out flat and depressed, and she hoped he didn't notice. Thankfully, he just nodded his head.

"True enough, but you can't keep *treating* me like

your boss when we're with your mom. You're stiff and formal. You either have to fess up now or play this to the end and make it look real. I'm just trying to help you."

But he *was* her boss. "What exactly did my mom say to you?"

"She thinks you rushed into this marriage without being in love. That you did it for her."

"I *did* do it for her! Not that I really *did* anything. I mean, we're not married, right? So I didn't actually *do* anything."

Except lie, Meghann. Big time.

She let out a frustrated huff. "But *whatever* it is I did, I did for her." She shook her head.

"And you act like it. Your mother thinks this is a one-sided relationship—"

"It's not any kind of relationship at all!"

His expression was patient. "I know that, and you know that, but for now, you mother doesn't know that. And I'm sure you don't want your mother to feel guilty for pressuring you to marry someone you didn't love. You care for her too much for that. I think you would probably give up everything for her." The last statement was said with compassion and his look was tender. "Think back to the first time you were in love."

"This *is* the first time!" She stopped, horrified. How had she let that come out? She scrambled to explain her words away before he could do or say anything that would make her humiliation total. "What I mean is, this is the first serious relationship I've ever had. Or *supposedly* had. Oh, you know what I mean!"

She risked a peek at his face and saw he was just

watching her, considering her words. *Please, please don't let him realize what I said was the truth.*

Because it was. She'd never been in love before. Not even once. She'd had crushes from time to time, but never felt she'd met a man she loved. Really loved. As in forever.

Except for maybe now.

Why did Bruce have to be so nice about everything? Why did he have to be so wonderful and caring and beguiling? Why did he have to be the one man she'd ever fallen in love with? She should have chosen someone she didn't even like. Someone who made her skin crawl.

Then her heart wouldn't have to break when this was all over.

His silence unnerved her. She couldn't quite read his expression. A little smile curved up the corners of his mouth. Was he pleased? Or could he be laughing at her?

"Have you ever been in a school play?"

His question was so unexpected, Meghann could only shake her head.

"Pretended to be someone else?"

She continued to shake her head.

His soothing voice probed further. "You were never Dorothy landing in Munchkinland? Never played dress up? Didn't you do anything fun as a child?"

"I suppose when I was real young. After my dad died, I mostly helped Mom with the housework. In high school she wouldn't let me get a job to help. She was afraid my schoolwork would suffer. I studied extra hard to make her proud."

He studied her in silence. When he spoke, his voice was low. "It's hard for you to lie to your mother, isn't it?"

She nodded. "I'm not very good at it."

"Neither am I. Believe it or not, this is all a first for me as well." His eyes grew serious. "All of it."

She frowned. What was he saying? Before she could think it through, he went on.

"But I do know this much, if you are going to play a part, you should try to be believable."

"I can't make this believable…" She was too close to the edge as it was, too close to letting her heart get the best of her.

"I realize pretending to love me isn't easy—"

She glanced at him quickly. Was he offended?

"But I'd like to think it's not impossible."

"Well, of course not—"

"Just think of it as a game. You are acting out a part."

"I'm not sure how."

"For starters, take my hand." He held out his hand. She looked from it to his expression. Was he serious?

"Meg, are we or are we not supposed to be happily married?" He waited for her to nod. "Then *act* like you're in love. Newlyweds touch and hold hands and gaze into each other's eyes." His voice dropped to a low growl. "Like this."

Her breath caught in her throat. The look he gave her now bespoke of love and affection. So much so that it made her a bit dizzy. The man was good at this "game," as he called it. Could she play it as well?

Without losing her heart in the process?

Too late, a small inner voice mocked. Ignoring it, she took a step toward him and wrapped her hand around his.

"See, that wasn't so bad. I don't bite." Bruce's smile was pleased.

"How do you know *I* don't?" she said, turning up one side of her mouth. "You could be risking your very life."

"I'll take my chances." The reply was quiet and firm, and so full of conviction that she looked up in surprise.

He studied her face, and she felt caught by his searching. A cool breeze blew a strand of hair across her cheek. Bruce closed the gap between them and reached up with his free hand to brush the wayward lock back behind her ear. His hand settled on the side of her neck as he continued to gaze at her. Her skin tingled at his touch. She forced herself to breathe.

What was he going to do now? He was so close he could...no, he wouldn't do that! He wouldn't kiss her. Maybe she should just kiss him...just to see what it would be like...just to prove she could play this game with the best of them.

He lowered his head, his eyes still on hers, and touched his lips to hers with featherlightness. At least, she thought that's what happened. Either that or she reached up to kiss him....

She couldn't remember. But then, she was hardly capable of coherent thought at the moment. All she could do right now was float on the cloud of pure joy and pleasure of Bruce's kiss…the feel of his lips on hers…the faint awareness that he was shifting slightly, drawing her closer—

The sound of a throat being cleared behind them sent a shock through Meghann, and she jumped back and spun around.

"Perfect," Bruce whispered in her ear as she leaned back against him. The pleasure in his voice was nothing, though, compared to the approval on her mother's face.

Bruce wrapped his arms around her waist from behind and held her against him. "Hi, Mom," he said over Meghann's shoulder.

Even though she couldn't see him, she could hear the smile in his voice. And she was embarrassed for being caught kissing him. But she knew she shouldn't be, so she tried to slough it off. But her legs felt like jelly and she needed a moment to get her strength back. She wasn't sure she could stand on her own and was grateful for the support of his arms around her.

"I'm sorry, Mom. We—we didn't mean to ignore you." Meghann brushed at an imaginary piece of dirt on Bruce's sleeve.

Her mother waved off the apology. "Don't worry about me. I'm glad to see you kids having fun. I just wanted to say good night. I'm a little tired, so I'm going to bed."

"We're going to turn in soon as well." Bruce nuzzled against Meghann's hair.

She closed her eyes at the contact. If only she could stay there, leaning against his strength and warmth, his arms securely around her, his lips brushing against her hair. But as soon as her mother was gone, he released her and stepped away, moving back inside. Meghann stood at the railing, her hands clenching the metal fiercely, struggling to get her roiling emotions under control.

"Play the game," he'd said. Well, she had. And suddenly he was acting as though the touch of her burned him and he couldn't wait to get away from her.

Had he sensed how deeply their brief kiss had affected her? Was he embarrassed by that? Or maybe he'd been repulsed to kiss someone so inexperienced?

She waited out on the balcony for a few minutes, hoping he would come back out and invite her inside or say something encouraging. He never came.

She wandered in and found him in the bedroom. He had left the door conspicuously open. His dark hair looked mussed like he had combed it with his hands. He looked at her and frowned when she closed the door. Was he mad at her? What had she done?

He brushed past her without really touching her on his way to the door. He grabbed the knob.

Why was he leaving so suddenly? She knew her mother couldn't possibly be asleep yet. What if she heard him leave? "What—Where—"

He turned and looked at her, drawing in a deep breath. "I'll slip out quietly. She'll never know I've left." His voice broke with huskiness.

He stared at her a moment longer, then reached up to caress her cheek with the delicateness of a butterfly's wing. She sighed. He wasn't mad at her. His touch told her as much.

Then he was gone.

She readied herself for bed in a daze, then lay awake for a long time, feeling his caress and replaying his kiss. It might be the only time he kissed her and she wanted to cherish it. When this was all over, at least she would have the sweet memories.

Bruce carefully latched the apartment door so as not to make any noise, then sagged against it and raked a hand through his hair. He made it. He got out of there before he gave in to temptation and wrapped Meg in his arms and kissed her—*really* kissed her. With all the passion and emotion raging through him...emotions that had exploded into life when his lips met hers.

He thought kissing her would remove the mystique. It had only intensified it. And it hadn't been enough. Not by a long shot. He wanted to kiss her again. And again. Could he play this game without losing his heart? Did he even want to try to hold on to his heart? Or was it already hers?

You're fooling yourself into thinking this is something more than it is. You could have ruined it tonight. Tread lightly or you'll scare her off. She already thinks you're a cad, don't prove her right.

Dear Lord, help me.

For the next week and a half, Meghann made a conscious effort to hold Bruce's hand or put her arm around his waist in her mother's presence. It didn't take long, though, for the actions to become second nature. She was holding his hand without being aware of doing so, as though it were the most natural thing in the world.

Which it was. What wasn't going to be natural was stopping.

But she couldn't go back. As Bruce so often reminded her, appearance was everything. If only it didn't leave her heart unprotected and vulnerable. If only it didn't mean, in the end, the hurt would be that much greater.

Ten

EARLY THE NEXT MORNING, BRUCE WALKED IN THE KITCHEN and was surprised to see Meghann up already. She stood at the counter with her back to him. "Good morning." He kept his tone casual, trying to rein in his zealous emotions at the sight of her.

She straightened and raised her hands to wipe her face before turning around. The remains of errant tears on her lashes caused an iron fist to clamp around his heart. In an instant he was at her side. "What's wrong?"

"Nothing. I'm fine." She turned away from him.

He took a firm hold of her upper arms and turned her back toward him, then touched her cheek. "You missed one."

She gave up her denial and began to cry. "I didn't sleep well. She kept dying over and over in my dreams."

He tentatively wrapped his arms around her. When her tears had subsided, he smiled down at her, nestled against him. This was good. This was right.

But as though the intimacy of the moment were too much, she stepped back. A chaos of emotions thrashed around in him as they gazed at each other. He wanted desperately to wrap his arms around her and kiss her. Instead, he caressed a tear from her cheek with gentle fingers.

"Your mother will be fine. Why don't you go back to bed and try to get some sleep. Don't worry about coming into the hotel today." He tried fervently to calm the storm within.

With a sniff and a nod, Meg moved to do as he'd suggested.

Later after Gayle had gotten up and he saw she was looking better than the day before, Bruce slipped into his suit coat and picked up his briefcase. "Tell Meg I'll call her later."

She looked up from her tea. "I'm surprised she's not up already."

"She didn't sleep well. Bad dreams. See you later." He felt uncomfortable knowing...as though he were telling Meghann's secrets. He exited quickly, hoping her mother hadn't picked up on his discomfort.

He pressed the elevator button and waited, then the sound of an opening door caught his attention. He turned, and his pulse quickened at the sight of Meghann's hurried approach. The elevator door slid open. He held it with his hand until she reached him. Her honey-colored hair looked soft and luxurious against her violet sweater. His gaze continued down her jeans and landed on her bare feet. She darted inside the elevator and waited for him. Stepping inside, he released the door. What was she up to? She certainly wasn't going anywhere without shoes. The doors slid shut.

"I wanted to talk to you before you went off to the hotel." She looked a bit distressed.

His gaze slipped back down to her bare feet. "I figured as much."

She wiggled her toes. "Oh."

He waited through her silence. She fidgeted with her fingers. The elevator stopped on the fifth, third, and second floors to collect more passengers. Bruce didn't think she was going to tell him what it was that brought her out without her shoes in a small, crowded space. He had stepped closer to her with each group of new passengers until the two of them were tucked securely in the corner, and he drank in her sweet, soft scent. Had they been alone, he seriously doubted he could have resisted the temptation to kiss her. But had they been alone, he wouldn't have been standing mere inches from her, being enticed.

The elevator came to a stop at the garage level and emptied quickly. He held the door and waited.

He noticed her take a deep breath before starting. "I wanted to apologize for…well, for earlier…when I was upset and everything. You know, crying all over your shirt and all that. I really don't know why I let a silly dream upset me so much."

She was babbling again; it seemed to be a habit of hers when she was nervous. He set his briefcase in the doorway to keep the elevator doors open.

She shrugged, going on. "I was crying all over you, and I'm sure your shirt was all wet. I guess I just kept my fear of losing her all locked inside and it finally broke loose."

She only stopped chattering when he gently touched her cheek and moved his thumb across the soft skin. Her breath caught. Even without makeup she was beautiful. "Don't worry about it. It's already forgotten."

"Really?"

He pressed the button for his floor and stepped out of the elevator.

"Really." Well, in part. He'd forgotten about his shirt being wet. He could never forget her.

The doors closed on the vision of her, and he read—and understood—the quandary on her face.

This whole situation was nothing if not confusing. He leaned his forehead against the smooth, cold wall. "Meghann, what are you doing to me?" With a sigh, he turned toward his car.

Meghann stared at the closed doors, not seeing her own reflection in the polished steel doors, but Bruce's endearing face. *"Don't worry. It's already forgotten."* His words ricocheted around in her head. She stomped her bare foot.

"Already forgotten!"

Was she that easy to forget? She could have sworn he almost kissed her again this morning, that he'd felt the same, powerful pull that she had. Now…she shut her eyes against the dread filling her.

Was it possible she'd misread him? That nothing had happened between them earlier? Was the attraction between them all wishful hoping on her part?

Do I matter to you at all, Bruce Halloway? Do you ever think of me when we are apart, the way I do you? Apparently not.

The elevator stopped and she got out.

"I was wondering if you were coming back, the way you flew out of here after your husband."

Meg almost grimaced at her mother's knowing smile and the glint in her eyes.

Giving her mom a halfhearted smile, she held up one foot. "I forgot my shoes."

"Bruce said you had a rough night's sleep. Aren't you feeling well?"

"I feel fine. I just had a nightmare." But it was nothing compared to the ongoing nightmare she was living. That nightmare apparently had no end.

"Isn't it nice to have a big, strong, handsome man like Bruce to comfort you?"

Yes, it was nice, very nice. It would have been nicer if it had meant something to him. "I'm going to take a shower."

She'd been almost happy last night, lost in the sensations brought about by the kiss she and Bruce had shared. Then she had that stupid dream…and Bruce comforted her…then turned around and forgot her scant moments later.

What are you expecting here, Meghann?

She frowned at the internal question. What was she expecting? That Bruce would come to love her? That he'd turn into a knight in shining armor and sweep her away to live with him forever as his princess?

Yes, yes, and yes. She wanted it all. More than she

cared to admit. But even she knew life didn't turn out that way. Especially not as a result of going against what was right in God's eyes.

She and Bruce were not living a fairly tale. They were living a lie, and the longer she let it go on, the worse the consequences would be. It was simple cause and effect. The longer her mother thought they were married, the harder it would be for her to accept the truth.

"What a tangled web we weave...."

Cliché or not, it was painfully accurate.

"Let's go in here," Mom said.

Meghann followed in her mother's wake without paying attention to their destination.

Her mom had been eager to visit the local outlet mall. They had been in and out of more than a dozen stores already. It pleased her that her mom showed no signs of tiring. Just in case, she was keeping a close eye on her to see she didn't overdo it.

Meghann glanced around the store and couldn't figure out what could possibly interest her mother here. The walls were painted in bright primary colors, and a huge talking teddy bear occupied the center of the store. This was a children's clothing store. How odd. What could her mother be looking for in here?

"This is adorable," she heard her mom say from halfway across the store.

Meghann hurried over. Mom was holding a pink, lacy, ruffly infant dress. Meghann was aghast.

"Which do you like better? This precious ruffled dress or the cute little boy sailor suit?" Her mother held up the two outfits.

Meghann rolled her eyes.

"Do you and Bruce want to have a girl or a boy first?"

"Mother."

The older woman was not deterred by Meghann's obvious lack of enthusiasm. "Maybe I'll just get them both. You will probably have one of each, eventually."

She hated to dash her mom's hopes but knew it had to be done. She took the two outfits from her and hung them back on the rack. "Mom, don't spend your money on something that may never be used. I don't intend to have a baby for a long time." *A very long time.*

"Well, you can never tell. These things don't always go according to plan, you know."

"Can we just drop it for now?"

"Fine," her mother said, holding her hands up in front of her in mock surrender and heading for the door. "But you can't stop me from dreaming. I'm not getting any younger. I could go at any minute. I think my little episode proved that."

Little episode? Her mom had been in a coma, not expected to live through the night. That constituted more than a *little episode.*

The next store was safe. Not a baby item in sight.

Her mom wandered through the linen store and eventually picked out a picturesque throw with a lake nestled up in front of a tree-covered mountain. "Isn't this beautiful?"

"I love it." Meghann fingered the corner of it. "It's gorgeous."

"Good, because I'm getting it for you...and Bruce of course." Her mother headed off and rummaged through a large bin of throw pillows.

"You're buying it for me—uh—us?"

"For your house. It's a wedding gift."

"House?"

"It will go great thrown over the back of the couch or hung on that wall in the living room. You know the big one opposite the picture window? Push the couch from Bruce's apartment up against the wall, a couple of end tables with nice lamps, and these pillows will go great with it."

Her mother was already decorating a house that they weren't going to buy?

"Mom, I can't let you do this. You already sent me that punch bowl for a wedding gift, remember?"

"That was just a tide-you-over gift until I knew more what you needed. What do you think? The striped ones or these other pillows?" She held up a black-and-cream striped pillow and a paisley print in matching colors. "I think I'll just get them all."

"Mom, no! I don't want you to buy any of this for me—us."

Her mother looked stricken. "You just won't let me have any fun today."

"It's not that." What should she tell her? "What if Bruce doesn't like them?"

"Bruce not like them? What is there not to like? Of course he'll like them."

"Can't you just wait? We don't even have that house or any house."

"Fine. I'll buy them for myself." Mom pushed her cart toward the checkout stand. "I just wanted to help you and that cute son-in-law of mine to build your life together. You two obviously aren't making much effort on your own."

"Can we drop this subject, too?"

She paid for her purchase. "I won't mention it again to you. But if you or Bruce bring it up…"

"The only thing I intend to bring up right now is whether or not you have any aspirin. I have a headache." Meghann rubbed her temples. "Can we go now?"

"Maybe I should drive us home—"

"Somehow, Mother, I think letting someone drive who collapsed for no apparent reason is less than wise."

Her mother sniffed at that. "I was just trying to help."

Meghann put her arm around her mother's shoulders. They were still painfully thin. "I know, Mom. I'm sorry. I'm just being cranky today."

What can I say? I'm in love with a man who finds me easy to forget? A man I'm supposedly married to who will probably never speak to me again once this whole mess is over….

With a sigh, she led her mother to the car, where she put her mom's treasures in the trunk, then slid in behind the wheel. Her mom was only being so pushy because she thought Meghann and Bruce's marriage was shaky. Well, it wasn't shaky at all. It was nonexistent. So they were actually doing exceptionally well under the circumstances.

"Headache any better, dear?"

Meghann nodded absently, though it wasn't true. Her head was pounding like a drummer on speed. And Meg was pretty sure that the pain wasn't going anywhere until her mom went back home.

The drive was made in silence for the most part, until her mom came up with her next brilliant idea. "I think I'll move out here. This drier climate seems to agree with me."

Meg stared at her, her mouth working but no words coming out. It couldn't. She was too stunned to speak. Finally she managed to stammer, "You—you've got to be kidding! What about your job and all your friends?" Her mom just couldn't move out here. She couldn't!

"I can make new friends and get a new job. Maybe my son-in-law would hire me at the hotel. That way I would be closer to you and Bruce...and my grandkids." She beamed at Meg, clearly delighted at the prospect. "Wouldn't that be wonderful?"

Wonderful? No, that was not what it would be. Terrible, maybe. A nightmare come true, probably. The worst thing that could possibly happen, definitely.

But wonderful? Not in a million years.

Eleven

MEGHANN FOLLOWED AS HER MOTHER AND BRUCE WALKED through the room of display cases stopping at each one to read the Colorado history behind what was displayed there. The artifacts spanned from the early natives before settlers came to the present day.

"This is so interesting," her mother said. "I never cared for it when I was in school as a child, but now that I have vivid memories of living through some of this, it sends a shiver running right up my back. It makes me feel old to remember some of this stuff they call history."

Meghann had always loved history, loved imagining what people were like and how they lived. It was all so fascinating and somehow almost magical.

Mom moved on to the next display. Meghann started to follow but Bruce caught her hand and held her back.

"Wait for me," he said when she gave him a questioning look. "I'm not finished. I haven't read about the men and women from here who fought in the Korean War."

"I have. I was going to the next exhibit."

"Would you read it to me?" His eyes pleading.

"But...I—"

"Please. I love to hear the sound of your voice."

"That's so sweet," her mother cooed. "I'll just meet you two on the other side of the room." She moved on to the next display.

If there was one thing Bruce had perfected, it was the sad, puppy dog look.

Meghann sighed and tore her gaze from his to the case and began reading about the heroic efforts of a local boy. Bruce leaned against the glass and watched her, making it difficult to concentrate.

Good, she was done, they could move on and he could read for himself.

"Why me?"

Bruce's low question stopped her in her tracks. "What?"

"Why did you pick me?" He stepped up to her and slid his arms around her, locking his hands behind the small of her back. Her hands automatically braced against his chest.

She glanced around, self-conscious—and terrified he'd be able to tell how much she liked what he was doing. "Why are you holding me like this? Mom's moved on and out of sight."

"You're avoiding my question."

She gave him her own innocent, butter-wouldn't-melt-in-my-mouth look. "Which question would that be?"

His eyes scolded her gently. "Why did you pick me?"

She swallowed hard. "Pick you?"

His mouth curved up slightly at the corners. "Yes. Unless you know another Bruce Halloway who is assistant manager at the Palace Hotel."

"No. You are the only Bruce Halloway I know of." She made the meek admission in a low, hesitant voice.

"Soooo?"

"So, what?"

He gave her a little shake. "So why me? Was it because of my position at the hotel?" His gaze pinned her. "Or was it because you were interested in me?"

"Well-l-l..." How did she answer this honestly without revealing too much of her feelings for him? She couldn't tell him that she had been infatuated with him from day one; that, in a moment of pure frustration brought on by her mother's constant questions, she had hinted to her mom that they were sort of dating. No, she couldn't tell Bruce any of that. "I knew my mother would like the idea of me being married to an up-and-coming assistant manager who was being groomed for general manager."

A shadow crossed his face. "Ah, so George is on his way out. Shall I let him know? And it was my position you were interested in, or the position I would soon have?"

If his expression were any gauge, this wasn't going well at all. "No, I was interested in *you*—" Oh, good grief, what was she saying? "Or at least the idea of you that I had in my head. When I told my mom about you, I didn't know you. Not like I do now."

"And now that you know me better, do I meet with your approval?"

Met, exceeded, and left in the dust. "You're a little of what I thought you would be like." *And a whole lot more.*

"Is that a little in a good way or in a bad way?"

"Good." *Definitely good.* "We should probably go on." She pointed in the direction of the next display.

"I'm not stopping you." He raised his hands from where they'd been resting at his sides.

She looked at them in horror. Here she was still snuggled against his chest…and of her own volition! When had he released her?

She was always in a quandary when she was this close to him. Their connection felt so real at times. And her growing feelings for him were certainly real, but she knew the situation wasn't. He was only pretending. She felt divided.

A lie does that. It divides the heart from the soul. It hurts those involved.

Oh, Lord, let this be real. Let him feel something for me.

Bruce reached up and brushed back the hair from one side of her face while his other hand lightly touched her back.

The feel of his fingers on her skin was heavenly, and she realized her breathing was erratic at best.

"You two look so cute together."

Meg turned guiltily to find her mother beaming at them. She wagged a finger at Meg. "It won't be long." With that, she went off with a broad smile on her face.

Bruce glanced at Meg. "Won't be long for what?"

"Grandchildren." She rolled her eyes. "The woman is obsessed."

Bruce smiled before hooking his arm around her

waist and moving to catch up to her mother. "Where would you like to go for lunch, Mom? Unless you are too tired, then we can head back home."

"Lunch sounds great."

"But I haven't seen the rest of the exhibit," Meghann said.

"I'll bring you back another time, I promise."

His sincerity melted her protest and increased her feelings for him. She sure hoped he kept his promise because she looked forward to spending more time with him.

They picked a restaurant and ordered their food.

"What have you decided about that house?"

"Mom, you promised to drop it," Meghann said, exasperated at one of the only two subjects that seemed to interest her mother.

"I promised not to bother you about it any more, but I don't believe I was talking to you." She turned to Bruce and waited for his answer.

Bruce smiled, then raised his eyebrows. "I think our food has just arrived."

After the waiter left and they blessed the food, her mother stared at Bruce, still awaiting an answer from him.

Bruce glanced at Meghann for help. She had none to offer. After all, her mother wasn't talking to her. She shrugged her shoulders and abandoned him with a sweet smile.

"Well...we aren't sure yet. We don't want to rush into anything. Hasty decisions are often the wrong ones."

"You liked the place, didn't you?"

"Yes," he said reluctantly.

Meghann nodded with a congenial smile.

"Was there anything wrong with the place?" Mom asked, her eyebrows raised in determination.

Meghann shook her head. "It was perfect."

"Nothing that couldn't be remedied." Bruce seemed a little uncomfortable.

Meghann sensed he could feel himself being backed into a corner. How was he going to wiggle out of this?

"Then you have to move fast before someone else decides to buy it out from under you!" The woman gained inertia with each word. "You don't want to lose a find like that? To find a house you both agree on and like is nothing to be trifled with. Do you know how rare it is? Just like that—boom! You found your dream home."

Well, at least Mom has found her dream home, or should I say her dream home for us—or me—oh, whatever.

"So, what do you think? Are you going to let this pass you by, or are you going to jump on it?"

Bruce looked from his persistent pseudo-mother-in-law to his conspicuously quiet make-believe wife.

Meghann held up her hands in mock surrender. "She's not talking to, remember?"

He looked a bit stunned, then swung his gaze back to her mother. "I guess I'll call the realtor when we get back and get the ball rolling. I'm easy to please. If Meghann likes it, that's good enough for me. Any house where she is will feel like home."

Touché! She was sure her mom liked that little declaration of love and devotion. It wasn't what she'd expected him to say, and somehow she sensed he knew it. He'd said the opposite of what he knew she wanted because she hadn't gotten him off the hook. Well, she had tried at the start, but he refused to go away. Fortunately, he was good at thinking fast on his feet, even if he was sitting down.

"I hope you know you've only made matters worse," she said later that evening after her mother had gone to bed. "You're egging Mom on. She'll be impossible to live with now. She's like a dog with a bone."

"You could have spoken up."

"Yes. And you could have gone away on an imaginary business trip."

He fell silent at that, and Meg looked at him, surprised to see a hint of something—was it hurt?—in his eyes. His question seemed to confirm her suspicions. "Why are you always trying to get rid of me?"

She hugged her knees against her chest. "I'm not." At his pointed glance, she inclined her head. "Not really. It's just that lying to my mom is one thing, but I feel awful about dragging you into this. I never meant for you to know what I'd done, let alone have to take part in it!" She realized her voice was trembling and looked away from his gentle eyes. She gave a small laugh. "You probably think I'm a scatterbrained dimwit."

"Meg."

She didn't respond. She couldn't.

"Hon, look at me."

Even if she'd been able to resist the endearment, she couldn't withstand the utter tenderness in the request. She met his gaze.

"Meghann, it was my choice to get involved in this. Basically I knew what I was getting myself into. I can handle it."

She didn't doubt that in the least. Bruce Halloway could handle whatever came his way.

"As for you being a scatterbrained dimwit, I figured out a long time ago that women think differently than men and just accepted it. It's what makes women so interesting. You always keep us men guessing. I find it remarkable that a woman can have so many thoughts going in different directions and still remain functional. It must take a higher intelligence."

Hah! He could have at least said she wasn't a dimwit.

"I am only a lowly man, your humble servant, and cannot fathom the intricate workings of a superior mind." He concluded with a sweeping bow.

She laughed at that. The man was a nut sometimes but a charmer at all times. And for all that he was spreading his foolishness on thick, she was glad he wasn't eager to dash off the scene.

If only he would realize what she had...that this was the perfect point for him to kiss her.

Not unless he really wanted to kiss you, just to kiss you...after all, your mom's not here to impress.

He leaned toward her, and she felt her pulse jump. Reaching down, he cupped her face...his thumb caressed her cheek...and her eyes started to drift shut.

"I should be heading off."

Her eyes snapped open at that, and she watched, incredulous, as Bruce stood and stretched. "Your mother is probably asleep, so there's no reason for me to stick around." He glanced down at her, as though waiting for her to say something to prove him wrong. But she just shrugged. "Nope. No reason at all."

He nodded slowly, then made his way to the door. "See you tomorrow, then."

"Right. Tomorrow."

She watched him leave, then lowered her head until it rested against her knees, glad he hadn't wasted any time in leaving.

She'd hate for him to see her sitting there with her dashed hopes in a crumpled heap at her feet.

Twelve

Upon arriving home a few days later, Bruce parked his car in the underground garage and waited by the elevator. He had gone to the office early, so he hadn't encountered either one of the Livingston women this morning. He longed to see Meghann's face. He missed her.

He'd done his best to concentrate at work—he really had—but his mind kept drifting back to her. He relived their kiss over and over, her soft lips, the scent that was uniquely hers. He knew the experience would haunt him until he kissed her again. He wondered when he'd have his next opportunity.

When indeed?

Sorting out his feelings wasn't easy. He'd liked her before this charade, and his affection for her had now grown to where he cared deeply for her. Even—dare he admit it?—was falling in love with her. He'd always felt God would let him know, would show him when his heart was being given away forever. Now he realized it was something that happened slowly, gradually...and completely.

He thought about her all the time, wanted to hold her in his arms and kiss her again. Would she let him if her mother weren't there to see it? She seemed nervous and uneasy whenever they were alone. It was as though she were afraid to be alone with him and tried to make sure they weren't.

The elevator doors opened and Meghann stepped off, which was a pleasant surprise. She seemed taken aback to see him.

"You're home. I wasn't expecting you yet. Mom's still sleeping. Try not to wake her. She had a restless night." She was rambling; she must be nervous about something.

"Where are you off to?" He made the question as nonthreatening as possible.

"I'm just going to run a few errands. I won't be long."

That sounded like a dismissal. "Since your mom is sleeping anyway, how 'bout if I play chauffeur?"

If he'd hoped for a pleased reaction, he was in for a disappointment. A slight hint of red tinged her cheeks, and she shook her head quickly. "Oh. No. That's okay. I can manage. I don't want to trouble you."

She *was* trying to ditch him. Well, he wasn't going to make it easy for her. "No trouble at all. I insist." She opened her mouth; it looked like to protest. He wasn't going to give her the chance. "We'll take my car." He motioned for her to walk in the direction of the cars.

She reluctantly walked to his silver gray Infinity, stopping at the passenger door. She looked worried, biting her bottom lip.

Walking up behind her, he pointed to the cover hiding a sports car next to his other car. "I thought we'd take the 'Vette since it's only the two of us."

"The…what?" She stared at him, clearly perplexed.

He liked throwing her off balance. He went to the back of the cocooned car and pulled up the cover, exposing his red Corvette. Walking around the car, removing the cover, he freed the car of its wrapper. He drank in a deep breath as he stared at it. It was a beauty.

"1978 red special edition Corvette convertible with custom chrome mags, fuel injected L-88 engine with duel chrome pipes, hurst five-speed overdrive surrounded by smoke gray imported leather interior." He ran his hand along the sleek body. He glanced up at her, expecting to see how impressed she was; instead, she looked as if he had just spoken to her in a foreign language. Maybe he had, but this was his baby and he knew every square inch of her.

"How…? Where…? This is *your* car?"

He nodded.

Her eyes darted from one car to the other and back again. He pulled out his keys and dangled them in front of her. "You want to drive?"

She looked up at him, startled. "Me?" He raised his eyebrows in challenge. When would she ever have a chance to drive a car like this?

He saw a spark light in her eyes, and she was suddenly more agreeable to his presence. A smile slid across her lips as she snatched the keys from him and unlocked the door, no doubt before he could change his mind. Bruce smiled too as he rounded the car to the passenger side. This would be…interesting…and a challenge, a true test of his commitment to the Lord. He had mentally given over all his worldly possessions, this being the hardest. "Just take it easy, okay?"

She shot him a wicked smile. "What's the third pedal for?"

His stomach tightened painfully. "You're kidding, right? Please tell me you're not serious."

Her sudden laughter eased some of his anxiety. She deftly slid it into reverse and backed out smoothly.

Several small incidental errands later, his curiosity was burning. Why hadn't she wanted him along? Was she *that* uncomfortable alone with him? But why? Surely she wasn't still worried that he'd do something inappropriate?

Surely not, when you've been so circumspect? Kept your distance. Not pressed her on any front.

At the sarcastic thought, he felt an uncomfortable flush fill his face. Okay, so he'd been a little…assertive. So he'd kissed her. Pulled her into his arms a time or two. Was that so wrong?

What do you want from her?

The question took him by surprise. He frowned, turning to look out the car window. What *did* he want from Meghann Livingston?

The answer came clear and sure: everything. He wanted everything. Her heart, her love, her devotion…her. He wanted her.

She's My daughter, son. Do you deserve her?

The uncomfortable feeling in his gut grew more intense, but he ignored it. He'd treated her well, done what he could to help with her mother, covered for her, played the role...

Lied.

Well, yes. There was that.

"How can goodness be a partner with wickedness?... 'Therefore, come out from among the world, and separate yourselves from them,' says the Lord. 'I will be your Father and you will be my sons and daughters.'"

"Could we put the top down?"

Bruce jumped at Meg's question, turning back to face her. He took in her beauty, her sweet spirit, and his heart was pierced.

Make me worthy, Lord. Help me know what to do. And give me the courage to do it.

She arched her brows at his silence. "The top?" she repeated. "Can we put it down."

He nodded quickly. "Sure. No problem. After our next stop."

Said stop was a quick trip into a bakery to get some croissants they didn't need. She seemed to be making up errands as she went. Was she trying to buy time or just having as much fun driving his Vette as he did? The pleasure he had watching her enjoy his toy was unexpected. He was calm, even though someone other than himself was behind the wheel of his prized car. At least he could know without a doubt that God was working on him in the area of surrendering his possessions.

"I've never been in a convertible with the top down."

He glanced up at the sky. "It's a little cool."

"It's a beautiful day," she said, extending her hands

up to the clear blue sky to convince him.

"The wind makes it seem colder, but if you don't mind, neither do I." He showed her how the vinyl roof detached, and they were off. She wasn't a careless driver, and he marveled again that he trusted her with his car. But could he truly trust her or anyone fully? Could he confide in her and not have it used against him?

Meghann pulled into a strip mall a block away and parked in the first available space. "You can stay in the car. I'll only be a minute," she said in a rush as she jumped out of the car.

He stared after her as she crossed the lot. This was it. This was the secret errand. At least now he was sure her resistance to him wasn't personal. She had put the top down and got out in a hurry to make sure he stayed put. He smiled to himself. It would take more than that to hold him back. He quickly put the top up, retrieved the keys from the ignition, and took off after her.

Meghann's attempts to get rid of him amused him. He played dumb and remained her ever-diligent shadow, wondering what it was she wanted to do by herself. He figured he might not find out if he didn't give her a little space. Suddenly an ugly thought jumped up from the back of his mind: Did she have a boyfriend?

The wave of jealousy that swept through him was so strong it almost knocked him to his knees. For a heartbeat, his mind pounded with angry questions: Was she trying to meet him? How long had she known him? How could he have let her play him for such a fool?

Then reason whispered through his mind: If she

had a boyfriend, surely she wouldn't use Bruce for her make-believe husband. If Meg had a man in her life, she would have used him when trying to placate her mother, wouldn't she? The only way to find out was to give her some slack and follow her. He watched her walk halfway down the line of stores. Keeping her in sight, he took note of the store she ducked into at the far end.

The parking space she picked was as far away as she could get. He strolled down to where she disappeared. Nestled in between a bridal shop and a tuxedo rental store was the quaint jewelry store she entered.

He peeked through the window and saw her looking in a display case. She appeared to be waiting for one of the two sales people to be freed up from the customers they were helping. She was by herself so she wasn't meeting anybody. Unless *he* worked here. Bruce took a closer look at the two clerks; one was an older man in his fifties and the other was hidden behind a customer's head. But he could see her hand with long painted red nails and multiple rings.

He ruled out that Meghann was meeting another man, and his jealous tide evaporated. What could be so embarrassing about a jewelry purchase that she needed to keep it a secret? New earrings? A watch battery, perhaps? Top international spy stuff.

It couldn't hurt to find out. He opened the door and strode up behind her. "Those are nice," he said, looking over her shoulder into the display case of pearls.

Meghann jumped at his sudden appearance. "Wh-what are you doing here?" she said, catching her breath.

"I thought you were waiting in your car."

He leaned back against the display case, not taking his eyes off her face. "We could have parked closer," he said, raising his eyebrows.

She quickly looked back down to the display in front of her. "You could have stayed in the car," she retorted softly.

He gazed at the top of her head. "Are you looking to buy or just looking to avoid me?"

She didn't respond or look up. He wished he could see her reaction. Looking down into the case that had her rapt attention, he spotted a pair of delicate dangly pearl earrings and pointed to them. "Those would look nice on you."

She looked up at him in surprise.

"May I help you?" the older male clerk said.

"Oh…yes." Meghann rifled through her purse.

Bruce turned to face the man as well and gave him a smile in greeting.

"I would like to make a payment," Meghann said into her purse.

"Livingston, isn't it?"

Meghann stopped her pursuit. "Yes." She seemed surprised the man remembered her. Bruce wasn't. She was a woman who would stay in a man's memory. He should know. After their first meeting at work, he'd tried for months to forget her but couldn't shake her loose from his head. Or was it his heart? He'd resisted starting a relationship with a subordinate, and finally had decided the best thing he could do was just avoid her altogether. That plan had lasted all of a few days. He thought of her more than ever. So he gave up and decided to ask her out. If it was God's will for them to be together, then He would work things out. But then the Charmaine Altman Christmas fiasco happened, and she pulled back.

He studied her as they stood there, waiting. *She's not pulling away now...well, not often.*

Maybe things could work out for them, after all.

"I remember you," the salesclerk said. "It's not often the woman comes in alone to pick out a wedding set. The man, yes, but not the woman alone." The clerk turned to Bruce and asked, "I take it you approved of her choice, sir? She deliberated over it a long time. I told her she wouldn't regret spending the extra money."

"I definitely approve," Bruce said and gazed fondly at Meghann.

"Spoken like true love. I'm Nick Moss." He extended his right hand. "It's good to meet you."

Bruce clasped his hand. "Bruce Halloway. Nice to meet you, too."

Meghann produced the paper she was searching for. The man took the paper. "How does your ring fit?" He looked at Bruce. "She wasn't sure of the size."

"Perfect." Bruce glanced at his ring, then wrapped his arm around her shoulder. "Just like my sweetheart."

The man's smile broadened. "I see you two have already put those rings to good use." He unfolded the paper and looked from Meghann to Bruce then back to Meghann. "How much did you want to put on this?"

Meghann started to speak. "Uh—"

Bruce cut her off. "I'll go ahead and pay it off."

"But—"

Bruce squeezed her shoulder and continued as if she had said nothing. "And I'd like to see those." He pointed to the pearl earrings he had noticed.

Mr. Moss unlocked the display and removed the earrings.

"Is it all right if she tries them on?"

The man nodded and handed one of the earrings to Meghann. When she didn't take it right away, Bruce did. "Try them on for me, kitten, please." When she opened her mouth to protest, he gave her his most endearing smile.

She gave in and removed a gold stud from her ear. When the dainty pearl earring was in place, she looked in the mirror Mr. Moss provided.

"Beautiful," Bruce said softly. "And the earring is nice, too. Do you want them?"

"What?"

"The earrings. I'll buy them for you."

Her eyes widened. "No!" She quickly removed the earring from her ear and laid it on the counter.

Bruce could have kicked himself. Why had he done that? Of course she wouldn't accept jewelry from him. Was it his subconscious testing her?

"I guess not today." Bruce smiled at Mr. Moss and pulled out his wallet to pay for the rings. It pleased him she wasn't a money-grabber like so many people these days. So why did he feel like such a heel?

Outside the door he drew her to a stop and took her left hand in his, getting a closer look at her wedding ring. He had studied his many times but never hers. "Very nice." He gazed in her eyes. "I approve," he said huskily.

He glanced in the store window to see the clerks talking and pointing at them. "Mr. Moss is watching. Shall we give him something to talk about?"

"Something...to talk about?"

Her breathless little echo of his words—combined with the flash of anticipation he saw spark in her eyes—dissolved whatever control he'd been exercising. He drew her close, lowered his head, and did what he'd been wanting to do for days.

He kissed her. Really kissed her.

And he didn't intend to come up for air until it was absolutely necessary.

Thirteen

MEGHANN STILL COULDN'T BELIEVE HE HAD PAID FOR THE rings. She'd struggled with the idea, wondering how she could afford it, and finally decided it was the right thing to do. But she had only made her down payment on the rings. The gratitude inside her for Bruce's kindness threatened to overflow.

It had mortified her when he came into the jewelry store. She'd been so careful not to mention anything about it, so sure had she been that he'd tease her for buying such a thing. Instead, he had paid for them.

Appearances are everything, remember?

Maybe so, but she would enjoy them nonetheless.

As much as you enjoyed that kiss?

Just the thought of it made Meghann's toes curl. It had been sudden—and utterly wonderful. When Bruce had finally lifted his head and set her away from him, her heart was racing like a runaway train and she felt light headed. She'd wondered if her legs would support her. Embarrassed at how deeply the kiss had affected her, she glanced up at him—and had to fight not to burst out laughing. He looked like someone had smacked his head with a baseball bat. His eyes as he looked down at her were wide and dazed...and they'd stood there in silence, both too dazed to comment.

Bruce paused now at the door to his apartment. He looked down, then glanced at her. "I'm sorry for that stunt I pulled at the jewelry store."

Stunt? "I don't understand." Was he sorry he'd paid for the rings? Or was it kissing her that he regretted? "I'll pay you back for the rings."

"You don't need to. That's not what I'm talking about."

His eyes shifted away from her, and it was clear how uncomfortable he was. Her heart plunged. If he was feeling this badly about kissing her—

"I'm talking about my offer to buy you the earrings. It was inappropriate."

Relief so powerful that it made her giddy washed over her. She smiled at him. Actually, the offer had touched her. "Please don't feel bad. It was sweet of you, but I just couldn't accept an expensive gift like that."

"My point exactly. And if you thought I was insinuating anything...well, please know I wasn't. And accept my sincere apology for any offense to you."

"You have nothing to apologize for. I wasn't offended."

He cocked her a smile and bowed, every inch the perfect knightly gentleman. "In gratitude for the lady's graciousness, will you permit me to escort you and your mother out to dinner?"

She laughed, touched by his sincerity and gallantry.

Who could resist a man—and a smile—like the one before her? She made a curtsy. "Why, my lord, I accept with sincerest gratitude on behalf of myself and my mother."

Seemingly pleased with her response, he opened the door and followed her into his apartment. Her mother wasn't up yet, which made Meg wonder if she hadn't slept well last night. With a worried glance at the clock, she moved to go check on her.

"I'll make reservations for seven o'clock. Is that all right with you?" At her nod, Bruce left to make the arrangements, while she peeked in on her still sleeping mother. Nothing seemed amiss…her mother's breathing was deep and regular.

With a shrug, she went back to the living room.

"All set," Bruce said, hanging up the phone. "Reservations are for seven. We should leave here around 6:40. Is that enough time? I can make it for later."

"No, that'll be fine. I'll take a quick shower before waking Mom. Where are we going?"

He smiled and raised his eyebrows. "It's a surprise. Dress up a bit. I've got to run in to the office. I'll be back in an hour to change clothes."

"Thanks." As always, he made sure to be considerate of her privacy. Did he know how much that meant to her? She hoped so.

In the bathroom, Meghann flipped on the exhaust fan before stepping into the steamy shower. The water felt great against her tense muscles, so she lingered longer than normal, secure in the knowledge that Bruce wouldn't be back for a while yet.

Her tension started to ease away, and she wished her problems would do the same. Where was this emotional roller-coaster ride she'd put herself on going to end? She didn't know, but she feared it would be no place good. How could it? Yes, there were moments when she could almost let herself believe she and Bruce were growing close, but then she'd remember they were simply playing their respective parts—playing a game, as Bruce said.

They'd managed to pull it off so far, but how much longer could they keep it up? At least she felt fairly confident it couldn't get much worse.

She slipped on her lavender chenille robe and towel dried her hair to the hum of the fan. She wondered if her mother was up yet; with the fan on there was no way of telling. It would be best to go wake her now—if she wasn't already awake—and tell her of their dinner plans. That would give her mother plenty of time to get ready.

Meg glanced at the wall clock. Bruce wouldn't be back for another half hour, so she could wander through the apartment in her robe. She pulled the heavy garment tight around her. Even if he did happen to return earlier than he thought, she was covered from her neck to her toes.

She turned off the fan and reached for the doorknob. A rapping sounded on the door. Her breath caught, then she released it. Her mother, it had to be.

The knob turned, and she smiled, ready to greet her mother. "Oh!"

A strange man with shoulder-length brown hair stood before her, looking as startled to see her as she was to face him. A scream escaped her lips and she threw her whole weight against the door. It slammed shut and she fumbled to lock it. Her mind raced as fast as her heart. Terror swept through her as she wondered what the intruder wanted and who he was.

She put her ear to the door and listened for any sign of him. There was no sound from the bedroom. That's when it hit her…her mother was out there. With the intruder!

She grabbed the knob, then froze. What if he was waiting out there for her? What if they struggled and the noise woke her mother? She closed her eyes and leaned her forehead against the door.

Lord, what do I do?

Feeling trapped and sick to her stomach, she sat on the toilet to wait. But for what? The stranger to return? For Bruce? He would still be gone for a while. She wasn't about to just sit there like a ninny. Not when her mother might be in danger! She had to do something. She scanned her small surroundings, her heart still beating wildly.

She grabbed the hair dryer for protection, just in case he had ill intentions, and reached for the doorknob, then realized going out there in her robe was not a wise choice. She donned the jeans and sweater she'd had on earlier, took up the hair dryer again, and whispered a prayer of protection for her and her mother. She paused, listening with her ear to the door, but no sound came from the bedroom.

Taking special care to make no noise of her own, she filled her lungs with a breath of courage as she unlocked the door and eased it open, scoping out the room. No one was there. With her hair dryer drawn and at the ready, she went to the other door and listened. Was he out there? Or had he left the apartment all together, having already found what he had come for? She whispered another prayer for protection and grasped the doorknob with all the courage she could muster, then paused. What was that sound? Voices? Yes, voices. *Happy* voices!

Easing the door open, she cautiously stepped out and found her mother chatting cheerfully with another woman and a stately man, both of whom looked to be about her mother's age. With them was the younger man who had come into the bathroom.

Mom was the first to notice her. "Meg, come over and meet your in-laws." She barely noticed that her mother motioned her over to the dining room table where they were huddled.

In-laws?

The other woman turned adoring eyes on her and a friendly smile spread across her face.

"Olivia, this is my daughter, Meghann, your new daughter-in-law. Meg, this is Olivia Halloway. Bruce's mother."

The woman rose, all elegance and grace; she had an inviting warmth that reached out to touch Meghann, despite her astonishment. Meghann had the strong sense this woman accepted her fully, and her words confirmed that fact: "Meghann dear, welcome to the family." She gave Meg a quick but seemingly sincere hug. "I'm so glad to meet you."

Speechless, Meghann gaped openmouthed at the trio.

"I would like to say that Bruce has spoken so much about you that I feel as if I know you, but my son has been silent where you are concerned." There was a note of censure in her voice the woman couldn't hide.

What could she say? *"He didn't mention me because he didn't know we were married"?* Oh, that'd go over great. But to give any other excuse would be lying. Again. This time to Bruce's family.

She felt as though she were falling, spiraling into a dark, dark hole. *Lord, how much deeper are we going to get into this?*

"I...I don't know what to say." That, at least, was the gospel truth.

Bruce's mother regarded her quietly, then smiled. "Don't worry, my dear. I'm sure Bruce had his reasons and he will explain them to us in his own time."

That will be worth hearing....

The elegant woman turned to draw the man beside her forward. "This is Bruce's father, your father-in-law, Ivan Halloway." She said his name reverently.

The face studying her was hauntingly familiar; Bruce definitely favored his father. The same strong jaw-line, piercing blue eyes, aristocratic nose...but the resemblance ended there. Where Bruce's eyes over-flowed with kindness and humor, this man's expression was decidedly...aloof. That expression combined with his stiff posture and tailored suit made his reception considerably cooler than his wife's, but he wasn't altogether cold. Not really. Meg sensed his reaction to her was more like indifferent tolerance. As he gave her a critical looking over, she had the urge to call him *sir,* at the very least *Mr.* Halloway.

"And this is our son Brock."

Their son? That made him Bruce's brother. Where Bruce resembled his father, Brock took after his mother. He was tall and broad in his frame like Bruce and his father, but his face was a masculine version of his mother's.

"I'm sorry." He held up his hands in mock surrender, letting his gaze settle on her weapon. "I didn't know you were in the bathroom, honest. I thought it was Bruce."

Meghann looked down at the hair dryer in her hand, still poised to protect herself and her mother. Dropping it to her side, heat rose in her cheeks. If there were only a hole, she would gladly climb in.

"It seems my dear brother Bruce has been keeping secrets from us. But what a very pretty secret you are." Brock took her free hand and graced it with a light kiss.

By now Meg was so numb she scarcely reacted. She just stood there, mute, staring at them all. At Bruce's family!

So much for thinking things couldn't get any worse!

Bruce stepped through his apartment doorway, then stopped in pleasant amazement when Meghann came to greet him.

"Hi there," she said, smiling warmly.

He'd expected her to be in a dress for the evening and was mildly concerned that she was still wearing the jeans and sweater from earlier and her hair was slightly wet. He was looking forward to seeing what she had picked out to wear—but all thought of that fell away when she wrapped her arms around his neck and kissed him.

Mmm. This was nice! The kind of greeting a man could get used to. He knew her mother must be close at hand for such a display of affection, but he held her tight and made the most of it all the same.

He pulled back and held her at arm's length, smiling as his gaze took in her full attire. "This wasn't exactly what I had in mind when I said 'dress for dinner.'"

She smiled again, but he noticed this time that it seemed a bit forced. "I was distracted by our company, dear."

Meg was definitely tense, and a tickle of alarm shot through him. "Where's your mom? She is up, isn't she?"

"Yes, she's up," she said through gritted teeth, still smiling. "She's in the dining room." Her look was pointed. "With your *family.*"

"My...what?" He stared down, sure he had heard her wrong. What would his parents be doing here? The pleasure he had felt a moment before was sucked from him, and a gnawing panic gripped the pit of his stomach.

"Bruce, darling."

He spun at the sound of his mother's velvet voice.

Sure enough, she stood there, watching him and Meghann with raised brows. "I have a bone to pick with you, son." Her voice was light and without malice.

Bruce's focus went to Meghann's concerned face, then back to his mother's as she approached. She was really here. His mother was here, in his apartment, with—dread filled him—with his *wife*.

Oh, Lord…you've got to be kidding. "Mother, whatever are you doing here?" Still in a bit of a daze, he let go of Meg and stepped into his mother's embrace for a perfunctory hug.

"No hello? No how are you? It's great to see you?"

"This is just so…unexpected."

Now, that was an understatement! And the surprises just kept coming, for there, behind his mother, was the rest of the family: his father and Brock.

"You've been keeping secrets." His mother glanced at Meghann with adoration. "She's wonderful. I'm so happy for you."

Bruce's father held out his hand. "Congratulations, son."

"Thank you, sir," Bruce said, giving his father's hand a firm shake despite his confusion. There was nothing worse than a weak handshake, his father would say. Weak handshake, weak character.

Brock gripped Bruce's hand next and pulled him in for a back-slapping hug. "Congratulations, you sly old dog you. Sneaking off and getting married to the prettiest girl in town, no doubt." The approving look Brock gave Meghann sent a wave of irritation through Bruce. He'd seen his brother look at women that way before…too many times. Well, he could just forget it this time. No way they were going to repeat history. Meg was his, and he'd see to it that Brock understood that in no uncertain terms.

Maybe you should let Meg know first?

He cast a quick glance at the woman who stood at his side. He'd hoped to do exactly that tonight, at dinner. But now…

"Did I hear you say something about dinner?" Brock's smile was broad. "I'm starved."

Bruce watched with dismay as his family took charge. Before long, they were all heading for their rooms to change for dinner while Bruce—at his mother's direction—reluctantly changed the reservations from three to six people.

And as he dialed, he saw all his plans and hopes for the evening flying right out the window.

Meghann, the last to get ready, glanced at her watch and knew there was no time now to curl her hair as planned without making them all late. Though she preferred it in flowing curls and hoped Bruce would like it as well, she resigned herself to pulling it back in a French twist. A quick touch with the curling iron to her bangs and wisps she pulled out in front of her ears softened the look.

After exiting the bathroom, she stopped in front of the bureau mirror to put on a pair of black dangly earrings and the matching necklace. Twirling around so the full skirt swished out, she inspected her overall appearance in the full-length mirrors on the closet doors. She ran her hands down the side of her simple black dress and smiled approvingly. *The pearls would have looked great with this dress.*

Joining the others, she heard a wolf whistle and turned—a teasing smile on her face, ready to scold Bruce playfully for his forwardness. Her heart sank when she found herself facing Brock.

"Dahlink, you rook mah-velous," Brock said with a perfectly affected Caribbean accent. "May I escort you to dinner?" He offered her his arm, and she had no choice but to slip her hand into the crook of his elbow. His wavy brown hair was now slicked back into a neat ponytail.

"I'll escort *my* wife."

At the cold words, Meg jumped slightly. But before she could say anything, Bruce took her by the arm and all but carried her to the door.

Good heavens, what was his hurry?

And what was with that proprietary tone when he said *my wife?* What's more, did he have to keep such a firm grip on her arm? Appearances notwithstanding, he was carrying the game a bit too far this time.

She reached over to pry her arm free, and he released her immediately. Studying him, she realized he was angry! He probably hadn't even been aware of the hold he had on her. His displeasure seemed to be focused on Brock. But why? Brock had only offered to escort her.

"I'm sorry," he leaned down and whispered in her ear as they stood to wait for the elevator.

"It's all right," she answered quickly, but knew it wasn't. Something was going on between Bruce and his brother…something that made Bruce irritable and left her feeling as though she'd wandered into some kind of minefield.

And that was a feeling she didn't care for. Not one little bit.

Fourteen

As the maître d' at the Crystal Swan lead the way to their table, Bruce noticed Meghann's awe of the lavish interior. Ornate crystal chandeliers hung above the dance floor as music from the live orchestra floated around the room. Her quick intake of breath let him know he had succeeded in impressing her.

Of course, his father would approve as well. But that fact didn't mean near as much to him as the excitement he saw on Meg's face.

The hostess led them to a white linen-covered table. Three small candles flickered in a shallow bowl of scented water with spices and rose petals floating in it.

After seating Meghann, Bruce flinched inwardly when his father ordered an expensive bottle of champagne. This night would be better served without it. When would his father realize Bruce's days of drinking and parties were over? He'd found something far more rewarding in his faith…if only he could help his family understand that.

"This is a night to celebrate," Ivan Halloway said

when both Meghann and her mom declined the bubbly brew. He scowled when Bruce, too, deterred the waiter from filling his glass. "How am I to propose a toast with half the glasses empty?"

Bruce held up his goblet of lemoned ice water. "Our glasses aren't empty, Father. Propose away."

Ivan shook his head slightly but stood with his raised champagne flute anyway. "To my son, Bruce, and the woman who finally turned his head. After all this time, we figured him for a lost cause." He gave Meg a restrained smile. "Good to know we were wrong."

Glasses clinked, three drinking their champagne while the other three contentedly sipped water.

After they had ordered, Brock walked around behind Meghann's chair. It was all Bruce could do not to grab and shake his brother when he made a courtly bow and asked, "May I have this dance?"

Tell him no. Tell him to sit down and leave you alone. But Meghann turned to looked at Brock with a smile. "I—uh…" She glanced at Bruce.

The last thing Bruce wanted was for Meghann to be in his brother's arms, but when she gazed at him with that confused look in her big green-brown eyes, his anger melted. "It's up to you, darling, if you want to risk your feet to ol' elephant toes."

"Don't listen to him. He's just jealous because I'm better looking," Brock said with a smile and a wink. "And as for my dancing, let's just say I'm adequate. I promise not to run you into anything or step on your feet." He took her hand to assist her up. "And I won't take no for an answer."

Meghann stood and accompanied Brock to the dance floor.

Bruce knew it was irrational, but frustration washed over him that she was going with Brock. It took every ounce of self-control to stay in his chair, silent. What he wanted to do was stand up, pull her hand away from Brock's, and tell her she couldn't go. But he wouldn't hand out dictates as to what his wife could and couldn't do the way his father did—

Your what?

He swallowed hard at the reminder. Meghann wasn't really his wife. There was nothing that bound her to him. She could dance with whomever she pleased.

And that fact was driving Bruce crazy.

Of course, the fact that Brock's fun, relaxed attitude had always been appealing to the fairer sex didn't help at all. Any more than Bruce's painful awareness that his brother was not above stabbing him in the back.

Why hadn't Bruce persisted in asking Meghann out? Then he would have a solid foundation—a *real* one, not this farce they were perpetrating—to hold on to. They might even be engaged by now, and his brother wouldn't be a threat.

He watched as his brother put one hand around Meghann's back, then took her fingers in his other hand. Brock leaned close to Meg and said something, and she shook her head. Now he was talking again, but they weren't dancing yet. What could he possibly be saying? She smiled up at him, but why? His magnetic personality no doubt.

"What do you think, Bruce?"

I think I could lose her to my charming little brother.

"Bruce, are you listening to me?" The harsh, firm question pulled him from his morose thoughts.

Bruce straightened and turned to his father. "I'm sorry, sir. What were you saying?"

"Stocks, boy, stocks!" He slammed his drink down, sloshing some of the clear liquid on the linen tablecloth. "You haven't heard a word I've said. Which way do you think the computer market is going to swing? I heard Gates is going to…"

Bruce tried hard to concentrate on his father's words about the market. But he couldn't keep his mind on the subject. His attention kept drifting back to Meghann, the way she looked nestled in Brock's arms, the graceful way they moved together. They were laughing…and he wanted to pick up the champagne bucket and throw it at them.

Thankfully, the music ended as he was about to give in to that very impulse. He settled back in his chair, relieved that they would return to the table now. He took a sip of water and almost spit it out when the orchestra started the next piece, and Brock swept Meg into another dance.

Confound it, were they going to dance all night?

A touch on his arm broke his concentration. "Bruce?" At his mother's soft tone, he turned to meet her gaze. "Would you do me the honor of this waltz?"

"Olivia! I was speaking with him," Bruce's father said, clearly irritated.

"You can talk to him later. It's not often I get the chance to dance with my son."

Bruce stood up and held out his arm for his mother, relieved he didn't have to feign interest where none existed.

"What am I supposed to do while you two are frolicking out there?" His father waved his hand toward the dance floor.

Bruce and his mother turned simultaneously back to face him. "Talk to Gayle," his mother said. His father frowned. "You're an intelligent man. I'm sure you can think of something to say."

He was still scowling when they turned toward the dance floor.

Poor Gayle, Bruce thought. *I should go back. But what about Meghann?* He could keep a closer eye on her on the dance floor. "Maybe I should go rescue Meg—I mean Gayle back at the table?"

"Nonsense. Your father will behave himself." His mother gave him a calm smile. "Contrary to his behavior, dear, he is happy for you." She lowered her voice to a conspiratorial whisper. "He thinks you're back to *normal.*"

"Normal?" Bruce looked down at her.

"You know. That religion thing changed you so. But now you've got a woman in your life, and I must confess that the way you went about it, so sudden and secretive, makes your father feel like he has his son back."

He stared at her, nonplussed. They thought he'd been secretive, that he'd gone back to his old ways of doing things for himself, with no thought to anyone else. *Is it possible for me to feel any more rotten, Lord?*

With a sigh, he shook his head. He doubted it. "That 'religion thing,' as you put it, was a welcome change."

"Are we going to dance or not?"

He knew that was his mother's subtle way of saying she didn't want to talk about unpleasantries, that she preferred to move on to something more agreeable. She'd learned, as had their whole family, to avoid certain topics...topics his father was dead set against.

Which included anything remotely religious.

Bruce slid his arms around his mother and they waltzed around the floor. But even as he moved into the dance, he found himself keeping watch on Meg and Brock, not too close or obvious.

"I've decided to forgive you," Olivia Halloway said formally, like a queen pardoning one of her subjects.

Bruce felt bad he hadn't been paying attention, especially since he had no idea why he'd been granted amnesty. Or what for. "Excuse me?"

"I forgive you. For not telling us about Meghann or inviting us to your wedding."

He smiled down at his mother, the peacemaker. She hated strife between any members of the family.

"I like her," she was saying. "She's different from the other girls you've dated."

No doubt about that. Meghann wasn't like any woman he had ever known. For starters she was a Christian, but he didn't suppose his mother wanted to hear that. She was nice, not at all conceited, smart, and beautiful. He had dated attractive women before, but not one as beautiful on the inside as she was on the outside.

Pity she's not really yours. That she seems so content in your brother's arms, smiling at him. Ah, women. Every one as fickle as the last, eh?

He knew the thoughts weren't true, that Meg wasn't like that. But he couldn't seem to stem the jealousy welling up inside him again.

"Would you mind if we traded partners?"

Bruce glanced down at his mother in surprise. "I'm sorry, did I step on your—"

"No, dear, of course not. I'd simply like the privilege of dancing with my other son, as well."

Of course. Why not? Everyone wants to dance with the fun-loving Brock Halloway.

"Bruce, don't you want to dance with your wife?"

His mother's soft question drew his attention from his angry thoughts to her face and understanding dawned. She hadn't really wanted to dance with him. She probably hadn't want to dance at all. But she'd seen he was bothered by Meg dancing with Brock, so she was fixing matters in her own, nonoffensive, remarkably effective way.

A dimple peeked out on her cheek as she smiled at him. "Are you going to lead or shall I?"

"I'll lead," Bruce said with an exuberant smile. He guided her masterfully over to Brock and Meghann, reaching out to tap Brock's shoulder with a flourish. "Shall we change partners?"

"I'm rescued." Brock winked at Meghann, and Bruce fought back his irritation. But it flared even stronger when she blushed a slight shade of pink.

Rescued? Hardly. He looks more like the cat who ate the

cream than a man in distress.

"Or should I say, my feet are saved." Brock made an exaggerated limp as he took up the waltzing position with his mother. "She's lovely, dear brother, but you've been remiss in teaching her certain things. Not at all considerate of you."

The mockery was evident in Brock's tone and expression. But before Bruce could determine if it were he or Meg being mocked, his brother turned to smile at their mother. "Be gentle, Mother, my toes are tender."

With that, he swept her away, looking at Bruce only long enough to give him an altogether too-smug smile.

"I wasn't that bad," Meghann said, knowing an embarrassing blush was rushing up her cheeks.

"You stepped on his feet?" Bruce said with upraised brows.

"Only four times, well almost five. That's pretty good for a beginner."

"Beginner?"

She shifted from one foot to another. That dance had been bad enough; she'd be dipped if she'd let Bruce stand here and further humiliate her. "I've never waltzed before. It was so embarrassing. Can we go back to the table now?"

Bruce stepped in closer, putting his right hand behind her back and holding up his left hand for her to take.

Oh, please. "You're not going to make me step on your toes, too?"

"My feet were made for walking on, darling," he said with a smile.

"Not the tops!"

"Come on," he coaxed, wiggling his fingers. "How would it look if you danced with my brother but refused to dance with me, your ever-devoted husband?"

Appearances, appearances! Everything was how it appeared with him. Wasn't there a shred of emotion behind anything he did? Something to hang her hopes on? She guessed not. Well, then, he deserved bruised toes.

She reluctantly put her hands in position. "Don't blame me when your shoes get scuffed." She looked down at her feet. "I start on the left, right?"

"You start by looking up."

She raised her eyes to meet his and was rewarded with a breathtaking smile. Her heart beat faster. Could he tell the way a simple smile from him affected her?

"Keep your carriage straight," she heard him say but the words didn't register. She was too distracted by the tingle his warm hand around hers sent up her arm.

"Keep your back straight."

This time Meghann came out of her daze and threw her shoulders back and went rigid.

"No. You're as stiff as a board. Relax."

His cajoling tone eased her misgivings. "How am I supposed to stand straight *and* be relaxed?"

"Pretend you have a pole down your back. Your back remains straight while the rest of you moves. Relaxed, but not limp, sort of taut. My hands and body will guide you to where we are going. A press of my hand, the pull of my shoulder…just focus on me."

Like she ever did anything else.

Meghann closed her eyes, trying to organize her mental notes—relaxed, straight, not stiff or limp, his hand pushing, and his shoulder pulling. How did Fred and Ginger make it look so easy? How could she focus on learning to waltz with him so close and strong and smelling like a fresh spring rain with a hint of musk? *Get your mind back on the task, Meghann.*

"Don't think about where I'm leading you, just relax and it will come naturally. Okay, we'll start with a simple box step."

Meghann quickly dropped her gaze to her feet and concentrated on which way they were supposed to go. Her back was straight. She made sure of that.

"Head up," Bruce said softly.

She lifted her chin but kept her eyes downcast on their feet.

"Look over this shoulder," he said, moving the shoulder her left hand was on.

She glared at him, concerned. "How am I supposed to keep from stepping on your feet if I can't see them?"

Her only answer was a quirky smile accompanied by a squeeze of her hand and slight pressure on her back. "Left foot back, yours," he said as they began. "And if you look down, I'll pinch you."

They made a perfect box—stiff, but it was a box. Another box and another, and not one toe injured…yet.

"Relax and let me lead."

This time instead of the simple box she felt him press with not only his hand in hers but his shoulder as well. She moved back and back again. She almost stepped on his foot but recovered with a quick two-step. He smiled at her approvingly, and they went back and forth and made a box a few more times. Unbelievable, she was waltzing.

"I think you're ready for the next step," he said with a chuckle. "Pardon the pun."

"What?" She stiffened. Something different? Panic rippled through her. She'd been doing so well. Why did he want to risk his feet?

"Relax," he said. "Just *follow* where I lead you." He turned her with a press of his hand and the slight lift of his shoulder. Around they swirled on the floor.

This leading thing really worked. It was almost easier than dancing the tight little box. When her eyes flickered to his in surprise, he smiled and her breath caught, held captive by his gaze. He looked as if he might kiss her. She leaned toward him expectantly…and stepped squarely on his foot. *He was leading, not leaning, stupid!*

"I'm sorry. I forgot where my feet were supposed to go." A nervous giggle escaped. "I guess I wasn't paying very good attention. I got a little…"

"Distracted?" he finished for her.

A pleased smile captured his mouth, and she had the distinct sense that he knew—and was pleased—that he'd been the cause of her wayward thoughts. Or was he laughing at her? No. She wouldn't think that of him.

"Shall we finish this dance?" He continued to masterfully lead her around the floor.

"It's a good thing I danced with Brock first." She

tried to make light conversation.

"Pardon?"

She almost stepped wrong at the dark look on his face. "I—I got most of my toe stepping-on out of the way." She forced her tone to be light, hoping it would remove the frown from his handsome features.

It worked. His face relaxed again and he smiled at her. "You aren't a bad dancer. You catch on quickly."

"It's because you are good at this. I can really tell which way you are going to go." That did it. The frown gave way to an amused smile. "I always thought that leading was a figment of the man's—of someone's imagination."

The music came to an end, and they headed back to the table where hopefully their food would arrive soon.

Bruce's hand rested lightly at the small of her back. Meghann kept her pace slow so as not to lose him as they wound their way back to the table.

"I'm sorry about getting your family involved in my mess," Meghann said.

"It's all right. Don't worry about it. It makes my mother just as happy as it does yours."

"I was going to tell your brother the truth, but I was too busy stepping on his feet."

Bruce took her by the elbow and brought them to a sudden stop. "Don't. You can't tell them. Any of them."

"But this is my lie. They deserve the truth. I feel awful lying to them."

"Listen. My family…well…they just wouldn't understand. I need time to figure out how to explain this to them. My father has been out to prove Christianity is a farce for as long as I can remember. When my youngest brother, Brice, and then I, accepted Christ…well, he was far from pleased. Our father sees no need for a god of any kind. He views all Christians as hypocritical religious fanatics. This would just prove his point." He shook his head slightly. "I know this sounds manipulative, but I need time to think this through, to know how best to tell them what this is all about. And why."

"I just thought telling Brock might help—"

"The last thing Brock will do is help matters. Trust me, it's better he doesn't know anything for now." The bitterness in his voice when he spoke of his brother gave Meghann pause. What had happened to cause a breech between these two?

And how on earth had she landed smack in the middle of it?

By one little lie, Meg. That's how.

Touché. She'd gotten herself into this mess. And she'd gotten Bruce into it. The least she could do was respect his wishes where his family was concerned.

"They won't stay long, only a day or two. I'll call them and explain everything after your mom is gone."

"Speaking of mothers, I think your mom wants us back at the table." She nodded toward where his mother was watching them intently, brows raised.

"Are you going to say anything to them?" he asked as he fell into step beside her.

No doubt about it, Bruce was walking a tightrope where his family was concerned, and it was all her fault.

Her lie had become his lie and a stumbling block to his family. She hated to promise more lies, but she felt she had little choice. "I won't say anything."

Bruce seated her as their salads were being served.

"For a wedding gift I'm calling Christopher. He'll completely redo the apartment," Olivia Halloway said enthusiastically to Meghann. "Whatever you want."

"Redo?"

"Yes. Christopher is the decorator I hired to decorate the apartment when Bruce first moved in. Who knows what it would have looked like without him. But I'm afraid it is terribly masculine. Fine for a bachelor but not at all suited for a young couple."

So that was why everything matched so beautifully. "But everything looks so new," Meghann protested.

"No matter. Tell Christopher what you want. I'll have him send the bill to Ivan."

This was getting worse by the minute. Meg couldn't let Bruce's mother—or his father—spend money on a decorator when there was no real reason for it.

"They aren't staying at the apartment for much longer. They found a wonderful house." Meg's mother broke in, and to Meg's horror she went on to explain about their two places.

"Well then, we'll just have Christopher do the *new* place." Olivia looked positively delighted. "It will be all ready for you when you move in."

"No!"

"Meghann!"

Clearly her mother was aghast at Meghann's curt refusal, but Olivia laid a gentle hand on the woman's arm.

"That's all right, if Meghann doesn't want Christopher, we'll find a decorator she feels comfortable with."

"No, no, no. There isn't going to be any decorator or house or anything because—" The five stunned faces halted her. She clamped her mouth shut, realizing this was not the time or place to clear her conscience, but the truth screamed in her head all the same: *Because we aren't really married!*

Her words hung there in the silence, and Meghann looked at Bruce. *Do something!*

But for once his mind-reading abilities seemed to be on the fritz. He just sat there, watching her, looking as stunned as the others.

Oh, bother! She pushed away from the table, falling back on the only saving grace she could think of.

All out retreat.

"Excuse me," she said, standing, keeping her back straight.

The three men scrambled to their feet as well, and she cleared her throat. "I...I need..." She threw her hands up. "Oh, forget it."

With that, she marched away, leaving her so-called husband and his family standing there, staring after her, mouths agape.

Fifteen

MEGHANN ENTERED THE LAVISH RESTROOM, DESPERATELY longing for some peace and quiet. Like the rest of the restaurant, no expense was spared. An ornate vanity with plush stools graced the lounge that was separated from the stalls and sink. There were several women in the lounge chatting among themselves, but no one to make demands of her.

She moved to a sink, filling it with cool water. Dipping her hands in, she splashed her face gently, hoping to refresh her mind if not her spirit. Dabbing her face dry, she noticed the lounge had cleared out save one woman seated at the vanity. Meghann leaned toward the mirror to fix her lipstick and was on her way out when the woman spoke.

"That's a drab little dress. Is it off the rack?"

Meghann turned to the woman at the mirror, a beautiful blond with striking facial features and an iridescent red dress. What little there was of the dress was clearly expensive. The woman's eyes were a translucent sky blue and as cold as an arctic winter.

Meghann glanced around. There was no one else there, so the woman had to be talking to her. Meg studied her face again and frowned. She seemed vaguely familiar, but Meghann couldn't quite place her. Not her face, anyway. But her manners, well, there was only one person she'd ever met who was that rude and condescending…

"I see your taste in jewelry hasn't improved," the woman sneered.

Charmaine Altman.

Meghann fingered her black beaded choker.

"Don't think dressing up can change the fact that you are the hired help. Mummy and Daddy will see right through you. They'll put an end to this little tryst."

Mummy and Daddy? Good grief, the woman made it sound as though she were intimately acquainted with Bruce's family.

Maybe she is.

No. Meg didn't believe it. She lifted her chin a fraction. "Tryst? I don't think so." Charmaine Altman might be gorgeous, but her ill-mannered behavior marked her for what she was: common.

Unfortunately, the woman's sarcasm was anything but common. She all but raised insults to an art form. "When I say tryst, I *mean* tryst. Your engagement has never been announced, and no one who is anyone at all has heard about you or this illusion of a marriage. You, love, are a well-guarded secret. I daresay that will be easier that way when he turns you loose."

Meghann clenched her teeth so hard her jaw ached. Turn her loose indeed! She flung her left hand toward the contemptuous woman. "Does *this* look like a tryst?"

Take that! Meg thought with satisfaction.

Charmaine glanced in the mirror at the ring and laughed haughtily. "That? You think that little trinket means anything? The one he offered me was considerably more substantial. That practically isn't there. He obviously doesn't think much of you."

Meghann's anger boiled. "This is a wedding ring." She smiled sweetly. "Not a payoff."

Charmaine's eyes flickered at that. *Score a point for me,* Meg thought, but her pleasure was short lived.

The other woman shrugged elegantly. "Well, I admit I'm surprised he actually married you. He's carried this game a bit further than usual." She offered Meg a sympathetic smile. "But that is of little importance to me. He may be enamored with you for the moment, but he won't stay faithful to you. You're not his type."

"And *you* are?" Meg almost choked on the thought. Not in a million years. No, a *trillion* years.

Charmaine turned gracefully on the stool and bore her icy gaze at Meghann. "Oh, absolutely. Bruce and I are cut from the same cloth. We'll be together again before you know it." A slow smile pulled at her mouth. "And I do mean *together,* in every sense of the word."

Meghann stared at the woman. What was she saying? Surely she didn't mean…A smug smile slid across the blond's face.

"Oh, did your husband forget to mention the fact that we used to be lovers?" Mocking laughter twinkled in her eyes. She was obviously delighted to be the one to share this bit of information with Meghann.

It's not true. It can't be.

"Oh, my dear, dear child—" Charmaine touched her slender, manicured fingertips to her chest, where her ample cleavage showed—"you should see yourself. Your expression is absolutely precious. A mixture of shock and embarrassment with…what?… a hint of innocence. How unutterably quaint. No wonder Bruce is taken with you. You're simply too sweet for words."

Her mocking tone and chuckle rankled Meghann.

"But like anything sweet, you'll lose your appeal before long. I daresay I broke poor Bruce's heart when I left him. He begged me to come back. He's merely using you to teach me a lesson. It's like a game with him. He's gone overboard with it, but I have learned my lesson. And when we get back together—and we will—I will keep a short leash on him."

This couldn't be happening.…

"Don't shake your head at me, girl. Bruce said he couldn't wait for us to be together again." Charmaine turned back to the mirror and touched a slim hand to her hair. She looked at Meghann in the mirror. "Do you really think he's at the hotel all the time…alone?"

Against Meg's will, the mental picture of Bruce and Charmaine together formed in her head. The perfect match of tall, dark, and handsome with a blond beauty. The haunting image lodged in her brain. The restroom suddenly felt stuffy and confining.

Meg backed away, but in her rush to escape Charmaine, she nearly ran into a woman entering the restroom. After apologizing, she rushed out the front door of the restaurant.

She couldn't go back to the table. Not yet. Maybe not ever. But she at least needed a few minutes to compose herself, to clear her head. Hopefully fresh air would accomplish that.

"What did you expect?" she whispered to herself. "Nothing good ever comes from a lie." The young valet attendant looked at her expectantly. She shook her head and turned away from him.

Although the day had been pleasantly warm, the temperature had dropped considerably since sunset. She wrapped her arms around herself to no avail. It was as though the cold came from within as well as without. She drew in a couple of calming breaths. It would have to be enough. She turned to go back inside and nearly bumped into Bruce.

He steadied her, his hands on her upper arms. "What are you doing out here? It's too cold." He slipped out of his dinner jacket and wrapped it around her shoulders. His warmth, his fragrance, enveloped her.

She closed her eyes. "I was just going back inside."

He slipped his arm around her shoulders and walked her back in. "Your mom said you looked upset when you raced out of the lady's lounge, that she saw you almost run down another poor woman." He gave her a sideways glance. "She and my mother both think you could be pregnant."

"What?"

He chuckled. "They were going on about pregnant women getting upset for no apparent reason." His smile was filled with mischief. "We could just tell them you are, and they'll quit."

"*Quit!* You think they will quit? It would only be the beginning. It would be adding fuel to the flame. They would want to know when it is due. What names we have picked out and buy a boatload of useless baby stuff."

He held up his hands, laughing. "Okay, okay, I see your point."

"Then they would drag me around maternity clothes shopping and stuffing cigars in your mouth."

"You win." He put his arm around her shoulders and gave her a gentle squeeze. "It was a bad idea."

She hadn't meant to lash out at him.

His tender gaze settled on her. "Now tell me what upset you and sent you out into the cold without a coat."

What upset her? Tell him what upset her?

She fought the irrational urge to burst into laughter. Either that, or tears. How could she tell him what had upset her? There was too much to choose from! This had, without a doubt, been the worst day of her entire life. Bruce had caught her paying for rings to go along with her lie. A strange man nearly walked in on her in the bathroom. She was surprised by her "in-laws" and forced to compound lie on top of lie. She'd been humiliated on the dance floor, and then hounded by two mothers with one thing on their minds—babies that would never be. And last, but most definitely not least, there was the charming Charmaine Altman. How was she supposed to even *begin* to describe that encounter?

"*Oh, not to worry, dear. I just had an unpleasant run-in with a woman whose tongue is as sharp as razors and who minced no words about being after the man I'm in love with. But really, it was nothing."*

Upset? Oh no, she wasn't upset. She was ready to explode! But the last thing she wanted to do was tell Bruce all of that. So she just gazed up at him wide-eyed.

"What makes you think I'm upset?"

"For one thing, your hands are shaking." He took them in his. "And they're ice-cold."

"It's just from being outside. I'm fine." She freed herself from his grasp.

"Sweetheart, please—" His tone and the concern in his eyes were almost Meg's undoing. She couldn't resist when he took her hands again, tugging them gently. She was about to throw caution to the wind and move forward, letting him fold her into a comforting embrace and spill all her worries, all her fears...

But she was saved by the bell. Or rather, by a well-modulated voice from behind them.

"Bruce, darling. Fancy seeing you here."

He went stiff, as did Meghann, and he clenched his jaw at the sound of Charmaine's velvety voice.

Bruce turned and hooked his arm around Meghann's waist. "Charmaine." Meghann was relieved to hear how cool his words were.

"I hear congratulations are in order." She looked from Bruce to Meghann and back again, then held her hand out to him.

"Thank you," he said with a nod to her hand but made no move to take it.

If he truly disliked this woman as much as he acted, then why didn't he tell her to just go away? Why suffer her company a moment longer, unless…

Unless there was some truth in Charmaine's words.

The woman's coy smile slid to one of disdain as she looked from Bruce to Meghann. "All part of the game, sweetheart. Right, Bruce dear?" She batted her lashes at him and turned with a flare, making a grand exit to keep all eyes on herself.

"What was that all about? What did she mean by game?" Bruce's voice held a no-nonsense tone.

"It's nothing really. Let's go back to the table." She made a move to go, but he stopped her with a hand on her elbow.

"Was Charmaine in the lady's room?"

Meghann stared at the ground, her lips clamped shut. The last thing she wanted to do was get into this now. Here. In the lobby, of all places.

"She said something to you, didn't she? What?"

"Bruce, please. This is hardly the place."

"She said *game*. You didn't tell her what is really going on between us, did you? She could and would ruin everything."

Meghann had a sinking feeling something was going to come of her conversation with Charmaine, no matter how hard she tried to avoid it. And she wasn't sure she would like the outcome. "She…she sort of saw my ring."

Only because I shoved it in her face.

"So she thinks we're married?" He sounded relieved.

"Wouldn't you?" She noticed Brock approaching and added quickly, "Bruce, please, can we drop this? Here comes your brother."

"Smile," he said, turning toward his brother.

"There you two are," he said and came to a stop. "We were beginning to wonder if you skipped out on us for a secret rendezvous. I was sent to fetch you back." He wiggled his eyebrows. "I could always tell them I couldn't find you."

"But that would be a lie, and the last thing we want you to do is lie for us, brother dear. Would we, darling?"

Meg bit her lip at the harsh tone of Bruce's comment. He was frustrated that their discussion had been interrupted, that was obvious. But she couldn't do much about it now. Nor, to be honest, did she want to.

I wish this were over, Lord. I wish I'd never started it! I wish I'd kept my big, fat mouth shut, no matter how crazy Mom made me.

But wishing didn't change anything, so with a sigh, she shook her head. "No, of course not. Lying never works, does it?"

Bruce's eyes flickered at that, but she just turned from him and took Brock's arm. "Come on, brother Brock. Let's get back to the party."

By the end of the meal, Meg thought she'd go stark-raving mad.

The entire evening had been riddled with hints about grandchildren over broiled swordfish, duck à l'orange, and a few other food items that she couldn't even begin to identify. It didn't matter; her appetite had left her long ago, which only spurred yet another comment about morning sickness.

Meghann closed her eyes. She was sick all right, but morning had nothing to do with it. It had been bad enough with her mother's occasional comments, but now Mom had encouragement. *It will only be a couple more days. Bruce promised they won't stay long.*

She would just have to grin and bear it. After all, she was only reaping what she had sown.

"Meghann looks tired," Olivia said with concern. "We shouldn't keep her out late in her condition."

Meg's mother nodded in agreement, barely containing her grin.

Meghann looked from one woman to the other, fighting the urge to scream. Would they blame that on her *condition,* too? She sighed. "I do not have a *condition.*" She tried to sound calm. "And I do not *plan* on having a condition for a very long time."

The two mothers nodded at one another knowingly.

Bruce put a supportive hand on her arm. "Please, we've told you the truth. Meg isn't pregnant. We'd really appreciate it if you'd refrain from talking about this further."

Duly admonished, the two women fell silent. As usual, when Bruce spoke, he was obeyed.

At long last the time came for them to go home. Since they all couldn't fit in Bruce's Infinity, Brock had driven Meghann's mother in the Corvette.

"We'll take the 'Vette." Bruce exchanged claim tickets with Brock. "Would you take the others home? We'll meet you there."

The valet brought the Corvette first and Meg and

Bruce were off—but she realized they were heading in the opposite direction from Bruce's apartment. He fit well behind the wheel and shifted smoothly. He seemed to belong there and obviously enjoyed driving his toy.

"Where are we going?" Meghann asked.

"It's been a long day. I thought you could use a break from your mother and mine, and we should check on a certain black Lab."

"I would like to see Lucky."

"It will also give you a chance to tell me exactly what Charmaine said to you. This time without interruption." His tone left no room for argument.

Sixteen

MEGHANN SWALLOWED HARD. SHE THOUGHT THIS CONVER-
sation was finished. Evidently not. "It was nothing,
really." *Please drop the subject.* She didn't want to think
about that woman at all. She could still feel Charmaine's
icy stare and her haughty laugh.

Bruce reached over and took her hand. Meg looked
at him in surprise.

Why would he do that when they were alone?

"Meg, it's clear she upset you, and I want to know
what lies she is spreading."

Hope sparked inside her. *Lies? Were they lies?* She
hoped so…with all her heart. "Why do you think she
told me lies?" *Because I've lied?*

"Charmaine Altman is incapable of telling the truth.
Unless, of course, it gets her what she's after."

Do you think I'm incapable of the truth, as well?

His mouth was a thin, hard line. "She will say anything to get what she wants."

"And she wants you." Meg hoped she didn't sound
as jealous as she felt.

"Well, this is one time Charmaine is not going to get what she wants. I have absolutely no interest in her. All I want from that woman is her absence."

"She said you two were seeing each other at the hotel."

Maybe that's why he gave you the time off…so you wouldn't see them. She closed her eyes against the suspicions. *Shut up! Just shut up!*

"She said that?"

Meg opened her mouth, then shut it. Had Charmaine actually said that? She thought back…

"Do you really think he's at the hotel all that time alone?"

Don't embellish, Meg. You've done enough of that. Speak the truth. "Well, no…but she implied it."

The engine roared as he downshifted and made a quick turn into a grocery store parking lot. He parked away from the store entrance in a deserted section of the lot. His knuckles were white from the grip he had on the steering wheel.

"I take it we're not here to shop?" she asked, trying to lighten his dark mood.

He turned to face her. "Tell me every word she said." His words were forced like it was a chore to get them out.

He was not going to be dissuaded or put off. Fine then, she would tell him. He asked for it. This day had already gone from bad to worse, she might as well make a complete disaster of it. "Let's see, she started off by saying my dress was drab and that I am a lowly employee and beneath you."

His grip tightened on the wheel.

"She said she broke your heart when she left you and the engagement ring you offered her was much bigger than the ring you'd given me, so I was unimportant."

"Me, marry *her*?" His words came pouring out, like lava erupting from a volcano. "No way! I never proposed to that woman. She did all the chasing. But I knew before long that she was the type of person to get what she wanted, then stab you in the back and laugh while washing the blood from her hands. She's a user and a manipulator."

He leaned his head back against the seat, running a hand over his eyes. "What ever attracted me to her in the first place?"

The fact that he had once been attracted to her stabbed at Meghann's heart. "She's beautiful."

He was silent for a moment, and then he sighed. "I was an idiot."

She swallowed against the pain his words caused her. He had been attracted to her looks. He couldn't deny it.

"Meg, there is beauty—" his voice dropped a little and he touched her shoulder—"and there is *beauty*. Charmaine Altman is an ugly person where it counts."

"She was convinced she's going to get you back. That you were using me to make her pay for hurting you." She wanted to know the truth about Bruce's relationship with this woman, even if it irreparably wounded her, so she plunged ahead. "She said she would have you back, that you'd be together...in every way...and that she'd be sure to keep you on a short leash."

"I will never be in that woman's bed again!"

At Bruce's spat-out words, Meghann sucked in a quick breath. She felt as though someone had seized her heart in an iron fist and squeezed it until she wanted to cry out from the pain.

The look on Bruce's face told her he regretted the words, wished he could recall them, but it was too late.

Charmaine had told the truth. She and Bruce had been lovers.

Struggling for breath, Meg looked out the window, studying the darkness that seemed to be pressing in on her. "She said you two were…involved." With gritted teeth, she tried to swallow down her unwanted tears.

So much for your knight in shining armor. At least you know now your dream man isn't the man of character you thought he was.

"I'm sure the word she used was *lovers*." His heavy words were controlled and measured. "Meg, please let me explain."

She held up a hand, halting him. "You don't owe me any explanations. It's really none of my business. Can we go now?" She tried to sound cool and dispassionate, to somehow mask the wave of anguish washing over her and the tears struggling for release.

"Please, hear me out." He put his hand on her forearm. "I want to explain."

She turned to him, drawing her arm from his contact. She gave him a look she hoped said if-you-feel-you-must-I'll-listen, praying her features revealed none of her true, raw emotions.

He studied her for a moment, then looked down at his hands. "It was a long time ago with Charmaine. Over three years. I was a different person then. I wasn't a Christian, and I prided myself on the effect I had on women. I saw nothing wrong with using it to my advantage. I'm not proud of that, Meg, and I'm grateful I'm not that man anymore. But I won't lie to you about who and what I was."

His gaze came to meet hers. "But I want you to know I have not been with a woman in the two years since my thirteen-year-old brother showed me the way to Christ. God has changed me in so many amazing ways. I don't miss that partying womanizer I used to be. It was a lonely life, and I never want to go back to it."

Meghann stared at him blankly. A partying womanizer. The terms seemed as far from reality as possible when it came to this man. She didn't doubt his effect on women. How could she, considering the way he affected her every time they were together? But she couldn't, no matter how hard she tried, imagine him using someone that way.

Whatever else she thought, she knew this much was true: Bruce was no longer that man.

He turned back and gripped the wheel again. "'Therefore, if anyone is in Christ, he is a *new creation*; the old has gone, the new has come!' God reconciled the world to himself in Christ, Meg, not counting *my* sins against *me*.... God made him who had no sin to be sin for *me*, so that in him *I* might become the righteousness of God."

The passion and determination in his voice moved her deeply. Slowly, inexorably, the tears worked their way down her cheeks.

"I *am* a new creation. I've been given a second chance. Washed by the blood of Jesus. I messed up royally the first time around. I'm doing it right this time."

Stunned by his honesty, she didn't know what to say, how to respond. He wasn't the perfect fantasy she'd concocted in her mind...and he had a past, a history of mistakes. But so did she. And a present full of mistakes as well.

No, Bruce wasn't perfect, but he was doing his best. He was trusting God's promises and trying to live a changed life. And that was more powerful than perfection any day. In that moment, as she listened to him pour out his heart to her, Meg loved him so much it hurt.

Realizing her face was probably betraying her every thought, she turned away. She hated being so transparent to him. Could he tell she loved him? Probably. If he returned her feelings, he would have said something. But he said nothing of the kind.

"We should get going." His tone was weary, resigned. "They'll be wondering what happened to us." He turned the key in the ignition and hesitated. "Meghann?" He reached out to lift her chin with a light touch of his finger. The tenderness in his eyes was heart wrenching.

"Ah, Meg...what you do to me."

His hand cupped her face, and the gentle touch sent shivers coursing through her. She knew he was going to kiss her, and she was glad. She wanted him to do it. Now. Here. With no one around to see them.

But even as she leaned toward him, his hand fell away, and he turned back to grip the steering wheel.

Then, without a word of explanation, he turned the key in the ignition.

Mortified, Meg sat there, gripping her hands together in her lap. She was such an idiot! Why would he even think about kissing her? She was a friend, nothing more. Someone he'd promised to help.

The sooner she got that through her stupid head—and her foolish heart—the better off she'd be.

When they got back to the house, there was a big hulla-baloo about where everyone was going to sleep. The first option proposed was for Bruce and Meghann to stay at her place, but Meghann insisted on being near her mother. So she suggested she and her mother could go to her place. Wrong. It seemed everyone wanted to be around Meghann…everyone except Meghann herself.

She just wanted to get away. To be someplace where she wouldn't have to put on a front for a while. She felt like a favorite toy being fought over.

The final decision was made: Mr. and Mrs. Halloway would take the master bedroom; Meghann and her mother would be in the guest room; and the two brothers were assigned to the living room sofa bed.

The rest of the evening was interminable. Finally Meg saw her escape when Olivia turned to her, concern on her face.

"Dear, are you all right? You don't look well at all."

"I'm not." The first truth she'd uttered in days. "I'm sick."

No sooner were the words out of her mouth than she found herself being ushered to bed by two cooing mothers. But for all that, Meg was more weary than she'd ever been in her life—heart weary, soul weary—she couldn't sleep.

She spent a restless night sharing a room with her mother, thinking about Bruce's honesty that night. It gave her hope that he could have feelings for her—not love, at least not yet—but someday. But even that filled her with uncertainty, with dread.

Because she knew what she had to do. She had to get up the courage to tell him how she felt about him.

Seventeen

THE NEXT MORNING MEGHANN SAGGED ON JENNIFER'S couch. Jennifer had a cozy one-bedroom apartment not far from Meg's place. Meg had hurried over to catch Jennifer before she went off to work.

"I hope you don't mind my drying my hair. I still have a job to get ready for," Jenn said, flicking on the dryer and picking up her styling brush. Meghann got up and stood in the doorway to the bathroom.

"I have a job, too." At least, the last time she checked she did. After all that had gone on, the way she'd gotten Bruce's family caught up in this mess...well, she deserved to have him fire her.

"Yeah, but you're getting paid for staying home." Jenn worked the brush through her dark, shoulder-length hair as she angled the dryer.

"I'm still working on the ball. Believe it or not, it does take a chunk of my day." But Meg knew as well as Jennifer that the few hours she was putting in didn't warrant her pay. More guilt to pile on to her plate. "I didn't come to talk about work. I have bigger problems."

"What? Like wheedling a proposal out of Bruce?" She batted her lashes at Meg, then turned back to the mirror with a Cheshire grin.

"No. Bruce's parents and brother showed up last night."

Jennifer switched off the dryer and turned to her with her mouth in a surprised O. "Your *in-laws* are here?"

"They *aren't* my in-laws."

"Close enough. And maybe with any luck they will be someday." She wiggled her eyebrows.

"Jenn, this is serious. Now I'm lying to his family, too."

"Ah, yes, but apparently Prince Charming didn't tell them the truth, either." She seemed intrigued by this information.

"That's not the point."

"Oh, Meg, lighten up! Why are you taking all this so seriously?"

"Why don't you take *anything* seriously?" Meg snapped back. "What am I going to do now? I never should have let you talk me into this."

"Fine, blame all your troubles on me," she said, holding up her hands, waving her blow dryer and brush around. "See if I care. But answer me this, why did you take my advice if it was so awful? You could have told your mom the truth. I didn't exactly hold a weapon to your head and force you into this little charade."

Meghann opened her mouth for a retort…but there was none. Her friend was absolutely right. She was the one who'd given in to the urge to lie. She was the one who'd passed by opportunity after opportunity to set things right.

Nobody else.

Just her.

"I rest my case." Jennifer set down her dryer. "Now, answer me one more. Is your mom improving or not?"

"Well, yes." It was true. Her mother had most of her color back, and she didn't need to sleep as much.

"Well, then, I rest my case. Clearly what you're doing is for the best. Besides, you've only got a few days and Bruce's family hits the road. Then soon your mom will go home, and you and Bruce can go back to your lives. No harm, no foul."

Jenn looked so pleased with herself that Meg didn't have the heart to argue. But deep inside—where she felt the constant struggle, the tug to do what she knew was right no matter how terrifying it might be—she knew her friend was wrong. Flat wrong.

There was a great deal of harm taking place. To Bruce. To Meg's heart. Maybe even to her spirit.

She just didn't know what to do about it.

Later that afternoon, Bruce came home, opening his front door with care, wondering what kind of greeting he'd receive from Meghann. He had worked diligently straight through lunch so he could come home early to see her.

It hadn't been easy to tell her those things last night, to let her see his imperfections, his weaknesses. But when she'd listened so intently, when he'd seen the understanding in her eyes, he'd almost lost control. It was only God's grace that had held him back, kept him from taking her in his arms and kissing her senseless. Kept him from proposing to her on the spot.

All day long he'd thought about her, wondered what she was thinking, how she was feeling about what he'd said. And he'd prayed. Asked God to show them a way out of the mess they'd made for themselves. Asked him to salvage their relationship from the disaster they'd created.

Now what he wanted to do was see her.

Looking around, he found the usually over-crowded apartment empty, except for his pseudo-mother-in-law in the kitchen brewing some tea. "Where did everybody go?"

Gayle stirred a half a teaspoon of sugar and a dab of milk in her cup. "Your father had some urgent business to take care of. He dropped your mom off at the hairdresser's on his way and will pick her up when he is done. And Brock went with Meghann to the house to feed Lucky."

"Brock is with Meghann?" He didn't realize he spoke the words aloud until Gayle placed her hand on his forearm.

"Don't look so worried. He just wants to get to know his new sister-in-law. Those two get along great."

Her words hit him like a roundhouse punch. He had the urge to run after them and snatch Meg away from his brother, to take her somewhere remote out of reach of any man who would steal her from him.

"Relax," she said, giving his arm a gentle squeeze.

Gayle's expression told him she knew things weren't quite right between him and her daughter. If she only knew how wrong they were.

He couldn't relax. If he weren't careful, he would lose her. She could slip right through his fingers. He had to talk with her, tell her how he felt, ask her outright if there was anything for them beyond their little masquerade.

He hoped so. Prayed so. If not, he knew without a doubt that it would take a lifetime to get over Meghann.

But would confessing his love for her be enough? Not if she didn't feel the same way. He had to think of something else. But what? If only she loved him…. But as often as not, she was nervous and tense whenever they were alone, as though she'd rather be around other people.

Well, there were plenty of people to keep her occupied…not the least of which was good old Brock.

Bruce needed time….

"There's something I have to do." He gave Gayle a quick peck on the cheek and rushed out the door.

Meg shifted uneasily on the porch step.

Brock had asked if he could accompany her to check on Lucky. There had been a tense encounter between Brock and his father over the length of Brock's unruly hair. Meg couldn't understand why Bruce's father didn't just leave him alone. Yes, his hair was long, but that was hardly something to be ashamed of nowadays. Besides, he always kept it neat and it fit him:

unconventional, yet attractive.

"Tell me about Bruce," Meghann said to Brock as they sat on her back porch.

"Does your dog play fetch?" Brock toyed with a worn tennis ball.

"She loves it. But I must warn you, you will wear out long before she does."

If he didn't want to answer her question about Bruce, that was fine. She had noticed a strain between the two brothers.

He lobbed the ball across the yard. Lucky reached the spot before the ball and caught it after the first bounce. She raced back and he threw it again.

"What do you want to know?" Brock finally said to her.

"About his childhood. What he was like in high school. Stuff like that."

"I suppose he was a typical big brother, pushy, telling others what to do. I recall being forced to bow down to him a time or two," he said with a chuckle.

As an only child, Meg had pretended all the time that she had siblings. But even as a child she'd known it wasn't the same, that she was missing out on something. She'd watched her friends with their brothers and sisters, saw how they fought and called each other names, but at least they weren't lonely.

Not like she'd been.

Not like Brock sounds?

She frowned. It was true. Brock sounded lonely. She watched him as he went on, relating the glowing attributes of his older brother. "He was class president all four years of high school, quarterback and captain of the football team, valedictorian, and always managed to have the prettiest girl in school for his girlfriend." He took the ball from the dog and pointed it at Meghann. "I see he hasn't lost his knack for that."

She smiled self-consciously.

"I hope he appreciates you and tells you how lucky he is to have you and that you're pretty." He tossed the ball again. "Bruce is your basic all-American boy who excelled at everything he did. 'Nothing that's worth doing, is worth doing only halfway.' It was always all or nothing with him. He knew what he wanted, went after it, and got it. I envied him that. Knowing what he wanted, that is. I suppose if I knew what I wanted, I could get it too."

"Were you and Bruce close growing up?"

Brock shrugged his shoulders. "I guess so."

An uncomfortable silence fell between them. She sensed he had said all he wanted to about Bruce and probably more about himself than he'd intended to reveal.

In that, Bruce and Brock were similar. They both held their thoughts and feelings tightly to themselves. And Meg was starting to wonder if she'd ever break through Bruce's defenses.

The truth, Meg. The truth brings walls tumbling down....

She hugged herself tightly and wondered why lying was so easy, but giving someone she loved the truth was so hard. She didn't have the answer. She only hoped she found it before it was too late.

———— ∞ ————

"Back so soon?" George Phenton said, looking up from the work before him on his desk. "You just can't stay away from this place."

"George, how hard would it be to replace me?"

The older man lay his pen down on the papers and narrowed his eyes to scrutinize Bruce for a moment. "Is this where I'm supposed to tell you that the hotel couldn't possibly function without you?"

Bruce put both hands on the front of the desk and leaned toward the general manager. "No, this is where you tell me you have everything under control and so well organized that the hotel can run without either one of us."

George leaned back in his chair and laced his hands together behind his head, clearly undaunted by Bruce's boldness. "This place could run smooth as silk for a month without either one of us—but I wouldn't recommend it." He pursed his lips. "What is this all about, Bruce?"

"I need some time away. ASAP."

"Then take it."

Bruce paced in front of the desk and raked his hand through his dark hair. "I can't do that if I know it will leave you in the lurch."

"The hotel will survive without you. I promise it will be standing upon your return. How long do you plan to be gone this time?"

"I don't know. A couple of weeks…maybe indefinitely."

"Does this mean I should hire a real assistant manager?"

Bruce stopped pacing and looked at the man. Fifteen years his senior, George had always been an anchor for Bruce. "Was I really that much trouble for you?"

"You did quite well. You learned quickly and were surprisingly useful, when you were here. I kind of enjoyed getting to tell *you* what to do." George gave him a lopsided grin.

"And don't think I didn't notice."

Smiling fully now, George picked up his pen and went back to work, studying the file before him. "Have a nice trip."

Bruce turned to leave, then stopped. "One more thing, George. Give Miss Livingston a hundred dollar a week raise."

"Oh?" The general manager looked up from his papers and paid attention. "You realize she hasn't been in much for the last two weeks?"

"She's been…doing some special work for me." This time it was Bruce with a crooked grin.

"I see." George considered him for a moment. "May I give you some sound fatherly advice on employer-employee relationships?"

"No." Bruce turned to the door again and opened it this time. "And George, make that raise retroactive."

"Just how far back does this raise go?"

"Christmas." He knew he had shocked George, but he didn't care. He was doing what he had to: spending more time with Meghann and keeping her out of his brother's clutches.

"You're asking for trouble." George Phenton's stern look was the last thing Bruce saw before exiting.

"I've already got as much as I can handle," he said, as he closed the door.

This time when he returned home, he found Meghann and the others there. They were gathered in the kitchen as Meghann and Gayle prepared dinner; his mother was trying to help. She looked out of place even with an apron on. He doubted his mother had ever touched an apron before. This was new territory for her. And by the rigid look on his father's face, this wasn't territory he wanted her to cover.

Bruce came up behind Meghann and kissed her on the cheek. He held out a long, narrow velvet case to her. She stopped chopping the mushrooms and stared at the box. Slowly she set her knife down and took the box. Turning, she looked up at him. "What is this?"

"It's a present for you."

She looked down at it, then back up at him with a confused expression on her face. "Why?"

"Because he loves you, dear. Now open it," her mother said.

"It's for our two-month anniversary."

"That's not for eleven more days."

The fact that she was keeping track, even in make-believe, pleased him. "Open it." He was careful not to sound demanding, but he couldn't help sounding eager.

She seemed to prolong the act of lifting the lid. Or

was he just anxious to see if she liked what he'd brought her?

"It's beautiful," she breathed out. Then she did it. She looked up at him and gifted him with the most beautiful smile; her expression was warm, her eyes glowed…surely that was true affection he saw reflected in their depths? In any case, she enchanted him with that single look. It seemed as though they were the only two people in the room.

Bruce carefully removed the diamond cross pendant from its velvet case. "Let me put it on you." He held it up by its delicate gold rope chain and reached around her neck to fasten it.

She fingered it reverently as her tear-filled eyes swept up to his face. "Thank you," she whispered.

Though the others mistook her tears for joy, he could see a touch of sorrow in her eyes, and it broke his heart.

Why are you sad, Meghann? This was supposed to make you happy.

Would he ever figure this woman out? He hoped so. And he hoped it happened before he lost everything that really mattered to him.

Meghann stood before the mirror in the guest room she and her mother shared. The beauty of the cross sparkled in the light. She removed it from around her neck and turned the cross back and forth, watching the light dance within the carefully cut diamonds.

"It's beautiful," her mother said as Meghann carefully

laid the pendant in its velvet case.

All this attention from Bruce felt wonderful…until reality came crashing in. Appearances. That's all it was. His actions were calculated moves. She should be grateful he played his role so convincingly, but with each passing day, she found it only broke her heart.

"He loves you very much."

"Yes, so it seems." She touched it one last time before turning off the light.

Eighteen

THE NEXT EVENING, THEY SAT DOWN TO WATCH A MOVIE. The eight-foot screen slid down from its hiding place in the ceiling and dropped in front of the fireplace. Another box on the ceiling further back held the video projection unit. And the door off to the side of the fireplace housed all the other electronics.

Brock and Meghann had gone out to rent videos. But Meg hadn't been sure what the others would want to see. When she couldn't decide on a single movie, Brock insisted on renting all six that she was deliberating over.

At least having that many movies to watch would ensure her mother took it easy and didn't overtax herself.

Meghann came out of the kitchen with two large bowls of freshly popped popcorn. She stopped and studied Bruce as he played host serving up sodas and Perrier from his junk food stocked dry bar.

She was struck by wonderment at this man. He so easily stepped into the role of her husband, yet asked for nothing in return. He never acted inappropriately or carelessly. But then why should he? He wasn't even attracted to her. He did such a good job of acting, though, that it confused even her at times.

Who was she kidding? He confused her *all* the time.

She thought back to the last few days, to the way he'd been treating her, to his gifts and the way he'd take her hand in his, the way he'd look at her…. He was only acting so loving, so caring because…because, why? She stared at him a moment longer before she remembered the bowls of popcorn in her hands and moved to join the others.

Ivan, sitting in the overstuffed green leather chair on the far side of the living room, presided over what he considered this little annoyance. Olivia, Mom, and Brock occupied the matching couch. And Bruce sat in the chair that was twin to the one his father was in. With all seats taken, Meghann opted for a nice spot on the white plush carpet.

Brock stood and offered her his seat.

"She can sit with me," Bruce said quickly, taking her hand and gently pulling her into his chair.

Startled at first, she took up the challenge in his delicious brown eyes. She wasn't exactly on his lap, she was more wedged between him and the chair arm, except for her legs, which she immediately removed from across his, making herself as comfortable as she could.

The chair accommodated them both, but the feel of his arm against her, his leg against hers, sent her heart into somersaults. Here's hoping the movie was good enough to distract her!

Bruce pointed the remote and the show began.

Meg didn't realize just how comfortable she was until she drifted off to sleep before the movie was a quarter of the way through. Her mother had had a restless night last night, so she hadn't slept well, either. At least her mother had taken a nap, or Meghann would worry all the more. Soothed by the steady thump, thump, thump rhythm from within her pretend husband, she allowed herself to drift away on a dream and a prayer, serenaded by the sound of the movie and of his strong heartbeat in the background.

She woke sometime later to find herself being transported across the room by strong arms. "I can walk."

Bruce stopped by her bedroom door and released her legs but kept his other arm securely around her. She couldn't tear her gaze from his and licked her lips self-consciously. Her pulse quickened and her lungs didn't seem to need air at all. She swallowed as he leaned closer. Surely he would stop, pull back as he'd done so many times before...

But he didn't.

He kissed her tenderly, with a gentle reverence. Her mind scanned their surroundings for an audience. But there was no one. They were alone.

Her hope soared at the thought. And when his arm tightened around her and he deepened the kiss, her heart flooded with joy.

Bleak reality quickly came to light when the bathroom door clicked open and the sound of a throat clearing reached her ears.

Bruce tensed and broke the kiss, muttering something under his breath. He gazed down at her as if he wanted to say something, but Meg couldn't meet his eyes. She was too afraid she'd weep at what she'd been hoping and what she now knew was true. They hadn't shared a beautiful moment at all.

It had been the same as all the others. A kiss calculated to get caught.

"Why don't you two get a hotel room?" This from Brock who stood somewhere behind Bruce out of her line of sight.

A muscle tightened in Bruce's jaw.

Why did he look so upset? So they had been caught kissing. Wasn't that the point, after all? "Good night," she whispered.

"Good night, my love," he whispered back. "Sleep well."

His love? If only it were, this whole thing would be so much more bearable. She tore herself from his arms and escaped into the bedroom. Her eyes were awash with tears, her heart awash with the pain of dashed hopes. The lighting was dim enough, she hoped he hadn't been able to see the tears gleaming there when she turned from him.

She leaned against the door clutching her chest. *Father God, I love him so much. Why can't this be real?*

No answer came. But she knew the answer. It was all a lie. A lie can never be truth. And it stood between her and her mother, her and Bruce…and most important between her and God.

She slid down the wall, feeling hollow and alone.

The shimmer of unshed tears he'd seen in her eyes confused him. What had he done to hurt her? He had kissed her first of all because he wanted to, and secondly, to gauge how she felt about him. For one, brief moment, hope had coursed through him. She'd leaned into him, and the small sigh that escaped her as he kissed her had made his head spin.

But then...

Then she pulled away, looking at him with such sorrow. Obviously she didn't feel for him what he felt for her. Or was she already developing feelings for Brock and was sad he was the one to witness them?

"You're hopeless," Brock said lightly.

Bruce turned on his brother and stepped into the living room, away from the bedroom door. "Why don't you and Mother and Father get a hotel?"

"We all just want to get to know your new little bride. You certainly have been tight-lipped about her. We can't count on you to tell us anything. Which is hard to understand," he said, shaking his head. "If I was married to a beauty like that, I wouldn't hide her away. I would show her off to the world." Brock tossed the sofa cushions aside.

"Fortunately you don't have to worry about that, and the day after tomorrow I won't have to worry about it, either."

Brock unfolded the bed from the couch. "Sorry, bro. You're going to have us hanging around a little longer."

"What?" He ran a frustrated hand through his hair, unable to believe his parents would want to stay longer than a day or two. Six people cramped in his apartment was not their style.

"You know how Mother can be. She's like a child with a new toy. She finally has a daughter-in-law." His voice turned compassionate. "I think she misses not having a daughter."

They were staying. He couldn't believe they were staying.

"You're going to lose her," Brock said.

Bruce didn't have to ask Brock who he was talking about. Bruce glared at him. "Is that a threat?"

Brock shrugged a lone shoulder as he finished up with the bed. "Just an observation."

Snatching up a pillow and an extra blanket, Bruce went to sleep on the floor. He wouldn't likely sleep tonight anyway, so what did it matter where he was. He just couldn't lose Meghann.

Meghann sat at the two-person table at the Crystal Swan and forced a smile for her pseudo-mother-in-law. She had tried to get her mother to come too, but she insisted that Meghann and Olivia needed this time to get acquainted.

Meghann sipped her ice water with a wedge of lemon in it. "I'm sorry that the wedding was such a rush and we couldn't invite all of you. It was nothing personal. If we had more time, we would have invited everyone."

Olivia rested her hand on Meghann's forearm. "It's all right, dear. Bruce explained about your mother's health condition. But I insist on giving you and Bruce a grand reception this summer. We have friends that would be positively insulted if they were not invited to celebrate in Bruce's good fortune."

Why did she have the foreboding sense Olivia wasn't talking about a little gathering of their closest friends? "Please don't go to any trouble."

"It will be no trouble at all. I'm looking forward to it." Olivia leaned forward. "In truth, I've been looking forward to this for some years now. Oh, we tried to fix Bruce up with some nice girls, but he wasn't ready to settle down. Not until you that is." The excitement in her voice twisted Meghann's insides even more.

The waitress arrived with their food. Meghann stared down at hers, doubting she would be able to eat anything, her insides twisted and coiled into painful knots. Her chicken Caesar salad lay untouched on her plate. She thought it would be light enough for her turbulent midsection to take, but she feared she was wrong. Now it just stared up at her, mocking her, accusing her. She poked at it with her fork.

"Is everything all right?" Olivia dabbed the corners of her mouth with her linen napkin.

Meghann dragged her eyes away from the artistically arranged food on her plate to meet Olivia's questioning gaze. "Yes, fine."

"Is there anything wrong with your Caesar salad? We can send it back to the kitchen if you're not pleased with it."

"No, I'm sure it's fine."

"I understand, dear. If you don't feel up to eating, don't worry about it. It's only natural."

It's only natural? No, not this pregnant thing again.

Meghann picked up her fork and swallowed hard before taking the bite it held. She was going to eat every last leaf of this taunting salad, even if it killed her. Her tense stomach lurched in protest with the first bite. She swallowed carefully, forcing herself on to the next bite.

She already swallowed her pride, choked on her lies, and stuffed herself with humiliation. In light of all that, eating one stupid salad should be a snap.

Nineteen

A COUPLE OF DAYS LATER, MEGHANN FOUND HERSELF ALONE in the afternoon. Everyone was out doing one thing or another.

Finally, blessed, peaceful solitude.

She reclined in one of the soft leather chairs in the living room and propped her feet up on the ottoman to enjoy the quiet, filling her lungs with the stillness. A calm in the midst of the storm.

A certain pair of warm brown eyes came to mind, like soft melted chocolate...she had a sudden hankering for a Snickers bar. Bruce had a stash of little ones in his dry bar with an assortment of other junk food. If she recalled right, they were just behind the pop under the potato chips. She appreciated his penchant for junk food. He always had plenty on hand.

Bruce had undergone a transformation since his family arrived. The easygoing this-is-a-game-let's-have-fun Bruce had slipped away. In his place, a more serious Bruce who only smiled occasionally emerged...an echo of the staunch and stoic never-let-them-see-you-smile Ivan Halloway.

Jumping off the couch, she trotted over and opened the cabinet doors. She scanned the interior and noticed things had been moved around. Bottled water, pop, Doritos, Fritos, wine, and there they were, the Snickers, right next to the Scotch.

Meghann's hand froze in place. Scotch? Moving her hand slowly from the Scotch to the red wine, she noticed more: vodka, bourbon, and white wine. There must have been eight to ten bottles of assorted alcohol. When she heard the front door open, she quickly closed the cabinet doors with a double kathud and shot to her feet.

Bruce walked in and greeted her with a warm smile. Looking around at the empty apartment, he grinned at her. "How did you manage time to yourself?"

"Our mothers went off on some secret mission. I think they are up to something. I don't know where your dad and Brock went." She twisted her ring around and around on her finger. "I made calls from here, and everything's going smoothly for the ball."

He narrowed his eyes and studied her. "Are you feeling all right?"

"Yes, I feel fine," she said and nervously eyed the dry bar. She felt like a naughty child caught red-handed.

"You look pale." He came up to her with a concerned expression.

This was ridiculous; she had done nothing wrong. *She* certainly hadn't bought all that liquor. Besides, this was his apartment. He could have a hundred bottles of alcohol if he wanted to. "I'm fine, really," she said, waving away his concern.

He suspiciously eyed the dry bar. Meghann scooted away when he moved to open it. Letting out a heavy sigh, he shook his head and pulled out bottle after bottle of alcohol, placing them on top next to the clean overturned glasses. Gathering up as many bottles in his arms as he could, he asked her if she could get the rest and headed for the kitchen.

Meghann collected the last three and followed him, wondering what he planned to do with ten bottles of miscellaneous brew all at once. She set hers on the counter by the sink next to the other ones.

How was he going to explain all this alcohol to her? He'd made a point of not having strong drink at the hotel Christmas party. Most everyone at the hotel knew he wasn't a drinking man, but would Meghann think he was a different man in private than he was in public? The condemning evidence was in front of him…and her.

She looked so stricken at having found what she thought was his stash of liquor. Another strike against him.

"There is a corkscrew in that drawer next to you," he said as he opened the bottle of vodka.

She dug in the drawer and handed him the twisted utensil. "I know you won't believe this, but these are not mine." The ease with which he used the device to open the bottles bothered him. It was like riding a bike, you never forget. Both the red and white wine were opened swiftly. How would she believe his innocence now?

She reluctantly took the bottle of red wine he handed her as he took the white.

"Cheers," he said, clinking his bottle with hers, then began dumping it down the drain.

Meghann blinked and looked up at him questioningly.

"Bottoms up," he said with the raise of his eyebrows but couldn't blame her for being confused.

She slowly tipped the bottle over. The red liquid gurgled out and down the hole in the bottom of the stainless steel sink.

The alcohol was his father's subtle way of luring his son back to his old habits; party after party was his way of life back then. Well, he wasn't taking the bait—not now, not ever.

Father God, give me the strength to once again resist this temptation. In my own strength I will fail.

He poured with determination.

How can I make him see the changes in me are good? I don't know how to reach him.

Once Bruce emptied his bottle, he picked up another and poured it out. "My father bought all this. He does this every time they visit."

"But why dump it out? I'm sure this cost a lot of money."

"My father spared no expense, I assure you that. Only the best."

"You could return it."

"I don't want the money from it." He took a deep

breath. "I can't have it around. I'm ashamed to admit it, but it is still a temptation for me. Dumping it out gives me strength."

The first time his father stocked his bar Bruce had thought it wouldn't hurt to have it around for visitors. Surely he could stay away from it. Hadn't he seen how damaging it was for him? Some people might be able to handle liquor, but he wasn't one of them. He knew it and accepted it.

At least, he thought he did. Until he woke up the next morning with a headache and a boatload of regret. That was one hangover he vividly remembered; the others had been dulled by more alcohol.

The next time he found his father's "gifts," he took the bottles straight to the sink with shaking hands and prayed the whole time for God's strength to dump it all before he drank it. When the deed was done, he was wet with perspiration and shaking so badly he could hardly stand. Each time it got easier. Now, it was more a statement to his father that he wouldn't have it around even for him.

He looked directly at her. "My father has to know the changes in my life are permanent." He had to make sure she knew it, too.

If only he could be sure he had the time to show her. But with each passing day, the dread that plagued him grew stronger. He couldn't explain it, but he was fairly sure time was running out.

Twenty

BRUCE WATCHED AS BROCK, THEIR MOTHER, AND MEG'S mother occupied Meghann with merry chatter. Even his father was vying for a small piece of her attention.

Jealousy shot through him. He knew it was irrational, but he wanted Meg to himself. Wanted her to desire his company more than any other.

With a sigh, he studied his family and Meg again. Clearly, he was not likely to get any time with her. Not unless he remedied this situation.

Just then Brock reached over and touched Meghann's arm as he whispered in her ear. She turned and gifted him with a smile.

That's it!

Bruce strode over and took Meghann by the hand. She stood without hesitation, a fact that warmed his heart.

His mother, however, wasn't so compliant. "Bruce, what are you doing?"

"I'm commandeering my wife."

"You can't. We're having a nice talk with her, and I'm

not finished. I've barely gotten to know my daughter-in-law."

"Bruce, I—" Meghann began.

Bruce didn't let her finish. Instead, he swept her up in his arms and headed for the door. "We'll see you all tomorrow."

"Put me down!" Meghann's whispered command didn't bother him much, accompanied as it was by a broad smile. He held fast to her.

"Surely you're not leaving with her?" His mother's irritation was as evident as Meg's pleasure.

"Olivia! Leave the boy alone," he heard his father say in a stern voice.

"At least tell us where you are going," his mother said.

"Meg's place," Gayle said with a smile, and Bruce almost burst out laughing. Leave it to Meg's mom to suddenly seem pleased that they had two places.

Bruce shook his head. "Nope. I'm taking my bride to a place where we won't be found." He pinned Brock with a glare. "By anyone."

"I need to at least get my purse, so you can set me down," Meghann said.

He didn't budge. "Where is it?"

"On the table behind the couch."

He moved in that direction.

"Aren't you going to put me down?"

"No." He leaned over enough for her to grab her purse. He wasn't about to let her go and risk losing her to this crowd.

"What if we need to get in touch with you?"

"You'll just have to deal with whatever crisis comes up yourselves, Mother," he said over his shoulder. "Would you get the door, my dear?" He grinned at Meghann, bending far enough for her to reach the knob.

Her answering smile convinced him he'd done the right thing, and he walked out without any effort to close the door behind him. At the elevator he had her press the button with the toe of her shoe.

"You can set me down now." She attempted to lift her legs free.

"Not yet."

He stepped inside the elevator and waited for the doors to close before freeing her legs. As her feet touched down, their eyes locked. He wanted nothing more in that moment than to pull her into his arms and kiss her deeply, but instead he slowly released the hold his other arm still had on her.

Meghann started giggling. He loved to hear her laugh and feasted on the sound. His mouth, too, turned upward. She laughed all the way to his 'Vette.

"I don't think your mother can believe you did that," she said when she caught her breath.

His smile broadened and he chuckled. His mother's anger wouldn't last long. In fact, she'd probably be bragging on her forceful, obviously-in-love son to her community charity compatriots within the week. "I can't believe I did it, either. It was sort of a spur of the moment inspiration." He wasn't normally an impulsive person. Plan things out thoroughly to avoid potential failure; that was his motto. But he had never felt as possessive about a woman as he did about her. "I got tired of the crowd and figured you might be, too."

Her expression was grateful. "Yes, I was. I don't know how much more I could take. Thank you for rescuing me."

He glanced over at her after pulling into traffic. "My pleasure."

She leaned her head back and sighed heavily. "So where are you taking me?"

"How does dinner sound?"

"Isn't it a little early?"

"Not by the time we get there," he said wryly with the raise of his brows.

They headed north and an hour later arrived at Havana Street Station.

"Two?" the hostess asked and showed them to a table in the middle of the dimly lit restaurant. It was still early and the place was nearly vacant. Only one table was occupied with four little old ladies. Soft music wafted through the air, just enough to set a relaxing mood but not overpowering to distraction. Plants tucked in here and there gave the place a warm, earthy feel.

"Could we possibly get that table over there?" Bruce pointed to a cozy corner booth out of the line of traffic.

"Sure," the hostess said and seated them in the requested spot, leaving them with a pair of menus. Latticework between theirs and the adjoining booths gave it an air of privacy.

A few minutes later, a tall, lanky young waiter with sandy blond hair appeared next to the table. He took their drink orders—raspberry lemonade for Meg, iced tea for Bruce—and nodded. "I'll bring those right out."

They settled into their chairs, taking their time perusing the menu. Bruce felt himself finally starting to relax in the peaceful quiet between them. "How about we get a couple of appetizers for now and order our meals later?"

Meghann agreed readily, so Bruce ordered the appetizers a moment later when Scott returned with their drinks.

This, he thought as he watched the waiter retreat, is what he had wanted at Christmas. Just the two of them together, over dinner. Regret, sharp and painful, stabbed through him. If only he'd made sure it had happened. If only they'd been able to start back then, building a relationship. But now they had this deception between them. Though it brought them together, it also kept them apart.

Meghann's nose wrinkled slightly and she tilted her head, studying him. "Why are you looking at me like that?"

He raised his brows. "Like what?"

She pondered the question. "Like you've got something on your mind."

I do. You. Every minute of every day. He laid his napkin in his lap. "I was wondering why you moved so far away from your mother when it's only the two of you."

"Oh, I guess I needed to spread my wings. I love my mom dearly, but sometimes she can be a bit much. I needed some room to figure out who I was." She took a sip of her lemonade.

"So how did you end up here?"

"A friend had an uncle down here with a family camp ranch, so we came down to work for him for the summer."

"Is your friend still working for her uncle?"

"No." She twisted her glass around by its base. "It turned out she was allergic to horses, so she got a job in town, but I stayed at the ranch. When the summer was over, she went back home. I fell in love with it here, got another job, and started college."

"Your job at the hotel?"

"I wish." She abandoned spinning her beverage. "I worked many assorted jobs before I landed that one."

He watched her draw lines on her glass in the condensation. Was she nervous? Did she think he was prying? He only wanted to get to know her better, to know everything about her. "You must like it there."

Her head came up then. "I love that old hotel. It has so much charm and character. Like many of the employees, I was a little afraid of losing my job when the hotel changed owners. That was just before you were hired. There were so many rumors about staff cuts and the hotel possibly closing. But apparently the only one who lost his job was the manager. Some say he quit, others say he was fired."

"He resigned. There were irreconcilable differences between him and the new owner."

Interest sparked in her eyes at that. She leaned forward, a small smile on her lips. "You wouldn't mind divulging a little information on him would you? Or is it a her? Them?"

Oops, wrong subject. "I'd love to tell you everything I know, Meg, but I can't. I'm not at liberty to discuss it. The owner prefers to remain in the background for now."

She pouted for a moment, then sat back with an understanding smile. "Well, he or she must have a passion for the place, restoring it and all." Excitement danced in her hazel eyes. "I like to think of her as a sweet little old lady."

"Old?" He smiled at the idea.

She nodded, clearly entranced with her fantasy. "She spent her honeymoon at the Palace Hotel as a young woman desperately in love with her new husband. They had a long and wonderful marriage, and when she lost him, she decided she would do something to honor all they'd shared. So she's restoring the first place they were together to its grand old style." She sighed. "Her name would be Maud or Betsy or Cora Bennet." Yes, Cora Bennet. She liked the sound of it even if it was fabricated from her imagination.

Quite a little romantic, his pretend wife. He loved listening to her, seeing her like this. Reaching out, he covered her hand with his. "Will you be terribly disappointed if you're wrong?"

She looked up from their hands but didn't move away. "A little. It's such a wonderful story. But when it comes down to it, I'll like anyone who would go to the trouble to restore my grand old hotel."

He arched his brows at that. "Your hotel?"

The sweetest pink tinged her cheeks, and she laughed at herself. "In my heart, my dreams. I love that place." Her eyes shone. "I can hardly wait to see what it looks like when it's back to its original glory."

Bruce smiled, his eyes fixed on her glowing face, convinced that even the majestic old hotel in all its original beauty couldn't hold a candle to the glory he was looking at right that moment.

More than three hours later, after lingering over dinner and dessert, they headed back to Bruce's apartment.

"I can't believe we were at the restaurant for that long," Meghann said, but she wasn't the least bit sorry they'd taken so much time. It had been wonderful. "It went so fast. I feel bad we took up a booth for so long. Waiters and waitresses practically live on their tips. They depend on them. I know, that was one of my jobs in college."

"I don't think Scott, our waiter, minded. I left a very generous tip to more than cover any tip he may have missed out on." Bruce grinned. "Besides, he was quite taken with you."

"Taken with me?"

"He gave us far more attention than was necessary. Had I been there with a business associate, I wouldn't have seen him nearly half as much. Didn't you notice him flirting with you?"

She frowned, thinking back. The young man was very nice and always smiled at her. And her lemonade was never quite gone before he brought her another.... She angled a look at Bruce. "Am I to assume it doesn't bother my supposed husband that another man was flirting with me?"

"Not at all, for three reasons." He held up three fingers as he glanced over at her, then switched to only his index finger raised. "One, he was only eighteen or nineteen. Too young for you."

Well, the nerve! She sniffed at him. "How do you know I don't prefer younger men?"

He turned his gaze from the road, and the teasing laughter she saw in his eyes almost made her smile.

"Do you?"

She gave a careless little shrug. "I've never really considered age a major factor—" he arched one of those expressive brows, and she allowed a small smile—"but I confess I prefer men I date to be older than I."

Triumph filled his face and he focused his attention back on the ribbon of black highway stretched before them.

"And number two?" she prodded.

"This." He pointed out into the darkness. "There is more than an hour's distance separating the two of you. My guess is he's working his way through school. Both his time and money are limited. I doubt he would spend a fortune on gas, if he has a car at all, to come see you. Not to mention the limits of time."

So, he didn't think someone would go out of his way to see her. "Okay. What's number three?"

"The most important of all. You."

"Me?"

"You didn't seem to have the least bit of interest in him whatsoever."

Guilty as charged. She didn't even notice Scott's flirting. Her interest lay elsewhere—and she figured

Bruce knew that as well as she. But he could have at least acted a little bit jealous.

Why should he? There was no one around of consequence, so appearances didn't matter.

She turned to stare out into the darkness enveloping them. Why did it always come back to that? Why couldn't she just enjoy their time together for what it was?

Because you're not sure what it was, that's why. True enough. She sighed. "Where are we going now?"

"Your place."

"But you told your mother—"

"What's the point of escaping if we can be easily found?" He disarmed her with a heart-stopping smile. "Besides, I thought you would like to be at your own place for a change."

He was right again. It would be good to sleep in her own bed. She sighed heavily and leaned her head back.

"Are you tired?"

"No, not really. It's just nice to relax."

They pulled into her driveway. They slipped from the car and she followed him as he unlocked the front door of her house, holding it open for her to enter.

"Good night."

At the low words, she turned to face him in surprise. "Aren't you coming in?"

He studied her in silence, a slight smile on his lips. Then he shrugged. "I don't think that's a good idea."

Why ever not? This had been a lovely evening and she wasn't ready for it to end just yet. Disappointment swept her from relaxation into vexation. "Why are you doing this?"

His smile broadened. "Standing out in the cold?"

"No. Pretending to be married to me. I'm doing it for my mom. What do you get out of all this? And don't you dare say you have a mother, too."

He rubbed his hand on the back of his neck. "To be honest, I feel trapped in this now that my parents have arrived. I feel as if my family's openness to faith, to what I've been trying to share with them, somehow hinges on this. My father is looking for any excuse to condemn Christianity, to drive a wedge between my mother and siblings and faith in Christ. I know I'll have to tell them all the truth eventually..." He gazed out at the evening sky. "I'm just not ready yet. I'm worried about the distance it will put between us."

She blinked back tears at his words. If only she had known that careless little lie would lead to all this....

I'm sorry. Father, I'm so sorry.

He inclined his head and looked back at her. "Besides, I can't really back out at this point, now can I?" There was a trace of laughter in his voice.

Would you if you felt you could? Are you eager to be gone?

His gaze captured her. She couldn't speak or look away—or breathe for that matter. There was a spark of some indefinable emotion in his eyes. All she knew was that what she saw there made her want to throw herself in his arms for the rest of her life. His smile and the caress of his smooth voice made her heart beat faster. All logic and common sense flew out the window. She blinked, light-headed, feeling for all the world as though she were drunk.

Bruce Halloway was intoxicating.

The phone rang, startling her. She gasped in air and turned, staring at it in confusion.

Bruce grabbed her hand to keep her in her place. "Don't answer that. You're not supposed to be here. Don't answer the phone for any reason." He gave her hand a squeeze when she nodded.

The simple touch of his hand on hers sent shock waves jolting through her. Maybe he was right. Maybe it was a good thing he wasn't coming in.

His knowing expression told her he knew how she was feeling. He lifted one hand to cup her face. "Make sure you lock up." He ran a finger down her cheek to her chin, sending another round of shivers coursing through her body. "I'll see you in the morning."

She would look forward to it with great delight.

Twenty-One

MEGHANN WAS STARTLED AWAKE WHEN LUCKY SUDDENLY stood up and walked to the head of the bed. Pulling her hair out from under the dog's paw, she swatted at her. "Lie down. It's only six-thirty."

Surprisingly enough, Lucky obeyed and stuck her nose in Meghann's face. She rolled away from the dog breath. The Lab abruptly stood again, gave a little whine, and licked her cheek before jumping over her onto the floor. The whole bed shook from the movement.

Good riddance! Now maybe I can go back to sleep. She had found it difficult to get to sleep last night and snuggled deeper into the covers. Thoughts of Bruce danced through her mind, the little thrill she felt when he touched her cheek. If he could, by some miracle, feel half as much for her as she felt for him, they could live happily ever after.

Lucky's nails clicked on the kitchen floor, stopped, then clicked back. She whined at the front door, then clicked her way back across the kitchen floor.

"Oh, go lie down!"

Lucky raced to the bedroom and nudged her owner's hand. Meghann pulled her arm away and tucked it under the covers. "I'm asleep." The dog put her front paws up on the bed.

Meghann sat up. "Go...lie...*down,*" she said firmly, pointing across the room.

Lucky ducked her head and slunk across the room. Meghann watched as the dog stared at her as though unable to believe her owner really meant to send her away. Finally, the dog circled around once, twice, and then lay down with a heavy sigh. Meghann, too, settled back against the pillow.

Just as she was drifting off to sleep again, she heard Lucky trot back out to the living room. As long as she didn't pace in the kitchen, Meghann didn't care where the dog was and drifted merrily off to sleep.

Sometime later, she woke to hot breath in her face. She opened her eyes just in time to see a big black dog nose close up—much closer than she ever cared to. Lucky's tail started wagging, moving not only her head but jiggling the entire bed.

They stared at one another. "If I let you out, will you leave me alone?"

The dog's tail wagged more vigorously. Meghann sighed and threw back the covers. Lucky pranced backward. The clock read 7:25. "I hope you know I expected to sleep for at least another hour."

She put on her old blue velour robe—the one she had gotten in junior high school—and walked through the small house to the back door. Lucky sat at the front door.

"Come on, girl."

Lucky trotted to the edge of the kitchen, then turned around back to the front door.

Why was her dog being such a toad this morning? Punishing her, no doubt, for being gone so much. She threw up her hands. *Fine! If she wants out the front, I really could care less.*

She opened the door and Lucky bounded out. An inch of late spring snow covered the ground. A few flakes still drifted down, but the early morning sun was already trying to break through. By noon, the snow would all be evaporated.

Lucky stood with her front paws on the gate. Meghann looked beyond the fence to see what had captured her pet's attention. A red Corvette blanketed with snow sat in the driveway. Bruce!

Meghann ducked back inside, changed her clothes, and ran a brush through her hair.

She brushed the snow off the side window of Bruce's car and tapped on the glass. He started, then turned to her with a smile.

"How long were you out there?" she asked once they were inside her toasty warm cottage.

"Not that long."

Since about six-thirty by the amount of snow on his car—and judging by Lucky's suddenly explained actions.

"I woke up early," Bruce said. "When I realized it was snowing, I thought I'd better get over here before the roads got too slick." He thumbed toward the front door. "That car's not exactly designed for snow."

Meghann made them both some hot cocoa.

"I have something for you," Bruce said as she sat at the table with him. He laid an oversized, aged leather-bound book on the table between them. The old volume actually creaked when he opened it. "Look there. The third line down."

Her eyes lit on the names Bennet and Cora Jones. "Where did you get this?"

"There's a storeroom in the basement with all the old registry books and an assortment of other memorabilia that I imagine you would love to get your hands on."

"Could I? I would only go down there after work. I promise." Her mind raced with the first possible opportunity to go treasure hunting.

"I was thinking, after your mother leaves, how would you like to be the new hotel historian?"

Her eyes widened with excitement. "Really?"

"Would you like that?"

"Yes. A hundred times yes!"

Meghann dragged herself away from the small piece of history and made them an interesting breakfast: oatmeal without milk but with plenty of brown sugar, fried hash browns from frozen patties, and grape Kool-Aid. She had precious few ingredients left after cleaning out the refrigerator last night. It amazed her what could grow in a cold environment.

"You mind if I use your phone?"

"Go ahead," she said, clearing away the breakfast dishes.

"Your phone's dead."

"No, I just unplugged it last night." She set the dishes

down on the counter and reached over to reattach the plug.

"How many times did they call?" He said with one hand resting on the phone.

"Five before I pulled the plug. And they left three messages before that."

"Good girl." His words were almost a chuckle.

After Bruce finished with his calls, he rubbed his hands together. "Now what would you like to do today?"

"Do? Aren't we returning to your apartment?"

"Not right away. We can spend the day playing tourist if you like."

She was torn between wanting to spend more time with just Bruce and with her needy canine friend. "If we aren't going back to our families, I really should spend some of the day with Lucky. I fear she is woefully neglected."

"I think a walk in the mountains would do us all some good." He got up and headed for the door. "I have a couple of quick things to do, and I'll be back for you in an hour."

True to his word, an hour later, he returned in a rented 4-by-4 and hiking boots. They headed up into the mountains and parked at the side of a dirt road. Bruce seemed to know right where to go.

"Would you like to eat or walk first?" Bruce opened her door.

Lunch! She hadn't even thought about food until her stomach started growling on the way up. "You brought food?"

He pulled a basket out from the back end of the vehicle along with a tarp and a blanket. They found a sunny spot on the top of a nearby hill. Lucky raced up and down waiting for them to catch up to her while biting at the snow.

"What's the tarp for?" Meghann asked as they reached the top. "Are you planning on making a tent?"

He gave her a sideways glance but didn't dignify her smart-aleck question with an answer. He just handed her the picnic basket, then spread the tarp out over the thin layer of snow and laid the blanket on top of it.

With a graceful bow, he offered her a place on the blanket. "Milady, for your dining pleasure."

After they enjoyed the feast, Meghann wandered around the top of the small hill. The view looking down on the city was fantastic, and the view looking up at the mountains so close took her breath away.

She turned back to Bruce to find him gazing at her. Talk about breathtaking.... She returned his smile, even as emotions filled her to overflowing.

I love you, Bruce Halloway. Can you tell? Can you sense it?

He stood and walked to her. Her heartbeat quickened.

"Are you ready to pack it in and go for that walk?" he asked. "I know a great path up here."

She took a calming breath and nodded.

Lucky ran five times farther going back and forth than they ever walked. The path led them higher to a more spectacular view. Meghann felt energized in this setting and picked up a handful of snow. Bruce didn't notice until she was about to throw it at him.

He smiled and held up a hand. "Don't you dare."

Dare? Oh, now he'd done it! She never had been able to resist a dare. With a grin, she hurled the loosely packed snowball at him, hitting him in the shoulder. The spray splattered his face.

"I'll get you," he growled, and excitement thrilled through her.

I hope so...oh, I hope so!

Meghann squealed and took off down the path. A snowball whizzed within inches of her arm. She didn't expect the next one to miss and stopped, scooping up snow as she did. She turned, arm poised for the attack, but suddenly found her feet slipping on some loose rocks beneath the snow. Bruce's next snowball hit her square on the front of her coat as she went down.

Hard.

She lay there, staring up at the now clear sky, trying not to laugh because it hurt too much.

"Are you all right?" Bruce skidded to a stop next to her. "I'm sorry, Meg. I didn't mean to hurt you."

She waved her hand at him. "You didn't hurt me. I twisted my ankle on a rock." She eased herself up on one elbow, lifting her injured leg slightly, testing the motion of her ankle. At the sharp pain, she grimaced. Great, just great. She forced a smile to her face. "I'm fine. Really."

Bruce knelt beside her in one fluid motion, then took hold of her foot and proceeded to remove her shoe.

"What are you doing?"

"I'm checking your injury." He sounded so serious.

"I'm not injured."

"Does this hurt?" He rotated her foot gently.

Hurt? Did it hurt? She couldn't tell. The feel of his tender fingers on her skin had her head spinning. *Say something, Meghann, you dolt! Anything to keep him from looking at you and seeing that stupid grin on your face!*

"I—uh, I didn't know you were a doctor as well as a hotel manager."

He admonished her with a simple look. "You didn't answer my question."

Humor him. Maybe then he'd let go of her and she could catch her breath again. "No, it doesn't hurt, Dr. Halloway."

He ignored her teasing. "It's not broken, and I don't think you sprained it, either."

"How do you know about breaks and sprains?"

"I had my share of mishaps growing up and I saw a lot of injuries while playing sports in school."

"Brock said you played football." Why didn't the man ever talk about himself? Didn't men like to boast about themselves?

Bruce eased her shoe back on. "What else did he say about me?"

Though he tried to sound offhand, Meghann could tell by the sound of his voice, the way he'd gone slightly stiff, that it bothered him for her to mentioned his brother. What was it with these two?

"He said you were captain of the football team, class president, and valedictorian. An all-American boy. And that he bowed down and worshiped you."

Bruce furrowed his brow at her last comment.

"See if you can walk on it," he said, helping her to her feet.

She walked in a circle to show him she was fine.

"Does it hurt when you put your full weight on it?"

"I'm fine really."

"I just want to make sure." He brushed back a stray hair that danced across her cheek. "I could never forgive myself if I hurt you."

Held in place by his gaze, she stood silent. Her pulse raced as he leaned closer to her. She'd heard of higher altitudes making people dizzy, but this was ridiculous!

Relax. He's not going to kiss you. Why would he with no one around?

She couldn't answer that, but his nearness and longing look in his deep brown eyes told her so. She prepared to be wrapped in those big strong arms—

Lucky chose that moment to start barking like a maniac. The shattered spell drifted off on the breeze as Bruce turned to the dog, startled. Meghann took a slow, deep breath and waited for her heart to quiet. They both turned their attention to the dog. She had chased a squirrel up a tree and had a mind she could go up after it.

After a few minutes, they managed to get the Lab to give up on tree climbing and headed down the path.

"I'm still going to help you back down," Bruce said and put a supportive arm around her waist. "It could be weak and be injured more easily next time."

She didn't argue, and they walked arm in arm back to the 4-by-4.

When they finally returned to Bruce's apartment, it was empty.

"It looks like they didn't miss us much." Bruce picked up a slip of paper from the hall table.

"I hope everything is okay," Meghann said. "You don't think my mom had a relapse or something?"

"According to this note, they are all running assorted errands." He handed her the piece of paper.

She took the picnic basket in the kitchen to put the leftover food away.

He was once again alone with her. Should he try to kiss her again? There was no dog around to interrupt this time.

She held the empty basket out to him. "What do you want me to do with this?"

"I'll return it to the hotel." He put it on the counter so it no longer separated them.

He put his hands on her shoulders and stepped closer. Was that fear or anticipation on her face? He hoped with all his heart that it was the latter.

Please, let her care…let her feel what I do…

Just before their lips touched, the front door opened and voices filled the stillness. Meghann glanced away from him, suddenly nervous. He dropped his hands to his sides. He just couldn't get a break with her. Was the whole world against him?

Twenty-Two

THE NEXT DAY, MEGHANN STARED DUMBFOUNDED AT THE document thrust before her.

"Sign here." Ivan Halloway pointed to a line with his executive pen, then handed the instrument to her.

She stared at the contract before her, searching anxiously for the meaning behind the legal jargon. "What is this?" She looked up into the elder Halloway's stony face but could tell he had no intention of answering her...at least not until after she signed.

She looked to Brock, who sat at the far end of the table, hoping for an ally. He gave a noncommittal shrug. Some help he was.

Turning her attention back to the papers before her, she wished Bruce were here. His father was intimidating—purposefully so, unless she missed her guess—and seemed determined not to let her up until she signed.

If only Bruce hadn't gone on some errand with his mother and hers. She'd thought it odd that they'd asked him to go along. Now she wondered if they hadn't conveniently taken him away, out of her reach.

Brock finally spoke up. "It's sort of a post-prenuptial agreement."

Mr. Halloway shot his son a warning look. "Just sign it, then we can go over it if you like." She could tell even that was a compromise for the man.

She flipped back to the first page, determined not to sign something she hadn't read. She knew the basic idea of a prenuptial. But why would Bruce need one? They weren't married. Even if they were, in reality, considering that kind of a step, she certainly didn't need this kind of agreement. The only thing of real value that she owned—or cared about—was Lucky.

The legal jargon was thick, but she thought she got the gist of it. It seemed Bruce had some properties and investments that could one day yield a good sum of money. The least of which...

She stared at the words. Read them again. Looked up at Brock and his father, then read them a third time.

It couldn't be. But according to this painfully official document it was: The least of the properties Bruce owned was the hotel.

Bruce is the owner of the Palace Hotel?

There must be some mistake. He said he had the owner's ear, but she didn't realize he had them *both!* Literally. Sitting on the sides of his too-attractive head. She read on and nearly choked on the settlement amount being proposed for her in the event that their marriage, which didn't exist in the first place, should dissolve.

One... Her mouth formed the words silently; her

mind struggled to take it in. *One million dollars!*

She looked up and gaped open mouthed at Mr. Halloway. Apparently her reaction caught him off guard, for he momentarily looked ill at ease. He cleared his throat. "That is a very generous sum...for someone of your standing."

Someone of her... What was *that* supposed to mean? More than anything she wanted to stand up, to walk away—but not before she told this overbearing man what he could do with his prenup. But he looked even more determined than when he'd first led her to the table and plunked the papers before her.

She looked down at the figure again. If this was the settlement amount...She closed her eyes briefly. If they were giving her a million dollars, then Bruce would have to be worth several million.

"I don't understand. He's an assistant manager. How can he own the hotel?" Meghann's voice sounded thin and confused, even to her own ears.

Bruce's father harrumphed at that. "That's a mystery to me. Why he would want to work at all when he doesn't have to has always been beyond my grasp."

"He likes seeing how things run, getting down with the little people," Brock offered.

Little people? Like her?

"Ridiculous. You find trustworthy people, put them in charge, and let them make the money for you," Ivan said. "Any good businessman knows that."

"He didn't buy the hotel to make money."

Meg couldn't tell if Brock was impressed or disgusted with that fact. What she could see was that the gap between her and Bruce was widening. Fast.

Bad enough they had one lie to deal with. But now...

She shook her head. No wonder he could afford this grand apartment and his nice cars. He was rich. No, not just rich. The way his brother and father spoke, he was filthy rich.

What an idiot she'd been, thinking he could be what he said he was and still, somehow, afford all that he owned. What a fool she'd been to buy into his illusion. No wonder he'd taken to his role as her supposed husband so well. He was experienced at playing a part.

An acute sense of loss assaulted her, making her head ache, her chest feel tight.

Ivan turned back to the last page, indicating she should sign, clearly determined to get what he wanted. Her name, on the dotted line.

Setting down the pen, she shook her head. She couldn't sign this. She and Bruce weren't really married. Tears stung her eyes. Nor, despite all she'd been hoping and dreaming, would they ever be. The thought tore at her insides.

"You want more money?" Ivan Halloway's voice was filled with accusation. And loathing. "Fine. I'll double it." His comment held a note of impatience, and Meg looked up at the man who was so sure she was a money-grabber. But why? None of this made any sense.

Brock must have read the confusion on her face, for he leaned toward her slightly. "Our father is only trying to protect Bruce's assets. It's a sensible thing to do when your eldest son is worth twenty-seven million dollars."

"You *fool!*" Ivan pounded his fist on the table. "You

just cost Bruce several million dollars." He turned to Meghann. "Five million, not a penny more. It would not be wise to press your luck and cross me."

Meghann heard his menacing tone, but didn't react. *Twenty…seven…million…dollars!* Her head reeled at the figure. "You…you can't be serious."

Ivan's face hardened even further as he stared down at her. "I'm always serious about money. Five million, it's my final offer. And you'd be wise to take it."

Her mouth went dry under Ivan's piercing glare. Wise? No, what would have been wise was never getting mixed up with Bruce in the first place.

If only she'd known that before it was too late. But here she was, staring down an angry bully…

And desperately in love with a man she had just discovered she couldn't trust.

At the sound of a key in the door, Meg turned.

Bruce came through the front door, packages in hand, holding the door open with his foot for their mothers.

Liar! The word flew through Meg's mind, and she clenched her teeth against it.

As though he'd sensed her attention, though, Bruce looked toward the dining room. Taking in his father and brother standing there, over Meg, he strode directly over to her.

"What's going on?"

Meg didn't answer him. Let his family explain this little meeting.

Brock shifted uncomfortably, but Ivan stood proud and tall, unwavering. She suspected he was as nervous inside as Brock; he just had more years to perfect his apathy.

Bruce dumped the packages on the table, noticing the document in front of Meg as he did so. "What is this?" He snatched the document, scanning the pages. His features darkened.

All Meghann could do was stare up at the man she had come to love. *Tell me it isn't true. Tell me this is all some crazy mistake....*

But even she could see it now in the way he stood, the confidence and bearing...he looked very much the wealthy aristocrat. The last of her hope dwindled with the revelation.

You can't have him. He's out of your league. He's wealthy and out of reach. This is only a game to him. Hold on to your heart, Meg, hold on tight. Even as she counseled herself, she knew her heart was gone. It belonged to him.

"It's for your own good, son. I'm sure you didn't think of this. I'm only looking out for your best interests. You can't be too careful."

He thrust the agreement at his father and turned to Meghann.

She stood slowly, halting whatever he'd intended to say. Holding his gaze, she drew a deep breath. "You *own* the Palace Hotel. *You* are the anonymous owner?"

She was demanding an answer she already knew. But she wanted—no, *needed* him to admit it.

A long, brittle silence stretched out between them.

She felt as if a hand were closing around her throat.

"Yes."

With that single, reluctant word, her dreams were crushed. Shattered. Left in a pile on the table between them. Meghann turned and walked from the dining room, to the front door. She pulled it open and walked out, closing the door behind her.

Smothering a sob, she ran. To the elevator, then out, onto the street. She fled from him as if her life depended on it. And it did...or at least her heart did. Though she could hear Bruce calling out to her, she kept going. She couldn't face him in the wake of all she had just learned. All she had lost.

God...oh, Father, how can this be happening?

Only silence answered her anguished prayer.

I wanted to tell him how I feel, that I love him. How could things have gone so terribly, totally wrong?

Still no answer. No sense of peace, no calm settling over her. Only a silence as bleak as the reality of all she'd just lost.

Rubbing her hand over her eyes, she supposed she should be thankful she hadn't told Bruce how she felt. At least she'd avoided *that* humiliation. She could just see his reaction as he laughed at her, telling her she was a romantic little fool, that she'd confused reality with the fantasy they created. Her fantasy. After all, it was only a game.

"Quite a hoot pulling this off, don't you think?" he would say before going back to his life and his money and forgetting about her. Except for those rare moments at parties when he pulled out the story. *"Oh, listen, you think that's good? Wait till you hear about a woman I knew once..."*

Thank heaven she'd never told him. As painful as it had been to keep her feelings to herself, it was nothing compared to having them flung back at her.

The only saving grace in all of this was that he couldn't take her memories away. No one could. She would always have them to look back on and smile.

Small consolation for a decimated dream. But what did she expect from something that started because of a lie? She should count herself fortunate she'd escaped with as little emotional injury as she had.

Another lie, Meg? You're destroyed, and you know it.

Maybe so, but she'd never admit it. Not to herself. And certainly, never, ever to Bruce.

Meghann sunk into the passenger seat of Jennifer's yellow Hyundai. It was a safe haven in the midst of an emotional storm. She knew her best friend had a million questions for her—*no, twenty-seven million,* that small voice inside her mocked—but thankfully Jenn was silent. For the time being.

Jennifer pulled into the flow of traffic. "This is a switch. I'm usually the one bumming a ride from you." Seemingly uncomfortable with the silence she went on. "I'm not sure whether I have more miles on the road or on the rack."

Meghann had bought her used Honda at the same time Jenn bought her new car. Unfortunately, Jenn's car had not been nearly as reliable. She'd said her choice of colors was prophetic: lemon yellow.

"Is everything okay, Meg? Nothing has happened to your mother, has it?" Jenn asked the question, keeping one eye on Meg as she checked traffic and changed lanes.

"Mom's fine. But as for everything being okay?" She dropped her head back against the headrest. "No. My life is a mess."

"Aren't things going well with Bruce?" Her friend's voice was filled with compassion, and Meg nearly lost it right then and there. She focused on the street signs as Jenn pulled into the left-hand turn lane and stopped, waiting for the light to turn green. "Your mom didn't find out the truth, did she?"

"No, I found out the truth."

Jenn blinked at her. "What? Don't you already know the truth?"

"Evidently not."

Jennifer pulled into a strip mall parking lot. "I need to drop off a package, then you can tell me all about it."

Jennifer left and returned all too quickly. "Okay, spill the beans."

"I know you need to get back to work."

"You can tell me on the way to wherever it is I'm taking you."

"My place, please."

She pulled out and headed down the road. "Start talking. We haven't got all day. My bosses are nice, but there is a limit to how far I can push their patience."

Meghann told her about the flowers Bruce had brought her, about the cross necklace and the continued patience and kindness he showed her.

Jenn frowned, clearly confused. "It sounds to me like he could very well have feelings for you."

"That's what I thought, or should I say *hoped*, until today." She took a deep breath. What would Bruce want from her when all was said and done? She didn't know. And right now, she didn't care. "Bruce Halloway isn't just the assistant manager of the Palace Hotel; he owns it."

Jenn stared at her. "Owns it? The whole thing?"

"That and twenty-seven million other things." She met her friend's stunned gaze. "Green things. With numbers and George Washingtons on them."

"Are you telling me your boss is a millionaire?"

"Several times over. Here I was thinking he was this wonderful man who'd jumped in to help me out…" She shook her head. "When all the time he's just some aristocrat playing a game, seeing if he can get away with it."

"Poor little rich boy?"

"Something like that." She hung her head. Her misery was so acute that it was physically painful. "I'm such a fool." Her mind was languid, without hope. "When I try to pray, I get nowhere, like I'm saying nothing at all. I feel like I'm in front of a locked door; no matter how hard I bang, it won't open."

Jennifer pulled her car into Meghann's gravel driveway and stopped. "Are you sure you want me to leave you here alone?"

"I'm not alone. Lucky is already at the gate. I've got a key under the porch lip."

"I'll pray for you." Jenn squeezed Meghann's hand.

Meghann stared at her friend, surprised.

Jenn shrugged. "Let's just say I'm starting to understand there's more to this God thing than I realized. And I need to get more serious about it all." She smiled. "Besides, you're my friend, and I figure the best one to work all this out is God. Right?"

Meg choked back a laugh. "Right." But even as she said it, she doubted He would do so. Why would He? She'd gotten herself into this mess by going against Him. Why would He step in and make it all work out now that things were truly a disaster?

She squeezed Jenn's hand before getting out. "Thanks, Jenn. I need a lot of prayer now." And that was as true as it got.

An hour later, Bruce pulled his car up in front of Meghann's house.

She was there, sitting on the front porch steps.

The misery on her face cut him deep, and he wished again he'd never left that afternoon, never given his father the opportunity to pull that idiotic stunt.

Never given him the chance to let the truth come out?

Yeah. That too.

With a heavy sigh, he stepped from the car and went to cautiously sit beside Meghann on the steps. She didn't look up at him.

"Wouldn't you be more comfortable inside?" he asked after a moment of silence, pointing at the yellow door with one key, unsure of how she would respond to him after what she'd found out about him.

"I don't have my keys." Her tone was even, unemotional.

"And I have your spare." He handed her his key ring with her key on it.

She held up her hand to stop him. "I'm fine. I'll stay out here." Now her words were curt.

He fiddled with the ring of keys, outlining hers with his thumb. "Are you mad at me?" He closed his eyes. *Dumb, Halloway. Dumb, dumb, question.* "Let me rephrase that. How mad are you?"

"I'm not mad. Not anymore. But you make more sense now."

She was talking to him, which was a good sign. "How so?"

"Your car." She pointed to the red 'Vette in the driveway. "Correction, *cars*. Your apartment, or should I say penthouse. The way you talk about Mr. Phenton, like he's not your boss." She snapped her fingers. "That's right, he's not. You're his boss. Your clothes, your manner, Charmaine Altman…"

With each item, shadows of his past reared their vile heads to taunt him. He wanted to avoid it all—especially the subject of Charmaine—all together. "I blew it, huh? I guess I'm not so good at pretending, after all."

"Oh, I'd say you're very good at it. You had me fooled. On all fronts. You did a great job of playing the sincere worker, and of acting the devoted husband."

"I'm not so sure about that."

"I just don't understand why you weren't honest with me."

He took a deep breath. "Because of Charmaine

Altman—" he held up his hand at her sharp look—"and people like her. All my life people have treated me like a king when it suited their purposes because of my money. Fair-weather friends and all that. People aren't themselves. It doesn't take long before you question everyone's motive, every action and word. I let myself grow skeptical, and I sure didn't think I could trust anyone. I just wanted to be a normal guy struggling to make a living. I didn't want special treatment for once in my life. The hotel was my inspiration."

Father, how do I help her understand?

Tell the truth, son.

He sighed. *Of course.* There had been too many lies for too long. *Help me do this right.*

"Meg, I never meant to mislead you. Or anyone. I just didn't see any reason to announce to everyone that I was the owner of the hotel, or that I was a multimillionaire. Both of my parents came from money. And for some reason, my grandfather decided to leave the bulk of his estate to me. At the time, I was thrilled. I took that money and made more money."

She nodded in understanding. But could she truly understand? He had hurt her with his deception. He wanted to correct that, but how? Once trust was broken it was not easily mended.

"I should have been straight with everyone. Especially with you. But I was afraid…and it was easier to pretend I was just like everyone else. Just a guy working at a job he liked, doing his best to make a living. So I took the easy way out. It wasn't right, but I did it."

She met his gaze. He knew she understood that

part of it, at least. Wasn't that very fact what had gotten them into the mess they were in?

"Was I just stupid not to notice you were rich?" She gave a self-deprecating laugh. "And I worried you could be into something illegal."

She'd worried about him? That was good, wasn't it? "No, you are not stupid. You were distracted by your mom's illness."

"That's not all I was distracted by," she muttered.

"What was that?"

She huffed out a breath. "Nothing."

"Did you really think I was doing something illegal?"

"Well, not really. It didn't seem to fit you, but I didn't know how else you could afford all that stuff."

They sat in awkward silence for a few minutes, then Bruce turned to her. "Do you want to go back now?"

"No."

At the soft word, his hopes plummeted. She wasn't coming back? She was leaving? But how would he work all of this out if she didn't—

"But I will."

Relief swept him and he met her gaze.

"I don't want to go back there. I'm tired of the charade, tired of the lies. But you were right when you said we couldn't back out now. As much as I don't want to do this, I realize I can't just leave you in the lurch with your family. It's my fault we're in this—"

He started to protest, and she held her hand up.

"So the least I can do is play it out as long as your parents are here."

She stood and headed solemnly to his car. It was as though the whole thing had ripped the life, the spirit, out of her. He wanted to wrap her in his arms and make her smile again.

But at least she was coming back with him. That meant he had time. Time to be with her, time to talk with her, time to let her see he could be trusted. His task was enormous, but he would give it all he had. He would win her over before his family left.

He may have three strikes against him, but he wasn't out yet.

Twenty-Three

THE FOLLOWING EVENING, BROCK STEPPED OUT ONTO THE balcony where Meghann gazed out at the city lights. She'd come out to soak in the sights, determined to enjoy this panoramic picture—the majestic mountains to the west and the city lights glimmering to the north and east while the opportunity lasted.

Heaven knew she wouldn't see it again when this was over.

After a quick scan of the horizon, Brock turned and leaned his back against the rail. "Pretty impressive." Though he spoke of the view, he stood studying her.

"I'm going to go in now," Meghann said, uncomfortable with him staring at her.

"Don't run off on my account." He covered her hand with his. She tried to pull away, but he held fast to her and wouldn't let go, even when she tried to jerk free of him.

"Meghann, you are one beautiful woman," he said in a low, husky voice as his thumb caressed the back of her hand.

She looked up at him startled and yanked her hand from his grasp. What was wrong with him?

"Excuse me," she said, her voice cold. But before she could walk away, he caught her, pulling her back, trapping her against the rail with one hand on each side of her, caging her in.

"So, it's not me, eh?" His expression changed from endearing to a critical scrutiny. "Is it another man, perhaps?"

"What?" She kept her hands braced against his chest, providing some kind of barrier...though he wasn't pushing forward.

"I know it's not my brother's money, because you didn't even know he had any, did you?"

She shook her head. "Of course not!" What was he talking about?

"Or are you that good of an actress?"

The man was insane. "I don't know what you're talking about. Let me go."

"Something is not right here." Brock's words were cold, exacting. "I've seen it in Bruce's eyes."

"Well, bully for you. Why don't you go ask him, then?"

But for all of her bravado, Meg's heart sank. First her mother had seen things were not right, and now Bruce's brother was picking up on it. Trapped in her own lie, she felt defeated.

"It's there in his eyes, distrust. I thought maybe it was me, but you don't seem to be attracted to me. Or are you just playing at some kind of game?"

What had gotten into him? He was being ridiculous. "Let me go!" She pushed on his arm to escape, to no avail.

He held tightly to the rail. "Not until you tell me why Bruce doesn't trust you. I won't let you hurt my brother and get away with it." Meg stared at him, her mouth dropping open. So Brock really did care about his older brother. Oh, if only she could tell him the truth...tell him she loved Bruce with all her heart, that she'd never hurt him, that she was dying inside because she knew she'd never be with him.

But she held her silence. She'd promised Bruce not to say anything, and she wouldn't go back on that. All she could do was stare up at him, grasping for something to say to him to make him release her.

His gaze bore into hers. "What have you done to lose my brother's trust?"

"You don't have to answer that." Bruce's dark voice made them both jump.

Meghann looked from Bruce, who stood in the doorway, to Brock. The younger brother dropped his hands, then stepped aside. Bruce glared at the back of Brock's head.

Brother against brother. And she was the cause.

"I lied." The whispered admission came out before she could stop it.

Brock's expression changed from condemning to a surprised questioning. Before she gave herself away any further, she moved away from him, heading for the French doors and her escape. Bruce stopped her with a light touch on her arm. She waited, and he lifted her face until her eyes met his. "I do trust you."

How? After lies on top of lies, each one eating away at her soul. She could no longer stand herself. No longer trust herself, her integrity. How could Bruce possibly trust her after all the pain she'd caused him?

She searched his eyes for the truth, but it was useless. Sometimes she wondered if she would even know the truth anymore.

She went inside without a word. How could she say anything? How could he believe a word she said after all her deceit?

"How can you say that?"

Bruce turned to face his brother, pondering his frustrated question.

"Your wife just admitted lying. How can you trust her?"

"I understand why she did what she did." His patience was wearing thin with his brother. He saw the way Brock had Meg trapped against the rail.

"You're defending her, condoning her actions?"

He drew in a calming breath. "I'm neither condoning nor defending, only understanding."

"But trusting her? That is unwise, brother."

His use of the term *brother* rankled Bruce. "I'm not going to discuss Meghann with you," he snapped and turned to leave but stopped when Brock threw another curt statement at him.

"How does lying fit in with your religion? Your so-called faith?"

Bruce clenched his fists. Leave it to Brock to cut to

the heart of the matter. It didn't. It never had, and he should have known that. Should have known lying wasn't the way to help Meg, no matter how right it felt at the moment.

Lord, I've been a fool.

Tell the truth, son. Help Meg do the same.

Fear pierced him. *I'll lose her.* She would leave before he had the time to make things right between them.

Tell the truth.

We've got so much at stake. Her mother…my family…their trust in You.

That can't be based on a lie.

But could it be destroyed by one? That was the question he couldn't get past.

"I've seen distrust in your eyes." Brock said to his back.

Bruce flexed his fists. He wanted to continue on through the doors and leave his brother standing there alone. But his lack of trust was not directed toward Meghann, and he was loathe to go on letting Brock believe it was. Maybe it was time to let his younger brother know the source of his distrust.

Fine. If Brock wanted a confrontation, he would have one. It was long overdue. Bruce reached out to close the doors and swung around.

"You are the one I don't trust, Brock."

Amazement filled his brother's features. And confusion. "Me? What have I done?"

Bruce glared at his little brother. "Valerie." Bruce had dated a woman, Valerie Synclair, for a short time just after he had become a Christian two years ago. They had helped each other over some bumps in the transition from worldly to godly lifestyles.

"That was not my doing." Brock's tone was hard. "It was her."

"It takes two to tango, as they say. You were attracted to her. Don't deny it."

"Yes. I was attracted to her. But I never acted on that attraction. Not once. I can't help my feelings, Bruce. You can't condemn me for them!"

"She left me for you. She told me so."

"And she got nothing. I wouldn't have her. Couldn't trust her. If she dropped you so easily, why not me, too?"

Bruce stood there, watching his brother's face, weighing his words…and felt his anger begin to wane. Was it true? Had he been so hurt over Valerie's rejection that he'd laid the blame on Brock without reason? "I thought…I always assumed you two dated for a while and you just chose not to mention it."

Even as he spoke, Bruce began to understand. Losing Valerie had been hard. He'd really cared about her. But the worst part of it all had been thinking Brock had betrayed him.

Brock stepped toward him. "I know we fought, all kids do, but I always thought we were close. I knew there was a rift between us since Valerie, but I never imagined you thought I actually had something to do with the breakup. I wouldn't do that to you, Bruce. You're my brother."

Bruce shook his head. "I'm sorry. I guess I just convinced myself it was true. You were always tagging along and doing whatever I did while we were growing up. When you were ten, you refused to answer to your own name. You drove everyone crazy, insisting they call you Bruce. It was like you were trying to be me." He sighed at the memory. "I guess I figured what better way was there for you to do that than to take the woman I cared about?"

Brock looked away self-consciously. "Most of my life I wanted to be like you. I even wanted to *be* you. I figured if I stuck close to you and did everything you did, some of you might rub off on me, and I would be good enough…"

"Good enough for whom?"

Brock looked at him as though to say, *"Who else."* But he didn't know…and his patience was wearing dangerously thin.

"I'm not the firstborn son, made in his image, who can do no wrong," Brock said. "All the praise went to you. If he was in a generous mood, the rest of us would get an encouraging word to do better like Bruce."

Their father? He was talking about their father. True, Ivan Halloway was a hard man who worked hard to get where he was. It hadn't been easy for Bruce being the oldest. Always expected to do things right. Always expected to meet his father's standards. He hadn't realized it was just as hard for his siblings. He thought they had it easy because nothing was expected of them. He had often been envious of their ability to get away with everything. They could do what they wanted without having to account for themselves. He had been under constant scrutiny while their father had basically neglected the others.

"You don't have to keep striving to please him, Brock."

"You could do no wrong in his eyes. Even if you did something he disapproved of, like becoming a Christian, it was okay because you were Bruce."

Was that why Brock worked in their father's company and stuck so close to him, to gain his approval? "Is that what is keeping you from making a decision for the Lord? Father's approval? Don't risk your eternity on his acceptance. He may never change."

Brock turned from him. "I would be ostracized. *You* can do no wrong, and Brice is still a 'foolish' kid who will grow out of it! I wouldn't be so lucky."

"Our father is not an easy man to live with or without." Bruce said sympathetically.

"I don't want to talk about this anymore." Like Mother, he preferred peace to strife.

"Okay, but just let me say one more thing for you to think about. Is temporary acceptance here on earth worth risking eternity in heaven?"

His question was met with silence.

"Don't wait too long, brother. You never know when tomorrow will be too late." When Brock remained silent, Bruce turned to leave.

"Bruce?"

He turned. "Yes?"

"Can I ask you a question? About your wife?"

There was caution in his voice, and disappointment in Bruce's heart. This wasn't the question he'd been hoping for. "You can ask, but I reserve the right not to answer."

"Fair enough," Brock said with a nod. "She said she lied to you. Is that something you can live with?"

"She didn't say she lied to me, just that she lied."

"And you can live with that? Doesn't it bother you?"

It bothered him a lot. Almost as much as his own lies bothered him.

"Yes, it bothers me, but I also understand." He chose his words carefully. "None of us are perfect. We *all* make mistakes. We have to forgive one another and help each other to become stronger. Love covers a multitude of sins."

"You can forgive her, just like that?"

"I have to, or how can I expect my heavenly Father to forgive me? Why do I have the feeling this isn't about Meg?"

Brock shrugged his shoulders in silence.

"A woman?"

Brock didn't answer, but Bruce didn't need affirmation to know he was right. And he was sure he knew which one. "It's Valerie, isn't it?"

Brock cringed slightly at Bruce's guess. "I've been thinking about her lately. I don't know why."

"Have you talked to her?"

"No!"

"It's okay, Brock. She's a nice girl." He had held on to this for so long, he was surprised and relieved at how easy it was to finally let go. And forgive his brother. "Maybe you should talk to her and see where it leads."

"But she was your girlfriend," Brock argued.

"The operative word being *was*." He held up his hand with his ring. "I'm a married man now." At least he *felt* married. And he intended to make that feeling reality as soon as he could. "I'm certain Valerie and I would have broken up eventually. Our bond was because we were both new Christians in a new church. I have no interest in her, except for where she concerns you."

"How do I know if I can trust her?" Brock asked.

"You'll never know if you don't talk to her. I don't believe she meant to hurt either one of us. Sometimes you just have to let go and hope you haven't misplaced your trust." That sounded like advice *he* should take. It was time for him to let go...of a lot of things.

"I really do want the best for you. Tell me, Bruce, is my appeal to women so strong that you worry about Meghann, or is your hold on your wife so weak that makes me a threat?"

Both. "I'm only holding on to her by a thread." Bruce was astonished he was willing to confide in his brother at all. "If it weren't for her mother visiting, we wouldn't be together at all."

"It's that bad?" Brock's eyebrows rose. "You can't tell. You two look like lovebirds."

"It's all an illusion. I don't know what is going to happen when everyone leaves. I don't want to lose her."

"Have you told her that? Women like to hear that kind of thing."

No, he hadn't told her. Things had been different since the day she'd found out the truth about him. She had become aloof. Most people were attracted to his bank account. She seemed to be repelled by it. But then she was not most people, which was probably why he loved her.

All he had to do was figure out how to let her know that. And how to make her believe it.

The next morning while Meghann was in the kitchen cleaning up after breakfast, Brock came in. She nervously wiped the clean counter to keep busy, wondering what he wanted and hoped he got it fast and left.

"I was hoping we would have a chance to talk." Brock walked over to her.

Talk? No, she didn't think that was such a good idea after last night. "I need to…" She put down the dishcloth and turned to leave.

"Please. It will only take a minute. I want to apologize." He sounded sincere, but she kept her distance.

She slowly sank back against the counter. Her palms suddenly felt sweaty, and she bit her bottom lip.

"I'm sorry for my behavior last night. I acted inappropriately. Bruce explained things to me."

Her eyes widened in astonishment. "Everything?"

"Enough that I think I understand."

That meant Bruce most likely didn't tell him the truth, the whole truth and nothing but the truth. But what had he told him?

"Will you forgive my rude behavior and tactlessness?"

"Yes, of course."

"Thank you." A sad expression crossed his face. "But I'm afraid I may have irreparably damaged what could have been a pleasant family relationship between you and me. You've probably noticed our family doesn't have many of them. And if you haven't noticed, you soon will. I won't bother you any further, milady." He gave a courtly bow and turned to leave.

"Brock." She felt this whole misunderstanding was her fault and wanted to make amends. He was sort of charming in his own way. He faced her and she held out her hand. "Truce?"

He raised an eyebrow and hesitantly took her hand to shake. "Truce."

"We sort of got off on the wrong foot anyway. Let's start over. Forgiven and forgotten. I'm Meghann."

His smile broadened. "I'm Brock, the good-looking one in the family."

And the one with enough charm to sweep a willing woman off her feet.

Twenty-Four

"I DON'T KNOW HOW BRUCE COULD BE TAKEN IN BY THIS superstitious nonsense," Ivan Halloway muttered as he flipped the Bible in front of Meghann closed.

Rude. The man was plain rude. Meghann cocked her head, looking sideways at Bruce's father. How had she ended up alone with him? No, not exactly alone; her mother was asleep in the other room.

Bruce said his father never allowed anyone to bring up the subject of religion. So Meg had been surprised when the elder Halloway pigeonholed her, clearly trying to provoke her into a discussion on it. What on earth was Ivan doing? Was he looking for a fight?

Fine. She was tired of being intimidated by him.

Lord, give me the right words. Don't let me back down....

"It's not superstition or nonsense." She made sure her voice was even, calm. "The Bible is—"

"I will not have my son brainwashed by irrational fears perpetuated by fools. He's above all that."

Who was the one with irrational fears here? Ivan

was a formidable man who used intimidation masterfully to get people to bend to his way of thinking. So far
it had worked with her. And even now, she struggled
with feeling foolish as she sat there with him staring her
down, demanding she defend her faith.

Lord, help me. Use me. Speak through me.

"Wouldn't you like to sit down?" She felt uncomfortable with him towering over her, but she sensed he
liked the power and control it gave him. She fidgeted
uneasily. What if she said the wrong thing; made her
faith look ineffective, stupid?

Be still child

She nodded. Ivan may be a formidable foe in business, but God was the true powerhouse here. The One
with ultimate control.

She looked up into Ivan's cynical face and her
timidity fell away. This poor man was searching for ful-
fillment. He would never find it on his earthly quest
until he looked up. He didn't realize he had just closed
the book on the greatest treasure of all that no amount
of money could buy.

"Bruce is not brainwashed. This—" she reverently
touched the cover of the Bible—"is real."

"Enough! I'll not hear any more of this foolishness."

Foolishness? She pushed herself away from the table
where she had been reading Bruce's Bible and stood.
Her opponent furrowed his brows slightly. He hadn't
expected her to come up to his level. She needn't cower
with God on her side. *If God is for me, who could stand
against me?*

"I'm sorry, but now that you've gotten me started I

have a thing or two to say. God is no threat to your relationship with Bruce. He'll make it better. God loves you as much as He does Bruce or me. You can't deny the changes in Bruce. God did that. God made the difference."

"I can't say it's for the better."

"Then you're not really looking. Bruce is so much happier now; he told me so."

Confidence surged through her as she spoke…but only for a moment. For right on the heels of her words came a bitter thought.

What right do you have to be saying these things? How can you speak for God when your whole connection to this man before you is a lie?

Meg swallowed with difficulty. It was true. At least, in the world's eyes. But didn't God promise His strength in her weaknesses? God was the One who opened the doors for sharing about Him, about His Son. How could she not tell Bruce's father what she knew? Regardless of her worth, Jesus was definitely worth it!

"Jesus gave His life for you."

"Humph," Ivan grunted as he folded his arms across his chest. He looked as if he were daring her to go on. Well, if he was willing to listen, she would speak as the Lord led.

Picking up the Bible, she opened it to John chapter 3 and read of God's tremendous love and sacrifice for mankind.

"God is pure love and pure good. He is perfect in all ways. He has no sin and can tolerate no sin in His presence. We are sinful creatures. We could never be good enough to get to heaven on our own. So, in His abundant mercy, He provided the way to Himself. The only way to do that was to sacrifice His only Son. God can do for you what he did for Bruce."

Ivan stood unmoved, staring down at her, skepticism painting his features. But he didn't excuse himself and walk away. He stayed, waiting. She couldn't tell if he was waiting for more or for her to give up. She hoped this was more than just a power struggle with him, that his heart wasn't so hardened and closed that he really heard none of what she said.

It was like having a staring contest to see who would blink first. Was he testing to see if she would waver or if he would still have power over Bruce?

Though she stumbled on a couple of points and had to backtrack, she felt she had been clear, that God had used her. Still, he stood stoically with his arms folded across his chest, unmoved by the God of the universe who knew the ever-changing number of hairs on his head. He looked more like he was merely tolerating her than listening. But as long as he was going to stand quietly, she would continue for what little good it would do. For the first time in months she felt used by God.

Father God, I have sinned. I see that clearly now. I should have trusted You from the start, regardless of what others said. But I'm in so deep now. How do I get out? Show me the way to truth, to reconciliation with You, with Mom, with Bruce...and even with Ivan. Don't let my sin cause him to stumble and perish.

Ivan could have left at any time but didn't. Maybe his heart wasn't too hard, after all. Maybe he was ready to start listening.

⸺∞⸺

Bruce and Brock returned to the apartment in a shroud of silence. They weren't trying to be sneaky; there just wasn't anything to be said between them at the moment.

As they came in the door, Bruce looked up quickly. He could hear Meghann's voice, and she sounded…impassioned about something. Excitement resounded in her tone.

Exchanging a look of surprise with his brother, Bruce moved closer—and his eyes widened when he realized she was presenting the plan of salvation! But to whom?

He and Brock moved silently to the end of the short entry hall to get a glimpse of whom she spoke to.

When Bruce saw it was their father Meg was talking to, he was stunned. Meghann, in her innocence, had accomplished in a few short days what Bruce hadn't been able to do in two years! His father, the great and proud Ivan Halloway, was actually allowing someone to talk to him about God.

Bruce's throat caught with emotion. He had prayed for this many times. In his own arrogance, he assumed he was the only one strong enough to stand up to his father and make him listen. How wrong he was.

At first, he thought he could do it the easy way and get to him through his mother. She would simply pat his hand and say, "Your father wouldn't like it if I got religion." Ivan was her god and she would have no other god before him.

He'd decided long ago that his father would probably have to step across the threshold of salvation first. Maybe, just maybe, Meghann was the one God would use.

Could that be why they'd come together? Could God have intended this from the very beginning?

"God causes everything to work together for the good of those who love God...."

Bruce nodded. God wasn't responsible for the lie he and Meg had perpetrated. They'd done that on their own. But God *was* using the situation to work his will...in their lives, and in others' lives as well.

Thank you, Lord!

In that short three-word prayer, the floodgates of his heart opened up and the light shone in. It was all so clear. He felt the overwhelming love he had there for a particular honey blond. He hadn't felt joy like this since he asked Jesus to come into his heart and be his Savior.

"Your wife is something else."

Bruce didn't like the husky emotion in his brother's compliment, but he had to agree. And even as he did so, a prick of fear threatened to edge out his joy. *"Your wife..."*

If only that were true! But Meg wasn't. And Bruce could still lose her. His heart tightened painfully at the thought. Swallowing hard, he knew he must not allow that to happen. He just couldn't!

His father's voice shattered his consuming thoughts and emotions. "Bruce, son, you're home."

Bruce looked up, painfully aware his father had cut Meghann off in midsentence. And completely ignored Brock.

He felt his brother stiffen beside him, and he clenched his jaw. How could his father be so blind? So careless?

Obviously the man's heart was so hardened, he no longer saw how much he hurt the people who loved him. Despair nudged at Bruce, and he shook his head, wondering if his father had heard—really heard—even one word of the message of hope Meg had just been sharing with him.

Probably not.

And that fact hurt Bruce more deeply than he'd thought possible.

Later that evening outside his apartment building, Bruce and Meghann turned right and headed down the street. Within moments Bruce clasped her hand in his. His touch sent all her senses tingling, and for one, brief moment, she allowed hope into her heart.

Maybe Bruce did care about her. Just a little. And if that were the case, it was a start.

"I don't know how to thank you." Bruce's voice rang with intensity.

"Thank me for what?" The cool night air felt good on her warm skin.

"For talking to my father about God."

"I don't think I was very effective."

"It doesn't matter. You spoke the truth, and he listened."

"That's debatable."

"You don't understand. He would never permit

anyone, even me, to bring up the subject of religion, let alone talk about God."

But she hadn't brought up the topic, his father had. Ivan had seemed almost determined to goad her into the discussion. She had thought maybe he was testing her to see how committed she was to her faith…but now she hoped maybe he was searching and didn't know how to be so vulnerable as to ask.

"Bruce, can I ask you a question?"

"Sure."

"If your father is so dead set against religion of any kind, how did you and your brother become Christians?"

"My younger brother, Brice, who's fifteen now, went to a summer church camp with a schoolmate when he was twelve. It changed him. Really changed him. He said he met God. You could say when he returned, he infected me. Father wouldn't even let him talk about God or his newfound faith. It was so sad the way our father would cut him off and belittle him. It made me feel bad for Brice. So I listened, not because I cared about what he had to say but because I felt sorry for him."

There was a hint of laughter in his tone, and he gave her a sideways smile. "God gets us when we least expect it, you know? It wasn't Brice's words that caught my attention, it was Brice himself…something from within. At the time I thought it was youthful enthusiasm. But soon I saw it was something more. And I wanted it, too. I know now it was an inner peace and a love for the Lord that gave my brother his zeal. My father may regret ever allowing Brice to go to that camp, but I, for one, know it was the best thing that could have ever happened to our family. And you may be the key to my father. I think you might have unlocked the door to his heart."

He was giving her far too much credit. "If I did anything, it was simply to nudge the door a little. I think you had already unlocked it."

He stopped and turned to face her. "Whatever your contribution, I thank you from the bottom of my heart."

He held both her hands, caressing the backs of them with his thumbs, sending her heart dancing to a wild beat at his endearing gaze.

"I'm in your debt."

He dipped his head to kiss her hands, and her heart plummeted.

Gratitude. This was only about gratitude. She took a deep breath and her heart sat out the next dance.

While Bruce took care of some hotel business, Brock accompanied Meghann to her cottage again to feed and play with Lucky. On the return trip, they stopped at Macy's for a pair of earrings Bruce's mother had seen. Bruce had paid for them the day before as a belated birthday gift for their mother and asked Brock to pick them up.

Since the altercation on the balcony and his apology, Brock seemed to be more friendly and polite, like he was on her side now. Before he seemed to be judging her every move. Now, he accepted her without question. He seemed to want her to know that she was welcome in their family, at least by him. What had Bruce said to him to make him so accepting of her all of a sudden?

He said he understood when Bruce "explained" things, but just what was it he understood?

"There. That ought to make mother happy." Brock held up a floral gift bag with plenty of pink tinsel to cushion the purchase.

Meg watched him, frowning. Something was bothering her…something about the way Bruce and Brock spoke of—and to—their mother.

Brock's smile was tight. "Pink is Mother's favorite color."

Understanding washed over Meg. That was it. Both Bruce and his brother had a stiff, formal manner where their mom was concerned. *Mother,* they called her, not *Mom.* As though it were more a title without affection than a loving endearment.

Sadness touched her over how far this family was from each other. "I don't think your mother would care what color you chose."

"Oh, she wouldn't say anything, but she would be disappointed. She covers it well, but it's there in her eyes if you know what to look for. Mother can be wounded easily."

He winked at her as he handed her the bag. "I'll let you carry this. After all, it *is* from you and Bruce."

His attention to his mother's feelings warmed her. For all of his formality, he did care what his mother thought. She gave him her most pleasant smile as she received the bag from him.

"I see you've found a new playmate," a condescending voice shattered Meghann's happy mood.

She turned and stared unwavering into the face of Charmaine Altman. Meg's stomach turned at the prospect of a confrontation with the woman—and there would be a confrontation; Charmaine would see to that.

"Well, he is awfully cute. I wonder what Brucey will say when he finds out you are spending your days with another man? And that he's buying you expensive gifts. I best get over to the hotel. I'm sure he'll need a shoulder to cry on." Her smile was disgustingly smug.

"*Brucey,*" Meghann said with a forced smile, "already knows. And he vastly approves."

"I doubt that. He's a very possessive man. I know." She lifted her chin. "It's only a matter of time, my dear. Only a matter of time." With that, Charmaine spun on her spiked heels and left.

Meghann made a face at the woman's retreating form, then glanced up at Brock to see if he noticed her little unladylike act. He hadn't. He was still watching the blond bombshell saunter away.

"Meee-ow," Brock finally said, turning to Meghann. "Who was that?"

"Charmaine Altman," Meghann said through gritted teeth. "Can we go to my house now?"

When they arrived back at her house, she slipped from the car. "You can go ahead and go," she said. "I'll just stay here for a while."

Brock slid into the driver's seat, but his expression was hesitant. "Are you sure you don't want me to wait for you? I could just sit in the car."

"No, thank you." Meghann leaned on the open driver's side window.

Brock touched her forearm gently. "Don't let her get to you. I'm sure a woman like that could mean nothing to Bruce."

I wish I were so sure. She once meant something to him. "Thanks."

"Meghann...about our father, don't let him come between you and Bruce. He'll try to control your lives. What he can't control, he destroys. Don't let him do that to you. Bruce deserves better than a broken marriage."

Why was he telling her this? Why did he even care? It didn't matter anyway; there was nothing to destroy. His concern touched her. She just wanted a good cry. And she could assure him Bruce would not have a broken marriage over this because there was nothing there in the first place. How could you break something that never existed?

"I just need some time to myself. I'll be fine." She didn't even wait for him to reply or protest further and turned and walked away from the car. She let out a sigh when she heard the car slowly backing out, very slowly, reluctant to leave her with her flying emotions.

Bruce looked anxiously at the door as his brother came in, but without Meghann. Where was she?

"I thought Meghann was with you."

Brock didn't answer. He just took hold of Bruce's arm and pulled him aside. "She was. We ran into an old friend of yours. A Charmaine Altman. The witch had her claws out, and unless I miss my guess, she drew blood."

"Where is she?"

Brock raised his eyebrows.

"Meghann! I mean Meghann!" His brother couldn't possibly think he wanted anything to do with Charmaine when he had someone as wonderful as Meghann. Well, almost had.

"She asked me to leave her at the cottage. I guess she needed some time to lick her wounds."

Bruce was out the door before Brock could say any more.

Meghann, please don't believe that woman. A woman like Charmaine could make even the most secure woman have doubts. And the relationship he had with Meghann was anything but secure.

Please, Lord, don't let Charmaine's words cause Meghann to lose faith in me any further. He'd been working so hard to regain the ground he'd lost with her by not being honest about his financial situation. He'd thought it was working, that she was looking at him with more favor...

Charmaine's timing was, as always, perfect.

He was relieved when he saw Meghann outside playing tug-of-war with Lucky. The dog was getting the better of her, yanking her around the yard even though Meghann was digging in her heels. She looked happy. Bruce stood and watched for a moment, listening to the dog growls mixed with her laughter. He didn't want to be the cause of her smile fading, not just yet. He wanted to enjoy her for a moment longer.

Suddenly, Lucky's ears perked up and she let loose of the rope. He had been spotted. Meghann sprawled backward into the budding grass.

She was still laughing when he rushed over to her. He held out his hand and pulled her to her feet, surprised she let him near her.

"My dog has no consideration for me when you are around." Meghann brushed herself off.

She smiled at him. That was a good sign.

"I'm sorry. Would you like me to try to teach her some manners?"

"Naw. It probably wouldn't do any good. She only has eyes for you," she said with a wave of her hand.

And you, Meghann, who do you have eyes for?

"Would you like something to drink? Coffee, tea, cocoa?"

"Cocoa sounds good."

Lucky jumped in front of Meghann with a worn tennis ball in her mouth and dropped it at Meghann's feet. "No, I'm not going to play with you after you dumped me in the grass." She stepped around the dog, but the persistent Lab dropped the ball at her feet again nearly tripping her.

"I think she's trying to say she's sorry," Bruce said on Lucky's behalf.

"I forgive you." Meghann scratched the Lab behind her ear. "But I'm still not playing with you." She picked up the ball and tossed it across the yard. Lucky raced after it. "Hurry up," Meghann called to Bruce as she hurried for the door. "It won't take her long to retrieve it."

She reached the door a step before the panting dog.

"Ha, I beat you." Pulling open the door, Meg slipped inside. Lucky turned hopefully to Bruce, but he slipped in with an apologetic smile.

"Sorry, girl, but I'm much more interested in your mistress right now," he whispered. Whining, the dog tried to follow him in.

"Leave your ball outside."

The dog looked up at Meg with mournful eyes, but she was firm. "Lucky…"

The Lab dropped her head but would not relinquish the ball.

"Fine, then stay out." Meghann began to close the door, but Lucky dropped the ball and darted in the door at the last second.

Laughing, shaking her head, Meg scratched Lucky's ears. "Go lie down."

With a heavy sigh, the dog laid down in the middle of the kitchen. Meghann had to step over the dog no matter where she wanted to go in the small area.

Meghann started on the cocoa.

"I think someone misses you," Bruce said. *And she's not the only one.*

"She's a little insecure with me gone so much. She's not sure what's going on. My short visits just aren't enough to reassure her. The poor thing."

She set a mug of cocoa in front of Bruce and sat down at the table with him.

Bruce cleared his throat. "Brock said you two ran into Charmaine at Macy's." He put the mug up to his mouth and scorched the end of his tongue. "I'm sorry she bothered you."

"It was nothing, really." She raised her mug and blew lightly on the marshmallow-topped liquid.

Uncertainty accosted Bruce. The encounter with Charmaine wasn't in the least bit upsetting to Meghann? "What did she say this time?"

"Nothing of importance."

"Brock said she was pretty catty."

She shrugged her shoulders and took a sip of her hot chocolate.

"Then you didn't believe her?"

She set down her mug. "It's hard to ignore someone like Charmaine, but when it came down to it, I chose to believe you instead of her." Her gaze met his. "I hardly know her. I certainly don't have any reason to trust her. But I do think I can trust what you've told me about her. So that's what I'm doing."

His spirits brightened. She had *chosen* to believe him. He felt like a man pardoned at the last hour.

Meg shrugged as she lifted her mug for another sip. "I actually feel sorry for her. She's so unhappy. I even prayed for her."

Meghann was a better person than he. All he could pray regarding Charmaine was that she would go away. Period.

Twenty-Five

BRUCE AND MEGHANN HEADED INTO HIS BEDROOM TO DRESS for dinner. They were going to the Crystal Swan again, apparently the only acceptable restaurant in town to Ivan. Meg's mom even talked her into inviting her friend, "Jenny."

Meghann grinned. Jennifer did not like being called Jenny. But she had been thrilled at the prospect of dinner at the elegant Crystal Swan. And she was even a little pleased at the prospect of being a sort of date for Brock. She'd agreed to meet them at the restaurant. Though from the excitement in her voice when they'd talked, Meg figured Jenn would probably beat them there.

As always, Bruce grabbed his change of clothes and moved into the master bathroom—his "changing room." Then he pointed to a translucent garment bag. "You can wear this tonight if you want," he said apprehensively and quickly left. She had never known him to act the least bit nervous before.

Meghann approached the thin white garment bag hanging on the back of the closet door and unzipped it cautiously. Inside was a sheer, off-white dress. Clearly, this was no off-the-rack garment. She wondered whose it was but dared not ask, lest she burst her fairy-tale bubble. She held the dress up to herself and gazed at the crepe creation in the mirror. It looked to be a perfect fit. It would look great with her hair curled…and she had just enough time to do that.

After fixing her hair, Meghann slipped into the dress, then put on a string of fake pearls and pearl button earrings. Holding her breath, she turned to her reflection. The dress fit perfectly as if it were made for her. She felt like Cinderella going to the ball.

"Bruce, why don't you go hurry your wife up," Gayle said. Everyone was ready and waiting on Meghann.

Bruce leaned casually against the corner of the wall. "From my experience, rushing a woman is more trouble than it's worth. She'll be out soon." He hoped she was aware of the time, but more than that he longed to see her in the dress if she chose to wear it. He had bought it last week in a compelling moment and wasn't sure if he should give it to her.

"Wow!"

At Brock's breathless exclamation, Bruce turned toward the bedroom door. His breath caught at the sight of Meghann. He pushed away from the wall slowly. She looked like an angel, better than in any of his dreams.

He strode over to her. "You look lovely." He leaned closer and kissed her cheek, then whispered in her ear,

"And well worth the wait."

She looked up at him, eyes wide, a touch of pink on those smooth cheeks, no doubt wondering why he didn't make his second compliment public.

Because, my dear Miss Livingston, I love you and plan to win your heart.

As soon as they had given the waiter their orders, Bruce escorted Meghann onto the dance floor. She stared up into his face as their bodies swayed to the music. The clock would strike midnight soon enough, and she would have to go back to her ho-hum, average life. After living in the palace with the attention of the prince, normal life would seem dull...plain...colorless.

Her heart ached just thinking about Bruce going on with his life without her, of him once again being out of her reach. Would working with him at the hotel be enough? Assuming, of course, he'd even return to his job. The thought of losing all contact with him was too painful, so she pushed it away.

Yes, he'd return. He loved his job. But could she be that close to him knowing he was never to be hers? No. She didn't think she could. It was clear to her that she would have to quit her job and make a clean break. She would leave Bruce behind. It was the price she must pay for lying, but she would enjoy this moment while it lasted. Just like Cinderella, the spell wouldn't last forever.

His eyes were telling her something, but what? Or were they probing deep inside her?

She met his gaze, willing him to read what was in her heart. *I love you, Bruce Halloway. Can you read my mind tonight? Do you know how I feel? Would you kiss me if I thought about it hard enough? There are, after all, plenty of people around to see.*

He did indeed lean forward but not to kiss her. He rested his cheek against the side of her head as they continued to sway together. His telepathy definitely wasn't working tonight. Either that, or he was purposely ignoring the messages she sent because he, too, knew it would all be over soon.

His arms tightened slightly around her.

"May I—"

"No." Bruce kept them moving to the music.

"They want you two back at the table." Brock seemed to be their messenger of choice, or maybe he was just handy. "The food—"

"No."

"Okay." Brock held his hands up and moved away, a slight grin on his handsome face.

A thrilling tingle raced through her. She wanted to kiss Bruce for not wanting to give her up, even if it was for show. She wanted to stay in his arms.

Not until the music faded out after the orchestra's final note did Bruce walk her back to the table. When she saw the plates of untouched food, Meghann realized the others had waited for them to return before eating, and she slunk down in her chair.

She forced down as much food as she could, refusing to give anyone reason to comment on the possibility of impending motherhood.

"I'm so glad to see your appetite has returned, dear." Olivia took a sip of her wine. "Morning sickness can be so miserable."

Meghann heard Jenn choke and turned to her friend. "Are you okay?"

"Fine. It just went down the wrong way," Jenn said with watery eyes, patting her upper chest.

Meghann couldn't win. No matter what she did, they were bound and determined to interpret her every move in the way they wanted.

"I need to use the little girl's room." Jenn squeezed Meghann's hand under the table.

"I'll go with you." The two got up and headed across the restaurant.

"You didn't really tell them you were...?" Jenn crossed her arms. "That's taking this a little far, don't you think?"

"No." At Jenn's incredulous look, Meg held up a hand. "I mean, no, I didn't tell them I was pregnant. That was *their* idea. My mom just wants grandchildren so bad she interprets my every move as impending motherhood, and now she's convinced Olivia, so the two of them goad each other on. They are like a pair of dogs sharing the same counterfeit bone in ignorant bliss." She forced open the door of the lady's room.

Jenn was clearly relieved. She glanced around in awe as they entered the restroom. "This place is gorgeous. I always wondered what it looked like inside this restaurant." Her grin was cheeky. "*I* never dated anyone with the capital to afford this place."

It was the most elegant place Meghann had ever

been in to. They entered the restroom like a couple of schoolgirls, giggling.

"I was so surprised when you called and invited me. And Brock is quite a looker." She raised her eyebrows up and down.

Brock was handsome; he was Bruce's brother, after all. But there was more to him than his good looks and charm. And though she sensed Jenn wasn't Brock's type, she felt sure he would play the perfect gentleman with her.

"It looks like you've made Bruce pretty happy," Jenn said with a mischievous grin as they sat at the vanity reapplying their lipstick.

Meghann took a deep breath. "It's all just an act. He's good at this game."

"I don't know. If I were you, I would seriously consider holding on to him while you can."

"I don't really have him, so how can I hold on to him?"

"You were doing a pretty good job of it on the dance floor."

Meghann glared at her friend's reflection.

"Don't give me that look. I don't think your illustrious and handsome Prince Charming is in any hurry at all to get away from you."

"Believe me, if Bruce didn't already have all the money in the world, he could make millions as an actor."

"Humph," Jenn said with the shrug of her shoulders.

So what if Jenn didn't believe her, she knew better. Bruce's act was just that, an act. And the final curtain was coming all too soon.

Twenty-Six

BRUCE WAS BETWEEN PHONE CALLS WHEN A KNOCK CAME ON his office door.

"Come," he called out, and looked up in time to see Charmaine saunter in like a cat on the prowl.

"Bruce, I've been looking all over for you."

Bruce pressed his lips together tightly. She was the last person he expected to see today, which had suited him fine. In fact, he could quite happily go the rest of his life without laying eyes on this particular woman again.

He knew she'd been wanting to talk with him. After all, she had left twelve messages while he'd been out. He didn't see much point in calling her back. He'd said all he had to her. History had proven no good came of talking with her. Whoever said ignore a person and they will go away, never met Charmaine. But leave it to her to take matters into her own hands.

Why couldn't she just leave him alone? With the masquerade ball less than a week away, he had a number of calls to make. Having a face-to-face with

Charmaine Altman was definitely not something he wanted taking up his time today.

Or, for that matter, any day.

"Charmaine." He nodded his head at her, reaching out to straighten his papers and close his file. Maybe she'd get the point that he was busy. Then an even better idea came to him: He could make the calls from home, where she couldn't bother him.

Scooping the file up, he stood. "Sorry I can't stick around to chat. I'm in a hurry." In a hurry to get away from her. He did his best to keep the impatience from his voice, but even he could hear that he wasn't succeeding.

"Hurrying home to your little wifey?" Her tone was ever so sweet. Too sweet. "Oh, but then again, she's not really your wife."

Bruce froze, his hands tensing on the file he held. How in the world had she find out about that? He met her smug gaze. "What is that supposed to mean?" He tried to keep his tone level. The last thing he wanted to do was reveal his jumbled emotions.

"Quite simple, dear boy. The county courthouse has no record of your marriage."

So the cat thinks she has cornered this mouse. Not if I can help it. "And you assumed we married here?"

"Not at all. I never make assumptions. My man did a thorough computer search of all fifty states last week. You know what he found?"

Yeah, he knew exactly what he found…or didn't find.

"Nothing." She stepped up close to him and ran her finger down his tie. "But I can keep your little tryst a secret." Her voice dropped to a low, sultry tone.

He held his breath and clenched his jaw. Having this information in Charmaine's hands was bad. Very bad. She could and would ruin everything, given the chance. He needed time to think...to decide what to do about this new development.

Lifting his chin, he did the only thing he could: bluff. "I hope you get a discount for your man's incompetence. Maybe you should have him try again?" A new search would at least keep her occupied and off his back for a few days. This mouse was escaping, one way or another.

He walked away, leaving her standing there speechless, such a blessed sound.

Unfortunately, it didn't last long. "I will get to the bottom of this," she called from behind him. "I promise you that."

He turned, putting on the most nonchalant expression he could muster. "There is nothing to get to the bottom of, so don't waste your time." With a sigh, he stepped toward her. "Charmaine, please, I have tried to be polite, to be civil to you, but you just have to accept that what we had is over. It has been for a very long time. And I'd appreciate it if you'd leave me—" he gave her a pointed look—"and my *wife* in peace."

She didn't flinch. Instead she closed the gap between them, stroking his tie again. "I could make you happy if you would only give me a chance," she purred.

As calmly as he could, he removed her hand from his tie. "No, Charmaine. Not now, not ever. Now, please, I need to go."

She sniffled and looked away. "You don't have to be mean about it."

"Your false tears aren't going to work on me."

Her head came up with a snap; anger burned in her eyes. "You can't fool me, Bruce. I know you too well. You want everyone to believe you've made some miraculous change, but it's all just an act. I know exactly who you are—" her tone turned sensual—"and what you like."

"No, Charmaine, you don't. You don't know me at all anymore."

She blinked, staring at him. "Maybe we should test that assertion." Before he could react, she slid her arms around his neck and pressed herself close against him.

Repulsion swept through Bruce, and he reached up to take hold of her arms, then stopped. He looked down at her for a moment, eyes narrowed. Maybe this was the best way to convince her she was wasting her time. Show her she didn't affect him, not even a little, no matter how close she got.

He dropped his hands to his sides, arching his brows, letting her see in his expression how tedious her display was. "Charmaine, I'm sorry, but I don't have time for your games." He slid his hands into his pants pockets. "Or interest, for that matter."

Anger flickered in her beautiful eyes at that, and Bruce felt a surge of triumph. Thank heaven, he was getting through. He'd had to go to ridiculous lengths to do it, but if it ended this woman's assault on him—and on Meg—it would be worth it.

Meghann pulled open the door to the hotel offices hall-way, walking across the carpet with a spring in her step. Everything was coming together so perfectly for the ball. Surprisingly, there had been no major hitches. In fact, things were going better than she'd ever hoped.

This was going to be an extravaganza, a fairy tale come true. The news she'd just received was the crowning touch and too good to deliver over the phone. She wanted to see the look on Bruce's face when she told him Cora and Bennet Jones—one of the couples from the old hotel registry—were alive and well.

And that they were coming to the ball.

They had been at the masquerade ball fifty years ago. They'd been young and in love—and from vastly different families, both of whom had managed to separate them. But Cora and Bennet had found each other again the night of Cinderella's Masquerade Ball and had been together ever since.

Meghann sighed at the romantic tale. This time Cora and Bennet would have no trouble finding each other—they were going to be the guests of honor. The night would be special indeed.

Meghann rounded the corner, then came to an abrupt halt.

Bruce's office door was open, and what Meg saw as she stared, dumbfounded, almost stopped her heart.

Bruce holding Charmaine in his arms. He didn't see Meg, but Charmaine did. And a triumphant smile oiled the woman's face as she nestled her cheek on Bruce's chest.

As though sensing Meghann's presence, Bruce turned and saw her. His expression was one of utter horror. Evidently he was stunned he had gotten caught. Caught red-handed!

Or, more appropriately, blond-handed.

Her head spinning, Meg put her hands on her warm cheeks, then spun and dashed from the scene. She couldn't bear to see them together. Her shock gave way to hurt, then anger. Rage burned in her at the thought of Bruce using her to make that woman jealous. That was what he must have been doing all along.

How could she have been so stupid as to let herself be manipulated like that? She was a first-rate fool. And Bruce was a first-rate cad. *I guess a leopard can't change his spots.*

She had believed him when he said there was nothing between him and Charmaine anymore. She guessed that was accurate; from what she'd seen, there wasn't even room for air to separate them! How could she have been so foolish as to think he could possibly have harbored feelings for her when that woman was so obviously available?

She rubbed her eyes, trying to erase the sight of them in each other's arms. But she knew that image—and the picture of Charmaine's victorious grin—would haunt her for the rest of her life.

"Meg!"

Bruce pushed Charmaine away, but he was too late. Meghann was gone.

"Meghann!" he called out again, moving to chase after her, but Charmaine grasped his arm. He stared in disbelief at the doorway for a moment.

"Let her go. You don't need her. You have me."

He yanked free of her hand, spinning to face his tormentor. "I don't *want* you! Why can't you understand that? Stay away from me. Stay away from Meghann and stay away from this hotel. Haven't you done enough damage?" He saw again the horrified look on Meg's face and despair flowed over him.

He had never struck a woman before, but as he stared down at Charmaine, he was tempted. Oh, how he was tempted.

She must have sensed his rage, for uncertainty filled her face and she took a step back from him.

Clenching his fists at his sides, he spoke to her in a firm, even voice. "If you ever come near me or Meghann or this hotel again, I will have you brought up on harassment charges." With that, he turned and marched out to find Meghann.

He first ran out in the parking lot to see if he could catch her and was relieved to see her cream Honda snugly parked in its usual space. As he opened the door to go back inside, Charmaine was exiting. He gladly held the door for her permanent departure. "Don't come back."

She stopped directly in front of him and brushed her hand down his coat lapel. "You don't really mean that," she said with a flutter of her lashes.

He grabbed her hand. "Hands off, Charmaine. For good." He released her hand with a jerk. "Stay out of my life."

"You don't have to get nasty about it." She sashayed a few steps, then stopped and looked over her shoulder. "Don't think you've seen the last of me."

"For both our sakes, you'd better be wrong. I meant what I said."

She shrugged and strolled away, as though unimpressed with his ultimatums.

He tightened his hands into fists, then turned to head back into the hotel. Charmaine Altman didn't matter. What mattered was finding Meghann.

But where could she be? He checked in the employee lounge, then in the offices and workrooms, but to no avail. *Meghann, where are you? Let me explain, please!*

After a half an hour of searching, he checked the parking lot again. Gone! Her car had vanished. He should have waited out here by her car until she left, then he wouldn't have missed her. He jumped in his car and raced to the only haven he could think of: her home.

At her place, he knocked a third time on her front door. Pounded, would be more like it. "Meghann, open up. I need to talk to you." Still no answer. Lucky waited patiently beside him. If Meghann were here, wouldn't she have let Lucky in with her? He pulled out his keys, tempted to burst in on her, but thought better of it and pocketed them again. He had to admit the place seemed deserted.

But if she didn't come here, then where would she go? *Please, Lord, let me find her.*

Twenty minutes later, Bruce stormed into his apartment but halted at the sullen faces. By the silent stares he was receiving, he guessed Meghann had been this way.

Please, let her still be here.

"Your wife is pretty upset." Brock's accusing tone shattered the silence.

Bruce met his brother's reproachful gaze without flinching. "Where is she?"

Brock pointed to the guest bedroom that she shared with her mother. "She's packing."

The words took Bruce's breath away as effectively as if Brock had punched him. Hard. Drawing in a deep breath, Bruce gave his brother a curt nod and went to knock on the bedroom door. Meg's mother opened it. She shook her head, throwing up her hands.

"Bruce, thank heaven. Maybe you can talk some sense into her."

Gayle walked past him and he stepped inside, closing the door behind him.

Meghann didn't even look at him. Her focus was on the clothes she was cramming into her suitcase.

"Meg, it's not what you think."

She glared at him and snapped her suitcase shut. If that look had had substance, he would be mortally wounded. But he wasn't dead yet.

"Give me a chance to explain."

She pushed past him to yank the door open and marched out, suitcase in tow. He couldn't believe she wasn't even going to give him a chance to explain.

"What happened to 'innocent until proven guilty'?" he called as he followed after her.

She set down the suitcase and turned on him. "You can hardly claim innocence. Don't forget, I'm an eye-witness. And believe me, I have already seen all the proof I care to." Unshed tears glistened in her eyes. They were greener today, and he wanted to kiss her tears away.

"But—"

"You were holding her in your arms!"

"Not quite true. She held me. My hands were at my sides."

This bit of information only served to further anger her. She sputtered, as though she wanted to say some-thing, then clamped her mouth shut. Bruce shook his head. They'd been through so much together. How could Meg believe he'd do such a thing to her? "It sounds like your mind is made up and there is nothing I can say—not even the truth—to change it."

"You wouldn't know the truth if it came up and hit you on the nose!"

His eyes widened at that jab, and he felt the burn of anger in response. "Bit of the pot calling the kettle, don't you think, Meg?"

Tears shimmered in her eyes, and she looked away. "It doesn't matter anymore, does it? I'm leaving." Her voice was choked with tears. "This marriage is over!"

Her declaration was met with stunned stares from the others in the room.

"Meg, honey, you can't be serious," her mother said. "All couples have problems. You'll work this out."

"I've never been more serious!"

"She's right."

Meg looked at Bruce sharply, clearly startled by his agreement. He met her gaze firmly. "If Meg can't trust me, then what hope do we have?"

"But you're so right for each other," his mother said, jumping in to smooth ruffled feathers. "Your marriage is so perfec—"

"Our *marriage?* There *is* no marriage!" Meghann was nearly shouting now. "There never *has* been! It's all been one big, fat lie after another."

The stunned silence that met Meg's words lasted for all of a minute. Then the room exploded into chaos.

"You two are living together?"

Bruce wouldn't have believed anything could make him laugh right then, but the stunned expression on his brother's face almost did just that.

Almost.

Gayle gasped as the color drained from her face, and Bruce waited for Meghann to cave in to one of Gayle's well-timed spells and try to backpedal. But she didn't get the chance.

Brock stepped toward them. "What happened to your high Christian ideals? Or do you only hold to them when it's convenient?"

"Give it a rest, Brock. You don't know what you're talking about." Bruce knew his words were harsh, but he couldn't deal with his brother's outrage right now.

Meghann shook her head. "No, no, no! We are not living together. We aren't even dating! Bruce—" she rolled her eyes—"Mr. Halloway is only my boss. I made it up…I told Mom we were dating to placate her. Then, when she was so ill, there was a misunderstanding.

Suddenly she was looking at me, all excited about my marriage, and I didn't have the courage to tell her it wasn't so."

Bruce watched Meg with mixed emotions. He was proud of her for finally setting things right, but he was also afraid. The lie had kept them together. Now...

Now there was nothing.

"So...what? Were you blackmailing Bruce to play along?"

Bruce almost slugged his father for that comment, but Meg glanced at him, and the sorrow in her face cut him to the quick. "Of course not. He just got involved. I never intended for it to happen, but he was in the right place at the wrong time and took pity on me and played along with this farce."

She held her hands out in entreaty. "We didn't mean to hurt anyone. It just kept growing, and then you all came, and we were suddenly caught even deeper in the deception. But it's over now. I'm so sorry for all of this, but it's over. And everyone can go back to their own lives."

So saying, Meghann snatched up her purse and grabbed her suitcase. Bruce didn't want her to walk out like this. He caught her arm. "I *can* explain about Charmaine. If you'd just listen—"

A single, lonely tear rolled down her cheek, then she pulled free of him. "I've had enough lies to last a lifetime and then some."

His hand fell away, and she turned to walk out the door.

Pain filled Bruce...a pain more intense than he'd

ever known. She wouldn't listen. Wouldn't even give him the courtesy of hearing what he had to say. She had to be the most unreasonable woman he had ever met.

"Fine! Go! See if I care!" But they were hollow words, and he knew it. He did care. More than he'd ever cared about anything in his life.

He stared at the closed door she had slammed and thought he'd go mad.

What should he do? He could go after her, even force her to listen, but doubted it would accomplish anything.

But if he let her go, he'd be saying good-bye to more than just Meg. He'd be saying good-bye to his heart.

He raked a hand through his hair and turned around. Four faces stared blankly at him. "What are all you looking at?" He threw up his hands, marched off to his room, slamming the door behind him.

And so help him, if anyone came in and tried to talk to him, he would not be responsible for his actions.

Gayle's gaze went from the door Bruce had slammed to the one her daughter had just gone through, broken-hearted. Had she pushed too hard? Was she the cause of this? Her anguish was disturbed by laughter. Turning, she stared at Brock, who was sitting in one of the living room chairs.

"What is wrong with you?" Olivia scolded.

With an effort, Brock reined in his merriment. "Isn't it obvious?"

"Isn't *what* obvious?" Olivia looked as though she wanted to throw something at him. Gayle thought she might join her.

"They're in love."

Olivia huffed. "Of *course* they are! We know that."

Gayle nodded slowly. She was beginning to understand. "But *they* don't know it."

"Bingo," Brock said, smiling at her. And Gayle was surprised to find herself smiling back. Her daughter had certainly married into a charming family. No, not married—her smile broadened—not yet.

"So I guess it's up to us to make them see it." Brock stretched out his arms and tucked his hands behind his head.

Gayle turned to Olivia and the woman's conspiratorial smile made her laugh. "Indeed," Olivia said.

"I think you are all insane."

Gayle fixed Ivan Halloway with a hard look. She'd had just about enough of this man. "Fortunately, Ivan, what you think is irrelevant."

His mouth clamped shut, and Gayle looked to Olivia, then indicated the couch. "Shall we?"

Olivia didn't even glance at her husband. She just nodded. "Absolutely. We have plans to make."

Indeed, they did.

Meghann slouched on Jennifer's couch, her arm over her eyes. "Thanks for letting me stay with you for a day or two." She had intended to go to her place at first, then realized someone would come looking for her there. She just couldn't face any of them, not yet anyway.

"Hey, what are friends for? I'm sorry it all blew up like that. I can't believe Bruce was with another woman. He seemed so perfect."

Yeah. He seemed a lot of things. He was good at appearances.

Meghann sat up. "Would you do one more favor for me? Call Bruce's and see if my mom is all right? She looked kind of pale when I left."

"Sure." Jennifer dialed and she heard her asking about her mother, then she covered the phone with her palm and said, "Your mom is fine. She's being taken to your place."

It was a relief to know her mother hadn't collapsed again because of her foolishness. And what had she gained by all of it? Nothing but heartache and humiliation.

And the truth shall set you free.

She bowed her head, tears threatening again. *I'm sorry, Lord. So sorry for being weak, for getting everyone mixed up in this in the first place. If I'd just trusted you...just held my ground with Mom...*

The tears made their way down her cheeks, as the Scripture verse washed over her again: *"The truth shall set you free."*

Strangely, she did feel freer and an undeniable peace that made no sense at all wrapped around her. In spite of herself, though she had disappointed her mother, hurt all of the Halloways, and lost the man she loved, she knew God was pleased. And that he forgave her for the lies…for the foolishness…for her lack of trust…for everything.

She had finally told the truth, even if it was at a loud, impatient volume.

Rest in Me, child. I am with you. All things work together for good…

She drank in the thought…and the sense of God's presence. She could feel it for the first time in a long time. Though not happy, a quietness existed in her soul.

"Thank you, Lord," she whispered.

Jennifer raised the phone a little, but didn't cover the mouthpiece. "The lecherous snake wants to talk to you."

Meg frowned. "The…?"

"Bruce. Mr. Trustworthy. The jerk who used and abused your trust, the rat who made you cry…"

She was saying it all loud enough for Bruce to hear her clearly over the phone. Meg shook her head adamantly. She couldn't talk to him now. Maybe not ever. How could he have betrayed her that way…with that woman? Was everything he said and did a lie, too? Could she trust anything he said? His past, his money, his ownership of the hotel…

She dropped her head in her hands. Who was he anyway? She didn't even know who he was anymore. Had she ever? For a few, fleeting moments she'd let herself believe he cared about her. But he hadn't cared enough to come after her when she left. Nor did he try very hard to explain.

Maybe there was nothing to explain.

Jennifer plopped down on the couch next to her.

"He hung up on me. Do you think it was something I said?"

Meg gave a short laugh. "Just because you called him a lecherous snake and a jerk? Gee, I don't know." Jenn was loyal if nothing else.

"How about if we pig out on ice cream? I have some rocky road, mint chocolate chip, chocolate cookie dough, toffee, and dutch chocolate, a cupboard full of toppings, and I even have some monkey food. We could make some awesome banana splits and watch a Mel Gibson movie."

As they were digging out ice cream and toppings, Jennifer's doorbell rang. Meghann froze with her hand reaching for the jar of caramel topping. That couldn't be Bruce, could it? He didn't know where Jenn lived. He wouldn't come here, would he?

"Oh, Dan, they are lovely," she heard Jennifer say.

Meghann let out the breath she was holding hostage. They came into the kitchen; Jenn with a bouquet of flowers. How sweet.

"Dan, you remember my friend Meghann." Meg shook Dan's outstretched hand. "I'm sorry, Dan. I'm going to have to cancel our date tonight," Jenn said, filling a glass of water for her flowers. "Meg had a major jerk dump on her, and I can't leave her alone."

"Sorry to hear that." Dan looked more sorry for himself, but he didn't argue.

Meghann's heart went out to the big lug. "Jenn, you go. Don't change your plans on my account."

A spark of hope lit Dan's eyes, but Jenn shook her head firmly.

"I couldn't do that to you."

She put a hand on her friend's arm. "I could really use some time alone. We'll talk more when you get home."

"Are you sure?" Jennifer looked her square in the eye.

"Positive."

Reluctantly Jennifer left, and Meghann was alone with her pain and a big bowl of ice cream. With the works.

The next day, Meghann returned to her cottage. Her mother was there, waiting.

"Why, Meghann? Why would you lie to me about something like this?" Her face was filled with sorrow.

Meg sank onto the couch. "It didn't start out that way, Mom, honest. Remember in the hospital, when that nurse congratulated me on my marriage?"

"Of course I remember. It made me so happy…"

"But it was a mistake. You were in a coma. The doctor said to talk to you about happy things; things that would make you want to fight for your life; something worth living for. I told him the only thing that would make you happy was if I told you I just got married. All the nurse must have heard was just the 'I got married' part. Then she congratulated me when you woke up."

She met her mother's eyes. "You were so happy, so excited. It was the first spark of real life I'd seen in you for days…" Her voice choked off, and she cleared her throat. "What was I supposed to do?"

"You could have simply told her she heard wrong. I would have understood."

"Mom, you didn't see the look on your face. You got ten times better just with that news, and the doctor confirmed it and said whatever I told you was helping and to keep it up. I was going to tell you when you got here, but then Bruce showed up at the airport, and you perked up even more. I just didn't want to do anything that would hurt you. Emotionally or physically."

"Meg, sweetheart, when it's my time to go, I doubt there will be anything you can do or say to stop it."

"I know that, but I didn't want to push you there before your time!" Meghann drew a calming breath. "I've seen your hands shake and wondered when you were going to pass out again. I just wanted to make you happy for a change. I know you were really disappointed when I chose to stay out here and not return to Florida. I was just trying to give you what you wanted while you recuperated."

"What I want is for you to be happy." Her mother had genuine tears flooding her eyes.

"Why can't I be happy without a husband and a house and a baby?"

"I never said you couldn't—"

Meghann took a deep breath and let it out slowly. "But you did, Mom. Every time we talked, every time you asked if I'd found someone, every time you sounded so disappointed when I said no. You made it abundantly clear what you wanted for me, *from* me. And I just couldn't give it to you. Not in reality. I want to make you happy, and when I don't live up to what you want for me, I feel like I've failed you."

Her mother rose from the couch and went to stand by the sink. "You aren't suggesting that I'm meddling, are you?"

"What about the house thing, Mom? 'Jump on it. You don't want someone to buy it out from under you.' And you kept insisting I'm pregnant when I told you I wasn't." Meg was on a roll, and it was easier to just keep talking than to stop what had been building in her for years. "Did you ever listen to yourself, Mom? Did you ever think how it sounded? 'Meg, dear, do you have a boyfriend? You know I'm not getting any younger. I want to hold my grandchildren before I die. You are all I have in this world.'"

Her mother looked away. "It's just that you sometimes do need a nudge. Dreams don't come true on their own accord."

"Whose dreams, Mom? Yours?"

"Well, I thought they were your dreams, too." A tear slipped down her cheek and she brushed it away.

Meghann went to touch her mother's arm gently. "They are, Mom. But in God's time."

"I suppose you're right. I'm sorry, dear."

"I just want you to be happy for me just as I am, unfulfilled dreams and all. If none of the things you want for me ever come to pass, can you be happy for me?"

Her mother took a couple of hasty breaths. "I am happy for you and proud of you. I promise not to meddle in your life anymore."

"Thanks, Mom." Meghann was exhausted but also

relieved. They'd faced the truth about many things, and they'd survived. And despite the intensity of it all, her mother was fine.

Meg wished she could say the same for herself.

Gayle watched her only child, miserable and discouraged, walk out the back door to the back porch. She raised her hand and looked down at the crossed fingers she'd held behind her back. "One more time, then I really will stop meddling."

Twenty-Seven

THE NEXT DAY, WHEN BRUCE PULLED UP IN FRONT OF MEG'S cottage, there was a car he didn't recognize in the driveway. Meghann had left a few things at his place, and he'd decided to bring them to her.

It gave him a good excuse to drop by. He only hoped the extra day he had given her to cool off was enough for her to talk to him. Or at least to listen.

He was grateful she had spent only one night with her antagonistic friend, Jennifer. Gayle had called him yesterday to let him know Meg was there just in case he wanted to stop by. She all but invited him to go over right then. At least he had an ally in her. She was a far cry from Jennifer, who was probably out hiring a firing squad for him. He prayed the unknown car out front didn't belong to her. He didn't need her bending Meg's ear against him.

He opened the gate when Lucky came running around the corner. "Hey, girl." He petted the dog's head, then looked up—just in time to make momentary eye contact with Meghann before she disappeared around the corner of the house.

He followed her and found her leaning against the elm tree that stood in the middle of the backyard. Well, at least she hadn't run in the house and locked the door. The despondent expression on her face tore at his heart because he knew he was the cause of it. He held out the bag of her things. "You forgot a few things."

She took the bag. "Thank you."

"Meghann, I'm really sorry for the episode at the hotel."

"Stop. Don't. It's not necessary to say anything about it. It doesn't matter anymore."

But it does matter. He needed to explain. It wasn't his fault.

The back door opened and Brock stepped out. "Here's your tea, just the way you like it—"

Brock stopped halfway across the yard and stared at him. Obviously he hadn't expected to see Bruce here anymore than Bruce had expected to see him. And how did he know how Meghann liked her tea?

Bruce looked from Brock to Meg, and his jaw clenched. "I see you've moved on rather quickly." He turned and walked back around the house before he did something they all would regret.

"Bruce, wait!"

When he didn't even pause, Brock turned to Meghann. "Aren't you going to go after him?"

"What's the point?"

"He came to talk to you. Don't just let him walk away like that."

"He could have stayed if he wanted to. I don't want to hear his excuses about Charmaine Altman, anyway."

"I'm sure there is a logical explanation."

"He has you fooled, too. Your brother is good at knowing how to manipulate people and situations, at making everyone believe black is white."

"He loves you."

She stared at him, then turned away. It wasn't true, and she knew it. "He has a funny way of showing it."

"I think you've got him all wrong. You could at least talk to him."

"I have nothing to say. He's the one who was wrong."

"Are you so sure about that?"

Positive. She'd seen it with her own eyes and it still hurt. Bruce had put in a token appearance here—how fortunate he'd actually had an audience in his brother—to show he was properly sorry for all that had happened.

Now he probably was off to see that woman.

Brock was staring at her, and Meg lifted her chin and met his look.

"You know, Bruce could draw the same conclusions about you and me that you have about him and the charming Charmaine."

"Hardly." She hadn't been locked in a romantic embrace with Brock when Bruce showed up.

"You don't think me walking out of your house like I belong here, with a cup of tea made the way you like it, won't look the least bit suspicious?"

Why would it? Nothing was going on between

them. "Well, maybe he has cause to be suspicious. You said yourself, why stop with one brother when I can have two?"

Brock threw his hands up. "You're being ridiculous."

"Are you saying the thought of a relationship with me is ridiculous?"

"It is when you're in love with my brother!"

She opened her mouth to deny it, but he didn't give her the chance.

"And he loves you, though you both are too stubborn to admit it."

"I may have thought I loved him, but it was all an illusion. And any feelings I *might* have had are dead now."

"Right." The word dripped with sarcasm. "Which is why you're so hurt over what you think you saw; why your eyes are puffy and red from crying. Because you have no feelings whatsoever for Bruce."

She wasn't going to listen to this. "Why don't you just go away?" She stalked off toward the back door.

He followed right on her heels. "Because someone needs to talk some sense into you! Admit it. I must have hit a nerve for you to get so mad."

She went inside, slamming the door behind her, cutting off any further comments. She marched through her little house, holding up a curt hand to stall her mother's words before she could speak them, and stormed into her bedroom.

She slammed that door shut as well. If only she could shut the door on her feelings as easily.

———∞∞∞———

"To what do I owe the honor of you darkening my door?" Kurt stood from behind his desk and greeted Bruce. "I knew I'd get you to my church—or, in this case, my office—sooner or later. What's on your mind?"

"Trust."

Kurt's smile faded and his brows pulled together. "I hope I haven't done anything to damage your trust in me."

"No. It's not you, it's me."

Kurt inclined his head. "So what about trust interests you?"

"How do you regain someone's trust after they think you did something wrong?"

"Is this someone the Miss Right you're not dating?"

When Bruce didn't answer, a smile pulled at Kurt's mouth but he was good enough to keep it in check. "So this woman thinks you did something wrong? But you didn't do it?"

Bruce nodded.

"Just tell her you didn't do it."

"It's not that easy. She saw me."

Poor Kurt was clearly confused, and rightfully so. "Hold on. She saw you do this thing you didn't do?"

He was going to have to give him a few details. "She saw me with another woman and assumed there was something between us."

"Jealousy is a mighty enemy to battle, but if you explain the situation to her, I'm sure—"

"It's not that easy. I have a past with this other

woman. We were involved before I became a Christian. And she's been telling Meg we're still involved. Then she manipulated me into a compromising situation, and now Meg won't even listen to an explanation." He let out a frustrated huff of air. "To be honest, even if she did listen, I don't think she would believe me. Too much has happened between us for her to believe I am anything but the two-timing womanizing jerk I used to be."

"Pray for an opportunity to speak to her, and when it comes, make the most of it. Pour your heart out to her. Tell her how you feel."

How he felt? Would something as simple as declaring his love for her be enough? He doubted it, especially if she'd already turned her feelings toward Brock.

"She means a lot to you, doesn't she?"

Bruce sighed. "She does. I can't believe how much. I thought love was supposed to be a good feeling."

Kurt smiled. "There is no greater feeling than loving someone and being loved in return."

"That's just it. I think she loves me, but I'm not sure. And now...I'm afraid it may be too late. I may have already lost her."

"Because of this other woman?"

"That, and I think my brother is interested in her. I may not have a chance to explain at all."

"Talk to your brother. Tell him how you feel about Meg and ask him to back off until you have a chance to straighten this all out with her. If things don't work, well, then perhaps he can pursue a relationship with her."

Bruce closed his eyes at the thought. Brock and

Meg. He wouldn't be able to deal with that. Somehow, some way he had to work things out with Meg.

And he would. No matter what.

Meghann stood in her front doorway and stared down at the hundred-thousand dollar check made out to her from Ivan Halloway.

"What's this for?" Was he trying to pay her to reconcile with Bruce? Didn't they all know it was hopeless?

"Anything you want," Ivan said in a cool and dispassionate voice. "As long as it is far away from my son."

Her head came up quickly. He was bribing her to get out of Bruce's life. She held the check out to him. "Don't bother. There is very little chance of Bruce and me getting together."

"I leave nothing to chance."

"Don't you see it was all an act? Bruce doesn't care anymore for me than he does for the tree out in my front yard! It was all a game. Appearances."

Ivan just stood there, staring at her. "Keep it then, as sort of an insurance policy. If you and Bruce aren't getting back together as you say, what can it hurt to keep it?"

Why wasn't the man listening? "I'll say it slowly. Then maybe you'll understand. Bruce and I were never together in the first place, so there is nothing to get back to! And I certainly am not taking money from you, for that reason or for any other."

Poor Ivan. He looked as though he didn't understand her at all. Well, that was fine. She wasn't so sure she wanted a man like Bruce's father to understand her. One thing bothered her, though. The elder Halloway must be worried that something was going on with Bruce or he wouldn't have felt it necessary to pay her off. Ivan was threatened by her…

She paused, studying him briefly. Or was it her faith that terrified him? Was God knocking on this man's heart, and Ivan was trying desperately to block out the rapping?

She wondered, even as she laid the check on the table. "I can't and won't accept your money. That's final."

"I'll double it."

"You don't understand."

"Triple."

He upped the price without even batting an eyelash. "I don't want your money."

"One million dollars."

A million dollars! She could do a lot of things with a million dollars, for herself and for others. But this wasn't about money, it was about principle. And truth. She'd compromised both once before and look where it had gotten her.

She wasn't going to make that mistake again. "No. I'm not interested."

"Everyone has their price, name yours."

He thought she was greedy; she could see it in his eyes. Just how high of a price was he willing to pay to secure his son? Suddenly she knew just what to ask for. "I don't want anything from you. But somebody else does."

"Somebody else?"

She nodded. "God. And His price is you."

He pulled back with a scowl, but she went on.

"God is calling you, Mr. Halloway. You know it and I know it. And He'll accept nothing less than everything from you. Embrace God and become a Christian, and you'll discover what real riches are."

"You are a fool!" he ground out, and spun on his heels.

Meg fought a smile as he stalked away. Not getting his way didn't seem to sit well with him. The wheels of his rental car spun in her gravel driveway as he sped away.

She truly felt sorry for him. He was caught in so much turmoil and discontent and so very unhappy. He struggled to control everything, and yet he controlled nothing. *Lord, soften his hardened heart.*

After his car had disappeared from sight, Meghann realized she still had his check. She had never seen so many zeros, and Ivan threw them around like they were nothing. Well, technically zeros *were* nothing unless they were preceded by any other number, then the more the merrier.

And on that basis, this check was quite happy.

"Stay away from Meg." Bruce's words strained from his throat.

"What?" Brock shifted in the iron balcony chair to stare at his brother.

Bruce moved forward to grip the railing with both hands. The cold metal helped cool his anger. "You heard me. She's off-limits."

"Off-limits? What are you talking about?"

"Meghann. I love her like I've never loved any woman before. Just give me a chance to work things out with her."

Brock was staring at him as though he'd gone round the bend. "You think I'm trying to steal Meghann from you?"

"Maybe not steal, but in her vulnerable state she could be easily lured away spending time with you."

"You got it all wrong, brother." The metal chair scraped the floor as Brock pushed himself to his feet. "I'm trying to talk her into listening to you. I'm on *your* side. In spite of the low opinion you *still* hold of me." He marched inside.

Bruce ran a hand over his aching eyes. *Great. It's not enough to ruin my witness to my family. No sir, I've got to alienate Brock, too.*

With a heavy sigh, Bruce bowed his head and took his fears—and his failures—to the only One who could help.

Bruce stood in Meghann's house, waiting for her in the living room.

Gayle had let him in with a broad smile and promptly took the dog for a walk. His confidence was bolstered by Gayle's smiling support. But he didn't think it would be right for him to make himself comfortable when Meg didn't even know he was here, so he stood near the kitchen counter, pushing papers back and forth.

A large manila envelope had been waiting on his desk when he got to work that morning. Opening it he found all the work she had done on the ball: What still needed to be checked on at the last minute, the schedule of what would arrive when, and what should be done by what time. Along with the ball information was a neatly typed resignation, which he was here to refuse. He tore it up as soon as he read it.

He looked up expectantly when he heard her footsteps as she entered the room.

She stopped when she saw him and narrowed her eyes. "What are you doing here?" She looked around for her absentee mother.

He dropped his gaze—and frowned. His attention honed in on one of the papers he'd been shuffling…the one with a signature he recognized all too well. He turned and picked it up. "A better question would be, what is this?"

She strode over and glanced at the check he held. "It's a check from your father."

"I can see that. What are you doing with it?"

"It's made out to me. Why else would I have it?"

"Why, may I ask, did he give this to you?"

"Well, it seems my absence from your life is worth a great deal to him."

"And you accepted his money?" He struggled to stay calm, to still the voices of condemnation that screamed out at him. It took all his willpower to refrain from crumpling the detestable piece of paper into a small, little wad.

"No. I did not accept his money. He wouldn't take it back."

"So you just decided to keep it."

"He didn't give me much choice. He left before I could give it back to him." She snatched the check from his hand and tore it in half. "I don't want his money or *your* money or *any* Halloway money. And if you don't believe me, then why don't you just leave."

He wanted to believe her, but how could he be sure? It was a fair enough question. Bruce just wished he had an answer.

Meg watched the emotions shifting across Bruce's face with rising frustration.

She stuffed the shreds of the check back in his hand. Enough was enough.

"If you're quite finished accusing me of being a gold digger, would you mind getting out?" She opened the door for him, watching in sorrowful silence as he complied.

He actually thought she would take a bribe from his father.

He strode outside and to his car, gunning the engine into life and racing off down the road. And, more than likely, out of her life for good. She closed the door and slid down to the floor.

If, as she'd so firmly told Brock, she really didn't care about Bruce any longer, why did it hurt so much that he thought she would accept a bribe? And why did she ache with the thought of never seeing him again?

God, help me. Take away this pain.

Bruce threw the two check halves at his father. "Stay out of my life."

"It's for you own good."

"*My* good? You haven't a *clue* what's good for me!"

"I was only trying to make this breakup go more smoothly for both of you. Everyone has their price, and she did name hers." His father's cool, dispassionate manner infuriated him.

His eyes narrowed with contempt. "And money wasn't it—" he pointed to the crumpled scraps of check—"was it?" His father's silence was all the confirmation he needed. None of this was Meghann's fault. He knew how his father worked. His father had pushed her and pushed her until she had no choice but to keep the check. "If you meddle in my life again, I'll walk away from you and never look back."

"You don't mean that, son."

"Don't push me," he ground out and stalked away.

This rift between Meghann and him was the worst pain he had ever felt. It ate at his heart. But what could he do to fix it when she wouldn't listen to or believe him?

Trust.

That's what it all boiled down to...trust. And Meghann obviously didn't trust him. But there must be something he could do to gain her trust again. To rebuild what Charmaine had ruthlessly torn down.

How could he go about restoring her faith in him when she wouldn't even talk to him?

Trust.

It wasn't his fault. Charmaine had taken advantage of the situation. No, he was to blame. He never should have listened to a word she said and simply called security as soon as she arrived.

Lord, forgive me for allowing a circumstance where Charmaine could manipulate me into a compromising position. Show me how to win Meghann back. I never wanted to hurt her.

Trust.

I do trust her, Lord. When I'm thinking straight. She is one of the most trustworthy people I know.

Do you trust Me?

Bruce was silent for a long while. He trusted God for his salvation, but did he really trust him with anything else? He was used to being in control, making his own way, solving his own problems. This time he was helpless. He had no control over the human heart.

He took a deep breath. *Okay, Lord. I give Meghann and this whole situation over to You. Whether I get her back or not is up to You, and I will find a way to be thankful either way.*

As he finished he realized he might have just prayed his love right out of his life.

Please bring her back to me.

Meghann answered the door to find a gray-haired delivery-man in a blue shirt and pants with several large boxes and garment bags. "If you would sign line 17, ma'am, it would make my day," he said with a wink and a nod to the clipboard resting on the box he held.

She signed in bewilderment and exchanged the clipboard for the cumbersome box.

"Thank you very much and have a great day." He was a little Johnny sunshine on a gloomy day.

"What is all this stuff?"

"It's from Costumes and More. Have fun."

Her costume for the ball tonight. She had forgotten all about it. Well, when they returned tomorrow to pick it all up, it would be untouched and still safely in its packaging.

"What's all of this?" her mother asked, fingering one of the two garment bags lying on her couch.

"They were supposed to be our costumes for the ball tonight."

A quick zip and her mother had exposed a green velvet dress. It matched her mother's eyes beautifully. "That was to be yours."

The dress was freed from its plastic casing. "It's gorgeous." She held it up to herself. "If this is my dress, yours must really be something."

"It's too bad we won't be using either of them."

"Why not? You've worked so hard on this event. You should be there."

"I can't go with Bruce there."

"As many people as will be there, you probably won't even see him."

Meghann closed her eyes and shook her head. "It's part of the program...I'm supposed to make a grand entrance, and we were going to dance together. How could I avoid him then?"

"Would it really hurt you to have one little dance with him?"

Yes, it would hurt. Deep inside she would cry out in agony and unbidden tears would come. Tears she was barely able to keep at bay as it was. "No, Mother. I'm not going." Absolutely, positively not!

"But—"

"No."

Twenty-Eight

BRUCE SAT AT HIS COMPUTER AND HAMMERED OUT INSTRUC-
tions for George. He couldn't believe the nerve of
Charmaine to show up here tonight for the ball. As if
the evening wasn't going to be bad enough without
Meghann to share it with. Charmaine thought she had
sufficiently destroyed all possibility of him and
Meghann getting back together, and that he would be
ready now to accept her advances, even if reluctantly on
the rebound. The thought repulsed him.

As he escorted Charmaine from the building, he
informed her that if she were the last woman on earth,
he wouldn't have her. He thought finally he might have
gotten through to her. Was it too much to hope for?

He looked up at the knock on his door. "Come."

"You wanted to know when Bennet and Cora Jones
arrived." The employee speaking to him was dressed to
look like a French servant from the early 1800s.
Meghann had worked to find suitable costumes for all
the people who would be working the ball, and she
pulled it off wonderfully with plain black trousers and a

white shirt with detachable ruffle collar and cuffs. The women had long black skirts, white blouses, and prim white aprons.

"Thank you. I'll be right out to greet them." As the young man was closing the door Bruce added, "They know to skip Cinderella's entrance, right?" No one would even know it had been planned and was now being edited.

"Yeah. It's just too bad she got sick at the last minute and couldn't find a replacement."

Sick of him was more like it. As for a stand-in, he could have easily gotten one, but he just didn't have the heart. How could he ever replace Meghann?

He finished his document and saved it. Grabbing his black mask, he fastened it in place and headed out to the ballroom. The huge room had been converted into a conference hall, but for tonight it was returned to its former glory. Meghann had done all the research and had it decorated much the way it would have been fifty years ago: elegant, glowing candelabras; silk banners; rented imitation King Louis chairs lining the walls; fresh flowers; and all the staff dressed in period costumes. On the far end of the festive room, near the seats reserved for Bennet and Cora, sat a large, red velvet chair: his throne to preside over the festivities.

He went over the program in his head. An hour after the ball got rolling when all the guests had arrived, the trumpets would sound, and the doors would swing open. Meghann, dressed as Cinderella, was supposed to sweep in and they would dance. But she wasn't coming....

So they would skip that little spectacle, and no one would be the wiser.

He ushered Bennet and Cora to their reserved seats. They were a cute old couple and still very much in love. He ached to have a love like theirs—one to last a lifetime—and had had hopes with Meg, but now it seemed an impossible dream. He sauntered through the room, greeting people and dancing with a few women, the wives or daughters of influential men. Then he took his seat and watched over the proceedings, but his heart was not in it. He would rather be anywhere but here without Meg. But she was too angry with him to even speak, let alone come to this public forum.

It wasn't right! She should be here instead of him. She was the one who'd put most of the work into making sure this night happened.

He watched dully as people mingled and couples moved around the dance floor in a swirling mass of color. If he kept a watchful eye, he could probably slip out unnoticed in a little while, work in his office, then return for the final waltz; not that there would be anyone special for him to dance with.

Glancing at his watch, he realized it was almost time for what would have been Cinderella's arrival. He hoped the band leader had gotten the message and remembered to can it. He held his breath as the music faded away. The band director was saying something, then the trumpeters raised their horns. He closed his eyes, praying they wouldn't give the signal for something that wouldn't happen. But they softly built into the next melody and the other instruments joined in.

His captive breath left him in a rush. They were playing another piece, everything was fine.

He eyed his watch, hoping for an opportunity to escape.

Placing his hands on the arms of the chair, he pushed himself halfway up when the band cut the tune short. Not really standing and not really sitting, he stared as the trumpeters stood, raised their instruments, and blew the announcement of the fairy tale arrival.

Oh no! Bruce looked up at the double doors at the back of the room—as did everyone else in the room. But he knew nothing was coming. What a disappointment for everyone. And what a sad way to end Meghann's perfectly planned party.

Suddenly the doors burst open, but the threshold was empty. This was not good; embarrassing, at the very least. People were already glancing his way, expecting him to give some kind of explanation after the fanfare. He stood, opened his mouth—and halted when a collective gasp filled the room.

Turning, he followed the rapt gazes up to the double doors. There, like a vision from a magical time, stepped a masked figure. Framed in the doorway, she stood, smiling, her flowing gold gown fit for a queen. Her hair was pulled up, and ringlets fell in a silken cascade all around her head. Jewels sparkled in the ringlets, glittering under the room's bright lights.

Bruce's breath caught in his throat. Whoever this was, she was stunning. She inclined her head to those gathered before her, and the action held a strange familiarity. There was something in the way the woman held herself, in her bearing, in the way she waved her hand…

He fell back into the waiting throne. *Meg? Could it really be her? Or had she sent someone in her place?* He dared not move, or the beauty of this mirage would vanish as surely as he lived and breathed.

As he and Meg had so carefully planned, the crowd stirred and every eye was locked on her as she entered the room. People parted a way for her as she reached them. *Was it really her?* There was no way to tell from this distance and she was wearing an iridescent mask.

"This is your cue," someone whispered beside him.

"What?" He kept his eyes glued to the vision before him. *Was it Meg? Had she come? Was there hope after all?*

"You're supposed to walk to her, like you're surprised at her arrival."

Right. That would be easy enough. He *was* surprised. Stunned, in fact. He stood and strode with calculated calmness to where the vision stood poised, near the doorway. As he drew closer, the certainty within him grew.

It was Meg!

But why? They stood facing each other and murmurs rose from the crowd. The band flowed into a familiar waltz. After she curtsied and he bowed, he held out his hand to her. She placed her palm in his, and he wondered at the perfect fit. Slowly, he escorted her to the middle of the floor.

She moved into his arms, fitting in them as though she'd been made to do so. He gazed down at her, drank in the sight of her eyes, the emotions he saw there.

Wordlessly, still scarcely able to believe she was here, he moved his feet, and they began waltzing around the room. At first the only sound in the room was the music, the rustle of Meg's dress—and the pounding of Bruce's heart. Then, slowly, others joined them in the dance.

He dared not speak lest the spell they had created would float away on the music.

After another dance, he escorted her off the floor, her hand still nestled in his. When they were apart from the crowd, he looked down at her. "Thank you for coming. I didn't expect it."

"I didn't want to disappoint everyone. A lot of people put a great deal of time and energy into making this night a success." Her voice was flat and passionless.

He couldn't help the stabbing disappointment that she had only come out of obligation. "I appreciate your sense of duty." He guided her near the red velvet throne to the elderly couple seated holding hands like a pair of schoolchildren. "May I introduce Cora and Bennet Jones. This is Meghann Livingston, the person responsible for all of this splendor." He motioned toward the room.

"I am so happy to finally meet you." The spark of energy was back as she spoke with their honored guests.

"This is all so beautiful," Cora said. "It's taken us back fifty years. It's almost exactly the way it was then."

"We feel like kids again." Bennet raised Cora's hand to his lips and kissed it. "I don't know why you chose us out of all the couples that were here that night, but we thank you for recreating one of the happiest nights of our lives."

It was all Bruce could do to not turn and walk away in defeat. Too bad he and Meghann wouldn't have any happy memories of this night as well.

Meghann wandered around the ballroom barely aware of the beautiful decorations and cheerful voices. This was supposed to be a night of dreams and fairy tales...and love. Instead, it was one agonizing moment after another, dragging on and on. The night she looked forward to for months, she now wished would just end.

In a moment of weakness she had let her mom and Brock persuade her into coming. It was hard being here, painful, in fact, but she knew it was the right decision. She had a responsibility, and she would play her role to the bitter end of the evening.

She looked to Cora and Bennet, longing for the lifetime of love they shared. The elderly couple didn't dance much thanks to arthritis and a bad hip, but they seemed to be the happiest couple in the room. Their faces glowed with the love they shared.

Meghann, on the other hand, had a steady stream of dance partners: Brock heading the list.

"You did an excellent job pulling this all together," he said, twirling her around the dance floor.

She smiled. "Thank you, but I didn't exactly do it all by myself."

"You and Bruce make a good team. I look forward to your next endeavor."

"I'm afraid you will be disappointed. There won't be a next endeavor. Our collaboration was short lived."

"That's too bad; you two make a wonderful couple."

Meg held back a frustrated sigh. Brock was forever putting in a good word for his brother, and it was getting tiresome. She didn't want to think about what could have been with Bruce. She wanted to salvage what she could of this evening and didn't want to spoil it with could-have-beens. Bruce had had plenty of opportunity to explain himself, but he chose not to.

"You've occupied her long enough." Meg turned in surprise to look at Ivan, but before she could refuse, she had changed partners.

She didn't really want to dance with Ivan Halloway and couldn't imagine why he should want to dance with her. As with everything else, he was accomplished and skilled, making him a smooth and elegant dancer.

Meg only hoped she didn't embarrass herself by stomping on his million-dollar toes.

"Do you think that your showing up here will somehow win you favor with my son?" His belittling tone rankled her. "Do you think he is going to beg you to come back? He has never begged for anything in his life."

She stopped cold and brought herself up to her full height. "I came because I have a job and responsibility, nothing more." Not caring who was staring at them, she turned and walked away from him. She'd told the truth. She was there because of her job, and for that boorish lout to think otherwise was ludicrous.

An immovable force suddenly stopped her progress. Bruce slid his arms around her, moving her back into a dance. The glare he shot his father's way gave her the chills. Or was it being in his arms again that made her shiver?

"Are you cold?"

"No." In fact, she was suddenly quite warm, as though she'd stepped out into a hot August day. His eyes held hers and she was unable to pull away from his intense gaze.

Her mind swarmed with memories like a tornado going round and round and round. She could hear his declaration floating around in her head, "I'm a new creation."

She thought of the cross he'd given her, which was even now safely tucked in her glove, like she used to do with her milk money on cold school days...she remembered the flowers he'd brought her with an endearing smile...

His smile, just the thought of it made her heart beat faster.

"I am a new creation."

And then her own words drifted through her mind: *"I chose to trust you."* But did she, did she really?

"I am a new creation."

Dazed by his nearness, her thoughts jumped about and her emotions collided with one another. All her senses seemed to be on alert. Being so close to him was suddenly overwhelming, and she tried to pull out of his grasp, but he held on tightly to her.

"We'll finish this dance, Meghann. Besides, it's a little too early for Cinderella to be running out on me."

His cool words—and his firm grip—left no room for argument.

—◆◆◆—

"Do you think it's working?" Olivia peered around Gayle Livingston.

Gayle shook her head. "I don't see how, when they insist on being on opposite sides of the room."

Olivia saw what Gayle meant. Meg was dancing with a tall, slim man; Bruce was sitting on his red throne sulking.

"I'll just have to put a stop to that." Olivia marched over to Bruce and soon he was escorting her to the dance floor. Her plan was obvious, even to Meg, who excused herself from her dance partner before Olivia could trade partners with her.

Olivia watched the object of her son's affections sweep away and smiled. *Point for you this time, Meghann, dear. But the evening is far from over.*

And their plan was far from over, as well.

Meg was avoiding him. Bruce was sure of it, and that fact told him all he needed to know; she'd been telling the truth. She hadn't come for him at all, but out of a sense of duty alone.

Lord, help me know what to do now.

As though in answer to his prayer, the last waltz of the evening began to filter through the room. He jumped on the opportunity, moving to Meg's side.

"This is our dance, sweetheart," he said, capturing her arm and leading her to the floor. He held her arm firmly to keep her from escaping. "And it's no doubt my last chance to explain myself to you." Like everyone else, he and Meghann had removed their masks during the evening, so now he could see her whole beautiful, sorrow-filled face without any obstructions.

He had put it off until now for fear of sending her fleeing, but to his surprise she didn't try to get away or object. She simply looked up at him, as though waiting to hear what he had to say.

She's ready to listen!

His heart all but sang the realization, until another voice threw the cold water of reason on his hope: *Either that, or she's reconciled to having little choice in the matter.*

He drew a steadying breath. Whatever the case, she was here, looking up at him. The time had come.

Meghann waited, praying she would be able to bear what Bruce had to say. The hurt she'd felt that day when she saw him holding Charmaine had been so deep. What if Bruce was prepared to tell her he and Charmaine were back together, or that he still cared for her…?

Give me strength, Lord.

Bruce's voice was low as he began to speak. "Charmaine came to my office with the news that she knew that we weren't really married."

So she was blackmailing him into getting back together with her? He could have told her no. Take a hike. Get lost.

"I told her she was mistaken and to go back and check her facts. I told her what we'd shared was long ago, that it was over, never to be resurrected. That I wasn't the same man. Apparently she felt she could prove me wrong by—" Meg watched in surprise as faint pink tinged his face. He cleared his throat. "She felt she could get a response from me by embracing me. I started to push her away—"

And well you should have!

"Then I realized the only way to get it through to her that she didn't appeal to me any longer was to let her pull her stunt and see that it didn't work. I figured even Charmaine wouldn't be inclined to pursue a man who reacted to her embrace with as much enthusiasm as a dead fish."

He smiled slightly. "So that's what I did. I didn't hold her. Didn't put my arms around her. In fact, I had my hands in my pockets, telling her I didn't have time for or interest in her games when you came to the door. After you left, I told her in no uncertain terms that if she bothered either of us again, I would have her brought up on harassment charges."

"She was here tonight," she said softly. She was sure he didn't think she knew about that since it happened before she came. Soon after a woman matching Charmaine's description had arrived, several people had seen them go off...together! Would he admit it?

He took a slow, controlling breath. "I told her she had better leave of her own accord unless she wanted a police escort out of the building. And she did leave, hopefully for good."

His gaze roamed her face, and when their eyes met, Meg saw only sincerity there.

"That's it, Meg. The gospel truth. I'd swear to it on a Bible if you wanted me to, but bottom line, you're just going to have to decide whether or not you believe me. And we're going to have to decide whether or not we can trust each other. I hope we can."

She opened her mouth to reply, but just then the dance ended. As the music faded, Bruce squeezed her hand and moved to make his closing comments to the crowd.

When he finished, he came to escort Meghann from the ballroom to rousing applause. When they were in the hallway, away from the crowd, she turned to him.

"Bruce—"

But he stopped her. "I'm sorry. I have to go someplace right now." With that, he turned and hurried away. She stood there, staring after him, speechless, then took a step to follow him.

"Miss Livingston?" She halted and turned. A fellow employee stood there, his expression beseeching. "We could use your help here, if you don't mind. We're not sure where things are supposed to go…"

With a sigh, Meg followed the man back into the emptying ballroom. For the next hour, she supervised cleanup duties and handled minor catastrophes.

Bruce's long strides couldn't get him out fast enough. He pushed open one of the side doors and drank in a long cool breath of fresh air. She didn't trust him. She just plain didn't trust him. It was on her face and in her question about Charmaine's presence earlier this evening. Not that he could blame Meghann. He was no saint, and even though he counseled himself against it, his hopes had soared with her being here tonight. Logic told him to give up, it was a lost cause, but everything else in him cried out to never let go.

He knew she was reluctant to dance with him, but holding her felt so right. No other woman could ever fill the place in his arms meant for her.

Even as the anguish rode through him, he was devising a plan to win Meghann back. It would start with prayer and end with a proposal. He would marry Meghann or no one, and he had no intention of remaining a bachelor the rest of his life.

Meghann watched the staff and cleanup crew dragging around the room with service carts and garbage bags picking up the debris left behind. Most of the ball guests had left, except a few who were also guests of the hotel. Her mother had gone home early because she was tired. She'd promised to send the limo back for Meg, but a quick survey of the parking lot told her that her mother had forgotten.

Maybe Brock was still around and wouldn't mind giving her a lift home, but a search of the ballroom, banquet hall, and the other rooms on the lower level offered her no possibility for a ride. Well then, perhaps Brock had gone to Bruce's office.

The office door was closed but not latched, and she heard nothing from within its darkness. She knocked softly and pushed the door open when she heard no reply. The only light in the room was a small desk lamp, casting strange shadows around the room. Since no one was here, she decided to use Bruce's phone to call a taxi and crossed the room to the desk.

"This night was a raving success, thanks to you."

Meghann spun around at the voice in the murky dimness, clutching the receiver to her chest. The light from the hall revealed a form stretched out on the couch. Bruce was still here?

He sat up. "It's a little late to be making phone calls, unless you're calling Europe or something."

She glanced at the instrument in her hand. "I was just calling a taxi. It seems my carriage has turned into a pumpkin." She couldn't tell if he smiled at that or not.

"I'll drive you." He stood and strode across the room. Her heart took off on a wild dance. "It'll take too long for a taxi to show up. I can have you home and be back here before one would even show up. It's the least I can do for a loyal employee."

She glanced at the couch behind him. "You're going to sleep here?" She realized he'd done so many times before, during their mock marriage. She felt bad that he had slept on a too short sofa on her account. Why would he do that for her?

"I have to be back here in a few hours anyway and didn't want to disturb my family." He stopped in front of her, still in his prince costume minus the coat, and held her in his gaze. "I don't know if there will be room for the two of us in the 'Vette with all that gold satin your dress is constructed of."

She smiled at the thought of stuffing her full dress,

hoop skirt and all, into his little sports car.

"You have a nice smile. I wish I could bring it to your face more often." He sounded downhearted, almost defeated.

Entranced by his fierce gaze, she could neither breathe nor talk. He just stood there unmoving. Her heart thumped so hard against her ribs she thought it might break free.

"I'll warn you right now, I haven't given up on the two of us." His voice had a new earnestness, low and husky. "Meghann Livingston, you are the woman I've waited for all my life. I know it as surely as I know my name. And I'm going to hound you until you realize it, too."

"You are?" His ardent pledge sent her stumbling back into his desk chair. If not for the quick reaction of his strong arms she would have fallen backward into the chair and probably tumbled to the floor.

A slow smile pulled at his mouth as she stood there, motionless, nestled against his chest—the place she was meant to be.

"I am. Because I can't fathom living life without a young, vibrant woman with hair the color of honey and brown eyes that sparkle with green, sometimes so much there is barely a trace of brown. A woman with a spirit so sweet I couldn't help but be drawn to her."

His words washed over her, and she felt the final remnants of her doubts slip away. This was true. This was solid and real and what mattered most—Bruce's feelings for her; her feelings for him.

As for Charmaine...she was the fantasy. The mirage that deceived her into seeing things that weren't there.

Bruce had told her the truth; Meg was certain of it, deep inside.

He caressed her cheek with the back of his fingers and leaned closer. "I love you, Meghann Livingston, now and forever."

She basked in the feel of his hand on her face and covered his hand with one of her own. "I lov—" but her declaration was lost in his tender kiss.

And at long last, Meg felt as though she'd come home. Now and forever.

Epilogue

IN THE SIDE ROOM DESIGNATED FOR THE GROOM, BRUCE straightened his tie in the full-length mirror. This was a perfect day. Nothing could possibly go wrong. Today he would marry the woman of his dreams. The six months since the masquerade ball had seemed like an eternity.

Brock slammed through the door, out of breath. "Bruce, you have to come quick. Our father is at it again. He has Meghann cornered."

Bruce grabbed his tuxedo coat and swung it on as he rushed out the door after Brock. His father had been more agreeable since they had their altercation over his attempt to bribe Meghann to walk out of Bruce's life. And the last time his father visited, he hadn't stocked Bruce's junk food bar with liquor. He'd really expected his father to behave himself. He sure hadn't expected him to try and pull something today.

He followed Brock through the church to the bride's dressing room. He charged into the room without fear of catching anyone only half dressed. If his brother had been in here and his father was in here, it was safe.

"Bruce, what are you doing here? You aren't supposed to be in here."

He ignored the women's protests; he didn't believe that nonsense anyway and searched out Meghann. There, in the corner, behind his overbearing father. He crossed the room quickly and plucked the prenuptial agreement from her hands.

"I don't mind signing it." There was laughter in her voice as she gazed up at him lovingly.

She took his breath away, and for a moment he forgot why he was there. But the papers in his hand reminded him. "Our marriage is going to be based on trust. When I marry you, it is for life. We don't need this." Bruce held up the distasteful document in the air.

"I know. That's why I don't mind."

"I *do* mind." He tore it in half and handed it back to his father.

"It's your funeral, son," Ivan said brusquely.

Bruce looked his father in the eye and said firmly, "No, it's my wedding." Bruce turned to Meghann. "You ready?"

She nodded enthusiastically and took his arm.

"I hope that God of yours is as great as you believe," his father called after them. "You'll need it."

"He is and more." Was that really his father mentioning God? Maybe he was softening and there was hope for him after all. But he couldn't think about that right now; he had the love of his life to marry.

He slipped a paper of his own from his inside jacket

pocket and handed it over to her.

"Don't tell me you had your own prenuptial drawn up?" Her eyes sparkled with laughter.

"No, darling. It's your wedding gift: the deed to our home."

Her eyes widened. "The house we looked at with Mom?"

"Unless you want a different house?"

Her squeal—and the way she grabbed him around the neck in a hug—gave him all the answer he needed.

He would gladly give her the world if it made her happy. Holding on to her tightly, he kissed her soundly.

"Hey, you'll have plenty of time for that later, brother."

Bruce let go of Meg and smiled at Brock. "I sincerely hope so."

Brock shook his head, an indulgent grin on his face. "Newlyweds, can't live with 'em—" he winked at Meg—"and that pretty well covers it."

She laughed and batted at him. Watching them together, Bruce was thankful he didn't feel even a twinge of jealousy. Just gratitude that his soon-to-be wife and his brother were so fond of each other.

Meg came to loop her arm in his. "God has given us so much, hasn't He?"

"More than I ever dreamed possible."

"All things really do work together for good, don't they?"

He tucked her into the crook of his arm. "They do, indeed, my love."

"Promise me one thing, Bruce."

At the somber request, he gazed down at her. "Name it."

"No more games. No pretense. No lies. We do this God's way, all the way."

His heart filled with gratitude for the woman God had given him. "I promise. No more games. Just a lot of years of love and honor and remembering how blessed we are."

He cupped her face in his hands and bowed his head, reverently sealing his vow with a kiss.

"Well, I'd say our plan was a total success."

They looked up to see Olivia and Gayle standing there, faces beaming.

"Oh yes, indeed," Gayle was agreeing. "It worked like a charm."

"Your plan?" Meg tilted her head as she asked the question.

"To get you two back together."

"Mother!" Meg's hands came to her hips. "You promised not to meddle!"

Gayle didn't look the least bit repentant, and Bruce had to fight back a smile. "But I'll bet you're glad I did this time—" Gayle looked from him to Meg—"aren't you, sweetie? Just look at the lovely husband I found for you."

"Mom…"

Waving at her daughter, Gayle reached out to loop her arm with Olivia. "Now, all we need to do is work on the issue of grandchildren."

"We should have the first within the year, don't you think?" Olivia agreed.

"Mother!"

Bruce and Meg said it together, and both their mothers turned, grinned at them, and sauntered away.

Meg looked up at Bruce. "They're unstoppable. You know that, don't you?"

"Well, so are we," he replied firmly, and was rewarded by a beautiful grin. She took his hand.

"So, onward into the future."

"With you? Absolutely."

As they walked toward the sanctuary, he knew their life together was going to be wonderful. And blessed. And filled with laughter.

And never, ever boring.

Dear Reader,

When asked to write this letter, I didn't know what to say to all the unknown faces out there who would pick this up, my first published book, and choose to spend their valuable time with me. So, I will give you my heartfelt thanks! I hope you enjoyed getting to know Meghann and Bruce as much as I did. Their path from my head to the printed page was a long, drawn-out process. However, God was good, as always, and they made it.

When I was growing up, I was a terrible liar. I never could have gotten away with what Meghann and Bruce did. My stepdad could always tell when I hadn't coughed up the truth, so I gave it up at an early age. I truly believe honesty is the best policy, even when it hurts.

God works all things together for good, from our outright disobedience to our shortcomings. God can turn all things around and use them for His divine purpose. Where we see hopelessness and despair, He sees an opportunity to show His mighty power. In our weakness He is strong. I am thankful for a faithful God who is not limited by my mistakes or inadequacies.

May God's faithfulness be evident in your life today.

Mary Davis

You can write to Mary Davis:
c/o Palisades
P.O. Box 1720
Sisters, OR 97759

FBI agent Dave Richman never intended to fall in love. But when Kate O'Malley becomes the target of an airline bomber, Dave is about to discover that loving a hostage negotiator is one thing; but keeping her safe is another matter entirely.

Available at a bookstore near you.
ISBN 1-57673-608-3

Dave waited until Kate's brother Stephen disappeared up the stairs. "Why didn't you tell me yesterday? Trust me?"

"Tell you what? That I might have someone in my past who may be a murderer?" Kate swung away from him into the living room. "I've never even met this guy. Until twenty-four hours ago, I didn't even have a suspicion that he existed."

"Kate, he's targeting you."

"Then let him find me."

"You don't mean that."

"There is no reason for him to have blown up a plane just to get at me, to get at some banker. We're never going to know the truth unless someone can grab him; and if he gets cornered by a bunch of cops, he'll either kill himself or be killed in a shootout. It would be easier all around if he did come after me."

"Stop thinking with your emotions and use your head." Dave shot back. "What we need to do is to solve this case. That's how we'll find out the answers and ultimately find him."

"Then you go tear through the piles of data. I don't want to have anything to do with it. Don't you understand that? I don't want to be the one who puts the pieces together. Yesterday was like getting stuck in the gut with a hot poker."

He understood it, could feel the pain flowing from her. "Fine. Stay here for a day, get your feet back under you. Then get back in the game and stop acting like you're the only one this is hurting. Or have you forgotten all the people that died?" He saw the sharp pain flash in her eyes before they went cold and regretted his words.

"That was a low blow and you know it."

"Kate—"

"I can't offer anything to the investigation, don't you understand that? I don't *know* anything. I don't know him."

"Well he knows you. And if you walk away from this now, you're going to feel like a coward. Just what are you so afraid of?"

He could see it in her, a fear so deep it shimmered in her eyes and pooled them black, and he remembered his coworker's comment that he probably didn't want to read the court record. His eyes narrowed and his voice softened. "Are you sure you don't remember this guy?"

She broke eye contact, and it felt like a blow because he knew that at this moment he was the one hurting her. "If you need to get away for twenty-four hours, do it. Just don't run because you're afraid. You'll never forgive yourself."

"Marcus wouldn't let me go check out the data because he was afraid I would kill the guy if I found him."

Her words rocked him back on his heels. "What?" He closed the distance between them, and for the first time since this morning began, actually felt something like relief. He rested his hands calmly on her shoulders. "No, you wouldn't. You're too good a cop."

She blinked.

"I almost died with you, remember?" He smiled. "I've seen you under pressure." His thumb rubbed along her jaw. "Come on, Kate. Come back with me to the house, and let's get back to work. The media wouldn't get near you, I promise."

Marcus and Stephen came back down the stairs, but Kate didn't look around; she just kept studying Dave. She finally turned and looked at her brother. "Marcus, I'm going back to Dave's."

Dave gave in to a small surge of relief. It was a start. Tenuous. And risky. But a start, all the same.

The jungle drums are sounding…calling you to an adventure you'll never forget!

Not Exactly Eden
by Linda Windsor
Coming July 2000

When spoiled socialite Jenna Marsten journeys to the wilds of Brazil's Amazon rain forest, she thinks she's going to a beautiful place where she'll find her past—and the father she never knew. But the jungle has a mind of its own, and what Jenna finds there is a world beyond anything she'd ever imagined. A world that is *Not Exactly Eden*. Harsh, untamed, and too frequently savage…this is a world that pushes her to the limits of her faith and endurance—and brings her to the brink of love with Dr. Adam DeSanto…a man she keeps reminding herself she can't stand!

Listen to the drums…let the sounds and feel of the jungle sweep you away, teach you lessons you never knew you needed, and change your life forever.

A BATH OFF THE SIDE OF A BOAT SOUNDED REASONABLE IN theory. After all, a rope hung over the side would be simple for access and safety. Unfortunately, application of the theory was an entirely different matter.

First, Jenna lost her bar of soap. It slipped out of her hand while she was sudsing her hair and went straight for the river bottom, which she could not touch with her toes. But the water was heavenly, like a pool during a long, dry heat wave. She wished she could let the rope go, but the current was strong and her arms hurt too much from working the hand pump to test her swimming skills.

Feeling fully refreshed, or as refreshed as one could in water the color of a chocolate shake, Jenna wrapped her feet around the rope and pushed upward. To her surprise, beneath the water's surface the thick jute was slick, no doubt covered with the same greenish slime that coagulated along the nooks and crannies of the banks.

A fish jumped a few yards away and her breath seized. Reminded that she was not alone in the water, Jenna tried pulling herself hand over hand. She could get her shoulders up to the ship's side, but there was no strength left to get her bottom half over it. Her bare legs scraped the cracked paint on the planking, searching for a knee or even a toe hold, but all she got was sharp pain in the ball of her foot.

With a startled yelp, she slipped back into the water, panic growing by the heartbeat.

"Adam!"

Oh heavenly Father, help!

"Adam!" she hissed through her teeth.

I won't distress!

She didn't want to awaken her father, or anyone else for that matter.

And I won't despair!

As for Adam DeSanto, it didn't make much difference. He'd make fun of her regardless. Although, she thought, pulling on the rope again with renewed determination, she hated to give him more fuel for his warped humor.

There was a sliding sound from overhead and the light thump of elbows, or perhaps, knees. Adam's head appeared over the edge of the canopy, silhouetted dark against the moonlit sky.

"Jenna?"

He slid farther over and peered into the darkness of the deck beneath him.

Jenna swallowed the last of her pride.

"Down here...in the water."

"Ah!" He looked down at her over folded arms, head cocked sideways. "Are we skinny dipping?"

"In your dreams."

"In that case..." He yawned and rolled over. "I'll just go back to sleep."

"I *can't* get back in the boat!"

Something brushed against Jenna's foot. It was most likely more of the flotsam, but she couldn't keep the panic from her shrill whisper.

"And there's something in here nibbling on my toes!"

Dear God, please, no piranha!

With a smooth acrobatic curl, the irascible doctor dropped down from the canopy and onto the stern deck light as a cat. He moved like he was born to the jungle, quick and quiet.

"Grab my arms, Jenna."

With no quirky smile or taunt but simply raw grunting strength, Adam hauled her out of the water. Exhausted from fear as much as effort, she didn't resist when he pulled her to him and held her, trembling in his arms. He was warm, and his embrace felt like nothing could harm or threaten her. She savored it, knowing full well the risk she took was all her own. But recklessness was becoming a growing facet of her personality. For all she knew, it had always been there, leashed by the role of her former life.

Her nose twitched, tickled by the hair on his chest. Without warning, she sneezed. The captivating closeness evaporated. Adam released her. The cool rush of air that filled the void between them struck Jenna at the same time her left foot protested from her full weight upon it.

She gasped and dropped onto the bench, remembering the splinter. Her foot cradled across her leg, she felt for the offending object. It had broken off when she stood up. She shook off a tummy swirl of nausea.

"Let me see."

Seemingly from out of nowhere, Adam produced a small penlight and shined it on her foot. Wrapped around her toe was a piece of river grass. He pulled it away and tossed it over the side.

"I did see a fish earlier," Jenna managed in self-defense.

Adam touched the stub of the wood and swore. "My next project is to scrape and paint this boat!"

"Can you get it out?"

"Have you got tweezers? My bag is stashed forward and all I have is this." He produced a pocketknife.

Jenna nodded. "In the bag."

Ah, the leetle flowered bag on wheels! Adam didn't need to say it. His expression did. He picked it up and handed it to her. Inside an exterior zippered compartment, Jenna took out a leather-encased manicure set.

Adam examined it curiously. "Have you any lotion or an astringent with alcohol?"

"Will triple antibiotic ointment do?"

"For tonight."

Jenna contemplated the rugged profile of the doctor's face as he went to work with the tweezers. He was so gentle, she hardly felt it when he opened the wound a little more to extract a piece that remained behind. His application of the ointment afterward affected her far more than it had a right to.

Adam DeSanto might have the temperament of a jaguar, or *onça,* as Juana chided from time to time, but beneath it was the incredible tenderness that made his former nurse swell with pride. Jenna saw it when he was with patients, especially the children.

And now. With her.

"You continue to amaze me, Jenna Marsten." He shoved himself up from the squatting position in front of her bench.

"I'll take that as an apology."

"For what?"

"For trying to scare me away with that kiss."

Jenna regretted the words the moment they were

out, not just because she'd admitted that Adam's kiss had left its impression, but because they brought the onça back. Gone was the sweetness, the tenderness. In its place was a predatory, ebony gleam.

Adam tilted his head, like the cat contemplating the mouse.

"You mean, you want me to apologize for kissing you?"

Jenna rubbed her foot and slipped it into her canvas deck shoe. She could tell from the incredulity in his voice that anything of the sort was out of the question now.

"Forget it. It was a dumb joke."

"Well, I am *not* sorry!" He glanced up at the canopy and ran his fingers through his thick hair.

"Fine. It was nothing."

"In fact..." He swung his gaze back to her, jaw jutting in a neck-stretching jerk. "I am so *unsorry*, that I will do it again!"

Frozen like a cornered mouse, knowing there was no escape, Jenna caught her breath. The caress of Adam's skilled fingers along her chin moved her head back to receive his kiss. If the possessive, yet tender claim on her mouth could be called that. Its completeness spread through her veins with a jalapeño effect, warm, elusive at first, then demanding recognition of all her senses.

And she thought feelings like these existed only in romantic movies! She'd never known the like with her ex-fiancé, Scott. They begged her to abandon reason and will. The only course was to go into his embrace. Jenna moved closer until she could feel the counterpoint of thundering hearts.

Suddenly, Adam tore away, staring at her as if she'd grown two heads. He raised his finger at her and then dropped it as if he had second thoughts.

"And for the love of Pete sake, put some dry clothes on!"

Reaching up, he grabbed the lip of the canopy and curled up and over it.

If she weren't in such a twist herself, Jenna would have corrected Adam's misuse of the English expression. But considering the fire of his kiss still ravaged her senses, proper speech was the *least* of her problems.

Be sure not to miss these other releases!

Danger in the Shadows, Dee Henderson
ISBN 1-57673-577-X
In hiding from the man who kidnapped her as a child—a man who's still after her—the last thing Sara needs is a high-profile relationship. But former pro football player Adam Black isn't going away. But will his love—and faith in God—be enough to save her when her nightmares become all too real?

The Decision, Gayle Roper
ISBN 1-57673-406-4
When a car bomb kills nurse Rose Martin's cancer patient, she escapes into the arms of Jake Zook, a man struggling with his past and his Amish heritage. Can the living find God's forgiveness for themselves and gain justice for the dead?

Hi Honey, I'm Home, Linda Windsor
ISBN 1-57673-556-7
Kathryn Sinclair's husband, Nick Egan—an obsessive journalist who put his job before everything else—was reportedly killed in a terrorist attack over six years ago. So what's he doing on her doorstep, as impressive as ever, ready to take up where they left off? Can Nick and their precocious boys prove to Kate that God has truly changed Nick's heart?

Island Breeze, Lynn Bulock
ISBN 1-57673-398-X
The last thing ex-cop Cody North needs is more excitement. But when Bree Trehearn, a woman on the run from danger, stumbles into his life, he starts to wonder if she isn't exactly what he needed after all!

Reunion, Karen Ball
ISBN 1-57673-597-4
Taylor Sorenson is hiding wolves on her ranch; Connor Alexander is a wildlife biologist sent to find out if wolves have returned to Wyoming. But they're drawn together when they face angry ranchers, superstition, and an enemy who's determined to get rid of the wolves once and for all.

Searching for Stardust, Lorena McCourtney
ISBN 1-57673-414-5
When Jan and Mark Hillard, divorced years earlier, are thrown together in a search for a woman who may be carrying their grand-child, neither can deny their long-buried feelings of love. But can Jan believe that Mark's newfound faith has made him a new man?

Summit, Karen Rispin
ISBN 1-57673-402-1
Julie Miller's career as a rock-climbing guide is ascending smoothly until David Hales, an internationally recognized rock climber, shows up and gets all her jobs. When Julie uncovers a sinister plot that puts both their lives in danger, only trust in each other—and in God—will get them through alive.

True Devotion, Dee Henderson
Book One in the Uncommon *Heroes Series*—*Men of the military standing in the gap for honor…and love.*
ISBN 1-57673-620-2 (July 2000)
Kelly Jacobs has already paid the ultimate price of loving a warrior; she has the folded flag and the grateful thanks of a nation to prove it. Navy SEAL Joe "Bear" Baker can't ask her to accept that risk again—even though he loves her. But the man responsible for her husband's death is back—closer than either of them realize. Kelly's in danger; and Joe may not get there in time...

Unlikely Angels, Barbara Jean Hicks, Annie Jones, Diane Noble, Linda Windsor
ISBN 1-57673-589-3
Three old favorites and one delightful new novella by popular Palisades authors Barbara Jean Hicks, Annie Jones, Diane Noble, and Linda Windsor. See how four couples discover love thanks to the assistance of their furry, feathered, and four-legged friends!

Wilderness, Karen Ball
ISBN 1-57673-552-4
Mady Donovan and Jason Tiber have little in common. Then they end up lost together in the wilderness, where they discover the reality of faith in a broken world—and of God's sufficiency in even the most desperate circumstances.